Iron & Blood

Book Two of the Expansion Wars Trilogy

Joshua Dalzelle

©2017

First Edition

This is a work of fiction. Any similarities to real persons, events, or places are purely coincidental; any references to actual places, people, or brands are fictitious. All rights reserved.

*****

Edited by Monique Happy Editorial Services

www.moniquehappy.com

"The great questions of the day will not be settled by means of speeches and majority decisions but by iron and blood."

-Otto von Bismarck

Chapter 1

Planet Juwel

Juwel System, United Terran Federation

"Keep your damn heads down! They're still shooting over the ridge, there's nothing to see!"

Another series of explosions shook the ground and made Emil hug the dirt and scrunch his eyes shut so tightly he was seeing spots. The twenty-year-old had never felt fear like this at any other point in his life, so scared that he felt no shame for the whimpers that escaped his lips and the uncontrollable trembling. He squeezed the infantry carbine as if it was a life preserver and he was a drowning man.

"Emil! Get your fucking eyes open!" Finn Auer shouted, waving his three-fingered hand at him. "Keep tucked down but be alert! We only have to keep them from overrunning us into the town ... the Marines will be here soon!"

Emil had heard that before and knew there weren't enough Marines to go around. The old man was likely mouthing platitudes to keep his young charges from completely succumbing to fear, and Emil despised him for it all the more. Since the Darshik invasion three major cities had fallen; the armored troopers the aliens had landed made short work of the civil defense forces that were more in place for law enforcement and emergencies than for any real fighting. CENTCOM had managed to get two drop carriers through the Darshik blockade and land two full regiments on the southern point totaling seven thousand combat capable Marines. Unfortunately the support ship that would have brought their equipment was destroyed at the jump point, and almost all of their mobility, artillery, and supplies were lost before they could even make it into orbit. That left a lot of Marines with no way to get to where they were needed and most only had light infantry weapons. It was a disaster from the beginning.

Emil had been a child when the Phage had ripped through the Frontier worlds. He remembered his parents talking about it as if it were nothing more than an intellectual curiosity. After all, it was so far away ... not even New European Commonwealth worlds. They were safe on Juwel. While the adults dismissed it as an interesting, if abstract topic, he remembered the older kids at school whispering about it; the Phage were coming to wipe out all of humanity and no Terran world would be spared. The visceral terror he'd felt as a child was still vivid in his mind.

That fear was nothing like he felt now, however. The Darshik troops would land outside of major settlements, congregate for a time as they silently organized and deployed their force while only taking action to fend off any meager defense put up by the humans, and then march into the city to subdue it quickly and efficiently. They were nothing short of terrifying. Ensconced in their matte-black combat environmental suits, the only thing that could be gleaned of their appearance was that they were bipedal on short legs with long arm-like appendages and a head that was more squat and ovoid than a human's. Any of the aliens the human militia managed to kill were quickly cleared from the field by their comrades, so as far as Emil knew nobody on Juwel had ever seen a Darshik without the protective suit.

"Here they come!" someone shouted from down the line.

"Brace yourselves!" Finn called. "Don't let them get past this position!"

Emil risked a look up over the hasty fortifications they'd built and saw that the Darshik troops were now sprinting across the open field. They made no sound other than the pounding of their feet, creating an eerie spectacle. While the troopers were bad enough on their own, at least the fact they'd begun their charge meant that the bombardment from their ground-based artillery had ended. That was the good news. The not-so-good news was that their position was first in line and really only intended to slow down the advance so that the rest of the settlement's defense force could muster and get into position. In other words: They were a speedbump. From what he'd learned he knew that the Darshik would not simply bypass even such a small defensive position but would instead stop and eliminate them to the last man.

"Oh, God," Emil whispered, petitioning the God of his youth to give him courage. He'd already resigned himself to the fact that he wasn't going to survive this assault by an enemy he'd given no offense to.

The heavy machine gun that was on the opposite side of the line from Emil opened up, the single-barrel, chemically fired weapon spitting out 25mm shells at a rate of fifteen hundred rounds per minute. It was an antiquated anti-vehicle gun, but it still packed a hell of a punch. More importantly, it was all they had. The crew was firing in long, sustained bursts that would quickly destroy the barrel. Emil knew that they must have reached the same conclusion he had regarding their odds of survival and were hell-bent on doing as much damage to the enemy prior to the inevitable.

A new sound reached him, the spiteful buzz of the Darshik infantry weapons opening up on their position. Their handheld weaponry drew power from their combat suits via an umbilical and fired some type of concentrated plasma burst that acted like an incendiary projectile. From previous engagements the defenders of Juwel had learned that the weapons were devastating, but severely range-limited. They also weren't especially effective against even a moderately armored vehicle, creating a lot of light and noise but the charge dissipating before it could cause significant damage. The Darshik troops relied on the pinpoint accuracy of their field artillery and orbital bombardments to soften up Terran positions before they swarmed in to clean up anybody still left fighting. So far they had ignored any civilians not taking up arms.

"Right side! Fire your fucking weapons!" the shout came from somewhere down the line. He couldn't recognize the voice but knew it wasn't Finn. Emil sucked in a breath, steeled his nerves, and rose up over their hastily erected earthworks, sighting down his weapon. The leading elements of the Darshik force were stretched out and concentrating on where the heavy gun was still hammering their formation. A dozen dead aliens littered the field and the rest were crouched down, using the slope of the terrain to keep out of the gun's line of fire. They were stacked almost single file and completely exposed to trailing positions occupied by Emil and three other defenders.

"They're out of range, Emil!" the middle-aged man he shared the ditch with hissed. "You'll expose us!"

"You really think they don't know we're here?" Emil asked, the man's cowardice making him all the more disgusted with himself for his own hesitation. He saw that they were largely being ignored as the rear elements of the enemy were moving further away to try and flank around the large-bore projectile weapon that had momentarily fell silent while its crew hastily swapped the ruined barrel out for one of the two spares they had left.

Emil sighted through the optics of his rifle, an infantry weapon that was already outdated when it was built some eighty years prior. The ranging data showed that the Darshik troops hunkered down were just outside the effective range of the gas-powered 5mm rifle. The scope reticle would blink red whenever he sighted on the enemy, telling him there was no valid shot available.

"Scheisse!" Emil cursed in the tongue of his ancestors. He wasn't a soldier or even much of a fighter. But he was a hunter and a master marksman with weapons not nearly as powerful or accurate as the one he currently held. He ignored the prompts and warnings in his scope as the computer insisted he didn't have a shot. Observing the wave of the grass he saw he had two distinct crosswinds and estimated he'd have to put his point of aim at least a half a meter over his target to get the proper elevation.

He squeezed the trigger and barely noticed the pop into his shoulder as the weapon fired, the report being completely lost in the cacophony of the skirmish. Through this scope he could see the ground near one of the enemy troops kick up as his round hit a few meters short. Without a moment's hesitation he held his point of aim just a bit higher, relying completely on instinct even though the weapon was unfamiliar, and quickly squeezed off another round.

Emil watched, fascinated, as the second to last Darshik jerked and then slowly toppled over, a stream of vapor spitting from a hole in the neck of its environmental suit. The soldier fell and did not move so Emil assumed that he'd hit something vital. The elation of striking back broke through the wall of terror, the only emotion he'd felt since they heard the Darshik were on the move towards their settlement, and he got down to business.

The next target he picked was just behind the lead Darshik and appeared to be setting up some sort of portable standoff weapon or artillery. He applied the doping he'd learned from his last shot and squeezed the trigger, watching as the 5mm round tore the crown off the top of the enemy's helmet. After the same release of gas the Darshik fell to the ground, flopping like a fish out of water. The other troops seemed to be confused as to where they were taking fire from, their squat heads rotating about. Emil gritted his teeth against the adrenaline dump and began picking off targets at random. Time to make these *fickers* pay.

****

Sergeant Willard "Willy" Barton forced himself to remain calm as the truck bounced across the recently harvested field. The vehicle was a surprisingly capable eight-wheeled flatbed used in agriculture and its electric drive had more than enough power to haul him and his men across the flat Juwel plains. What was causing Barton so much consternation was the fact the vehicle was built for load capacity and torque, not speed. Even with the shortcut their local driver was taking they were covering the distance at an interminable crawl. The high-pitched whine of a turbine starting broke him out of his ruminations and he looked questioningly at the driver.

"Batteries were down to thirty percent," she said apologetically. "It's not good for them to get much lower than that or you start to get bad cells." Barton just nodded. They were out in the middle of nowhere still so he wasn't overly concerned about the extra noise the vehicle's tiny gas turbine generator would make as it replenished the batteries. As a rugged farm vehicle at least it had its own generator, unlike its smaller, city-dwelling counterparts that needed to be hooked to a charge station. The driver, who had only introduced herself as Josie, had shown them a direct route to a medium-sized agricultural town called Westfall where the Darshik had been sending scout parties to begin softening up the militia emplacements before the main wave hit. Josie's route bypassed all the main roads and utilized cross-country travel and some unpaved, unmaintained dirt access roads.

Sergeant Barton's platoon had made landfall along with the rest of the two-regiment-strong force meant to repel the Darshik incursion onto a Terran world, but nearly all of their gear had been destroyed by the enemy blockade before it could be dropped to the surface. The result was a lot of Marines with no practical way to get to where they were needed and without the support equipment to fight for any real duration once they got there. Command had ordered four platoons from 5th Expeditionary Battalion to use whatever means necessary to make contact with the enemy, ascertain strength, harass when possible, and report back. The problem was compounded when the Darshik destroyed every satellite over Juwel, effectively blinding the stranded ground forces. Not even so much as a weather satellite was left in orbit.

Barton's platoon was pared down further as the lieutenant decided having everyone bunched up with limited coms and nonexistent real-time intel on enemy movements was tantamount to suicide. He ordered 2nd Platoon to perform their recon role and to not engage any superior forces unless absolutely necessary. While Barton normally had a less than flattering opinion of the LT's decision-making ability, he grudgingly had to concede that the fresh-faced young man was doing the right thing by not ordering his men into a buzzsaw in the face of no defined objective or coherent strategy to get the Darshik off of Juwel. All he knew for sure was that if the Fleet assholes didn't clear the skies this would be the shortest counteroffensive of all time. The Darshik might play hide and seek with a numerically unknown force for a while, but Barton knew that if the Marines became too much of a nuisance they could expect to be annihilated via orbital bombardment.

"Sergeant Barton," a skinny private first class called through the open back window. "We're close enough for the drone."

"Send it," Barton said over his shoulder. "Pipe the feed over the squad channel."

"Sure thing—*fuck!*" the PFC shouted, hitting the back of his head on the window frame as he pulled himself back through. The boy's name was Wilson … something Wilson, Barton had never gotten his first name. He was the stand-in tech operator for his squad and would control one of their two lightweight recon drones. The small unmanned craft were just under a meter in length and were powered by counter-rotating ducted fans, one on each of the stubby wings. In addition to being able to achieve an admirable forward flight speed as well as hover and loiter, they had nearly a twenty-kilometer signal range without the aid of an orbital repeater and an effective flight time of one hundred and twenty minutes. His people bitched about packing them along, but they came in handy when you wanted to see something over the next hill.

Barton heard the buzzing whine of the powerful little motors spin up even over the turbine of the truck and looked over his shoulder in time to see someone help Wilson ease the drone into the air. It followed along after the ground vehicle for a bit like a puppy before the mission parameters fully loaded and it zipped up and away along their direction of travel. He looked down at the semi-flexible, organic touch panel that was part of his battle uniform top and saw an icon for "Buzzard 1" pop up. When he pressed it the screen flashed to a live feed from the camera turret located under the nose of their drone. It didn't take long for the craft to get high enough to see there was a small skirmish kicking up along one of the border towns outside of Westfall.

"Wilson! I want to zoom in on that tussle up ahead of us!"

"On it, Sarge!" Wilson called back, manipulating the controls.

The video zoomed in and stabilized on what looked like two columns of Darshik ground troops engaging a haphazard defensive position that was dug in at the natural chokepoint the rolling hills provided. Barton shook his head as he watched farmers and industrial workers fire blindly into the hills and, in some cases, fire into the ground a few meters ahead of them as they tried to simultaneously remain fully behind cover and return fire to the enemy. He had to remind himself that these were militia members many, many generations away from any real fighting. Hell ... his own men were largely untested in battle so his disgust might be a bit premature. Just as he was getting ready to write the small engagement off as a total loss for the Terrans he saw Darshik troops in the leading column begin to drop.

He frowned as he couldn't make out why the enemy seemed to be dropping dead in the lead element as they weren't exposed to the militia's lone machine gun. It took two more dead Darshik for him to realize that someone was letting them have it from the far, perpendicular rise and from what he could see it was well beyond the effective range of the standard 5mm infantry carbines the militia was equipped with. He wasn't the only one who noticed the impressive shooting.

"Whoo! Some civvy is fucking them *up!* Get some!" someone shouted from the bed of the truck. "Hey, Sarge! We better haul ass or that kid's not going to leave any aliens for us!" Barton was torn between telling the unknown enthusiast to shut the hell up or to be in full agreement with him. The sharpshooter was sure to be sussed out soon enough and he still had a full element of Darshik that were hanging back to deal with. Despite the LT's orders, he had a chance to engage with relatively little risk and secure one of the major roads heading into Westfall.

"Listen up!" he bellowed, causing his driver to almost jump out of her skin. "We're going in hot! We'll stop the truck short of the last treeline and then we jump that trailing element along its left flank and drive the leading element into the militia's machine gun if we're lucky. You ready to kick some alien ass?" The shouts from the back of the truck were tinged with a sort of panic that concerned Barton greatly. He hoped it was just pre-battle jitters but it wasn't like he had any experience himself with such things. This would be the first time any of them had ever had shots fired in anger aimed their way.

"Here goes nothing," he muttered as he waved to the driver to veer off to the right to get his people better into position.

Chapter 2

The buzzing pops hitting the crest of the hill he was crouched behind told Emil that the Darshik had figured out where the incoming was originating from. He slid further down towards the shallow runoff ditch that he'd planned to use to escape since he could do no more good where he was. If he exposed himself again to be greedy and try for one more shot it was almost certain he'd be hit given the volume of fire directed his way.

"You happy now, hero?" a middle-aged farmhand everyone just called Cal hissed from where he knelt by the ditch, hugging his rifle to him. Emil couldn't help but notice the weapon wasn't even activated yet ... Cal hadn't fired a single shot during the entire engagement while their friends behind the other rise had been pinned down with withering fire. "They know we're here! You *killed* some of them! They're coming!"

"Shut up!" Emil snapped. He was disgusted with Cal's cowardice only because he felt the same crippling fear welling up in his own chest. It was one thing to pick off targets from afar when they weren't even paying attention to you, but now that they were surely advancing on his position he felt like his legs were made of rubber and he could hear his heartbeat pounding in his head.

"Why did you have to provoke them? There's only four of us here!"

"I said shut the fuck up, Cal!" Emil hissed. "Listen!" Sure enough, the sound of the enemy's fire had changed. It had increased in volume, but he could tell that it was no longer directed to their position. No more repeated *pop/hiss* sounds of their shots hitting the turf and burning as they expended energy. "They're moving away from the town."

"How can you tell?" Cal asked. Emil ignored him and, with a boldness that surprised even him, crawled back up the hill and risked peeking up over the crest. He raised up quickly until just his eyes cleared the obstruction and looked out over the battlefield in confusion. The Darshik were redeploying both of their elements in a way that made no sense. At least it made no sense to him until he saw the first two enemy troops get shredded by some sort of lobbed incendiary that looked like it originated about a half-kilometer further down the ditch line where the larger trees provided a natural break. He saw two more projectiles arc into the Darshik formation and take out another six before the remaining scrambled to get back and behind what sparse cover there was.

Before they could get set in a new defensive posture heavy weapons fire erupted from where the incendiary projectiles had originated. The *chug-chug-chug* of modern machine guns was unmistakable as more Darshik fell under the onslaught. The enemy was now pinched between the militia's defensive position and the overwhelming firepower of whoever the newcomers were. Emil took the opportunity to continue his own personal revenge, sniping targets of opportunity from an even more impressive range though it took him more rounds per target to put them down.

It wasn't long before there were only three Darshik troops standing, pinned down behind an abandoned bit of machinery. Under the cover of the heavy machine guns still hammering away, Emil watched in fascination as two humans in mottled camouflage uniforms charged across the field. He was impressed that the machine guns could so accurately lay down suppressive fire as their comrades ran through it. The pair paused around fifty meters away from the derelict bit of farm equipment while one raised a strange-looking short-muzzled weapon.

Foomp-Foomp-Foomp

What Emil now recognized as grenades arced away from the weapon and landed on and around the last bit of cover the Darshik could find. The fast-succession triple explosion ripped apart the rusted metal of the Terran machine and the bodies of the Darshik soldiers.

"Cease fire! Cease fire! Cease fire!" an amplified voice boomed from the treeline and echoed across the hills. The silence was deafening.

"Juwel militia! We are Terran Federation Marines; we will be approaching your position! Please hold your fire!" the voice rolled across the field to where they were hunkered down. In spite of what he'd just been through and the aftershock he was feeling from the adrenaline dump of battle, Emil turned and smiled to his companions.

"Looks like the Marines showed up just in time."

****

Barton approached the entrenched militia members cautiously, his weapon hanging loosely from its sling and his hands open wide and swinging where they could be clearly seen. Even though there was little physical resemblance between human Marines and Darshik soldiers he knew that the town's defenders, like his squad, had just had their first taste of battle. He wanted to make sure there were no mistakes or misunderstandings.

"I'm Staff Sergeant Willy Barton, TF Marines," Barton said, extending his hand to the older man who was standing ahead of the other civilians. "You in charge?"

"As much as anybody is in charge around here," the man said, grasping the proffered hand firmly. "I'm Finn ... Finn Auer. We can't thank you enough for showing up when you did, Sergeant."

"You did a hell of a job here," Barton said as he looked around. "Good cover, natural choke point, and you engaged a numerically superior enemy with overlapping fields of fire and allowed them to close enough to effectively engage ... you have any prior military experience, Mr. Auer?"

"Just call me Finn, everybody does," Finn said with a forced smile, wiping back his hair with a still-shaking hand. "I was a corporal in the New European Commonwealth Guard before it was disbanded, but I can't say that I intentionally placed people in position based on anything I remember from that."

"Good soldiers remember ... even if they don't remember that they do," Barton laughed. "Who is your sharpshooter?"

"That would be Emil over there," Finn waved back towards a young man holding a standard infantry carbine. "Don't listen for shit but he can pick a fly off the back of a keel deer at five hundred meters." Barton laughed dutifully, looking back to see that his men were helping direct their transportation through the drainage ditch.

"Okay, Finn," he turned back to the militiaman. "We're going to reinforce this position and build on what you have here. This is still the most logical point for the Darshik to try to secure a main artery into Westfall so they'll likely be back once they realize their probing attack was decimated here."

"What do they want?" the young man Finn had introduced as Emil said as he walked forward.

"We don't know, son," Barton shrugged. "They seem to have some definite goal in mind though; they're not just wiping out planets like the last aliens that came through. That at least gives us a fighting chance." Everyone jumped as white-hot flames erupted from an apparatus being manned by two of the Marines wearing hazardous material protective gear. Finn looked to Barton questioningly.

"Plasma," he explained. "That's a sort of self-contained, miniaturized version of a starship's engine. CENTCOM's eggheads say that after an engagement we need to burn the remains at the earliest convenience. They've not found any pathogens on the alien biological remains that could interact with human physiology, but they don't want to take the chance."

"So what do you need from us, Sergeant?" Finn asked, getting down to business.

"I need a tally of your personnel and weaponry as well as any machinery you have in the area that can be used to further enhance this position," Barton said.

"How long do you think we have until they return?" Finn asked.

"I wish I could say," Barton said with a frown, damning to hell the fact they had next to no aerial recon options available save for two underpowered, short-range drones.

****

"Sergeant Barton has checked in, sir. His squad has secured Objective Bravo and is requesting reinforcements to hold it."

"Send Charlie Company to relieve Sergeant Barton," Major Lucas Baer said to his com operator. "I want him brought back to HQ and debriefed."

"Yes, sir."

Baer squinted at the map again. A single company to hold that position wasn't enough, but he was spread so thin there were no Marines to spare. It didn't help that Command had absolutely no clue as to what the Darshik objective was with their invasion. They were committing large numbers of troops to secure highly populated areas, but were seeming to ignore key infrastructure and manufacturing centers. Once they subdued and were containing cities, they did nothing to threaten or harm the civilian population. They refused all attempts at communication and used their orbital superiority sparingly, only calling in strikes from their warships on the most stubborn human defensive positions.

If his superiors were to ask him, which they hadn't, he would swear he saw parallels in how the Darshik were approaching the opening battles to some of humanity's ancient, politically driven wars. In a way he found an odd comfort in that. He'd studied the Phage War extensively and what little declassified information there was had terrified him. At least the Darshik could be met in battle, killed, and definitely had a specific objective they wished to attain. That gave them options in that they could fight to deny them that objective or surrender it with concessions, a far cry better than the war of extermination the Phage had brought to them.

There was another aspect of the Battle for Juwel that concerned him; what would the newly formed United Terran Federation do if they couldn't break the blockade and get material support to the planet? From his contacts in Fleet that he trusted, Baer knew CENTCOM had been more than willing to sacrifice the Frontier planets to the Phage and pull vital combat forces back to the core worlds and hope the enemy just went away. Juwel, while an established and important colony world, might fall into the category of "acceptable loss" if Starfleet couldn't find a way to get past the Darshik warships in the outer system.

"Major, Alpha Company is reporting no enemy contact at the water treatment facility. They've secured the compound and are digging in," the com operator said. "Orders?"

"Tell Captain Anders to hold his position and keep us posted," Baer said, resisting the urge to shrug in exasperation. What the hell game were these aliens playing?

"Make sure all of our updates are getting back to Command."

"Yes, sir."

Chapter 3

"Helm answering all stop, sir."

"Thank you," Senior Captain Jackson Wolfe said absently, still working on something on his tile. "OPS! Have you recalculated our course yet?"

"I'm still working on it, sir," the OPS officer said nervously. "With all due respect, there's little precedence for what you're asking, Captain."

"Nonsense," Jackson said calmly. "It's a maneuver we routinely executed in the Ninth."

"This isn't a destroyer, Captain," the XO said gently from where he sat at the tactical station.

"This ship has more than enough sensor capability and engine power to do as required with a reasonable assumption that it will be successful," Jackson said, turning his full attention onto his squeamish bridge crew. "Let me be clear: We *are* doing this. The Darshik have figured out roughly where the jump points are into the Juwel System from the established warp lanes and have protected them accordingly. We've lost seven starships since they established their blockade. If we do not find a way to get our payload to the Marines fighting on the surface soon we risk losing the system. At this point, calculated risks must be taken. Understood?"

A handful of faces just stared back at him blankly.

"That was not a rhetorical question," he said, letting some of his frustration seep into his voice. "Am I understood?"

"Yes, sir!" a ragged chorus came back.

"Good. Let's get to work and deal with the problems as they arise," Jackson continued. "XO, how go the repairs in Engineering?"

"On schedule, sir."

"See that it doesn't slip; divert manpower if you have to, but we cannot be the piece that holds up the mission," Jackson said sternly. "Captain Wright is depending on us being where we need to be, when we need to be there. I do not intend to fail over a maintenance issue."

"Understood, Captain." The XO stood up. "I'll go down now and check on their progress."

The bridge of the *TFS Aludra Star* was cramped, not especially comfortable, and undermanned. The last observation was strictly her captain's opinion, of course, but he strongly felt the ship had too many tasks divided between too few people. He'd taken command of the *Star* when her former CO met with an unfortunate accident on the surface of New Sierra and CENTCOM could not afford for the ship to be delayed in its mission.

Circumstances had been such that just as Black Fleet Command was looking for a billet to put Jackson Wolfe into the *Star's* chair opened up. She was a *Vega*-class assault carrier though Jackson felt the designers may have been a bit too liberal with the term "assault." The ship was sturdy and only five years old, but there was little doubt her primary mission was to shuttle cargo from once place to another; she had been given only a smattering of armament with which to defend herself when dropping over a contested planet. He held no illusions about the ship going toe to toe with one of the Darshik cruisers and would be relying heavily on his destroyer escort to get the needed war-fighting materiel to the stranded Marines on Juwel.

It certainly wasn't the billet Jackson wanted, but it was the one he was expecting. Fleet Admiral Marcum, still serving as the CENTCOM Chief of Staff, wasn't going to put him back on the bridge of a mainline warship after he'd come out to the Arcadia System and yanked him back into service from retirement. Jackson assumed that Marcum, never one of his biggest fans, had been forced by political considerations and would do the bare minimum to honor the request. Hence, Jackson Wolfe was given command of a glorified cargo hauler.

No matter. He would perform his duty to the best of his ability and wouldn't give the clowns in Command the satisfaction of seeing him dejected or openly embarrassed by what could only be viewed as a demotion. Celesta Wright was turning down command of battleships; Jackson Wolfe wasn't even asked to relieve a temporary skipper on an obsolete Fourth Fleet frigate.

"Sir, I believe I have our first course plotted," the OPS officer said. "Would you like to look it over?" Jackson bit back his initial response. On the *Star* his OPS officer was also his navigation specialist. The ship wasn't normally required to navigate outside of established and well-mapped space so the designers hadn't felt a dedicated navigation specialist was required with the duties being divided between the OPS officer and the helmsman. It was an oversight he felt was almost criminal in its ignorance.

"Send it over, Ensign Dole," he said calmly. "And exactly how much experience do you have, Ensign? I don't mean operating your station, I mean how much astral navigation have you been exposed to?"

"I have completed all requisite post-graduate courses after the Academy and have completed all specialized training when I was assigned to Black Fleet and the *Vega*-class," Dole said somewhat stiffly.

"This isn't an interrogation, Ensign," Jackson said, catching the tone. "I need to know what the crew capabilities are on this ship ... all of our lives and the lives of the people on Juwel could depend on it. Just assume that nothing I ask is meant as anything other than a CO who's being rushed to get a ship ready for deployment without much experience with either the class or the crew."

"Understood, Captain," Dole said.

Jackson let his OPS officer escape back to his work as he reviewed the first series of flight parameters that would take the *Star* out of the DeLonges System and most of the way to the Jewel System. The nav plan was sufficient and only required a few tweaks to make it serviceable for the mission. The navigation computers aboard the *Star* were much more capable than those on the *Blue Jacket* and, in some ways, better than what he had had on the *Ares*. Fleet engineers seemed to have made a legitimate effort to take the human error factor out of spaceflight with the starships that were rolling out. He ruefully had to admit that any outdated systems that might have been in place on the *Starwolf*-class destroyers were likely done so at his specific request when he was consulting on the design.

"Captain Wolfe, New Sierra Control has informed us that we're to stand by for our cargo," his com officer said. "It's being ferried out from the Platform now."

"Thank you, Lieutenant Epsen," Jackson said over his shoulder. "Please inform Engineering and Flight OPS to be ready to receive the drop shuttles."

"Aye aye, sir," Epsen said sharply, turning back to her terminal.

The *Vega*-class assault carrier was designed specifically to rapidly deploy troops and material onto a planet's surface. The ship's hull had actually been laid over two decades prior, but had been moved out of the shipyard and parked in orbit over a moon for the duration of the Phage War. Once that had ended and CENTCOM slowly got back around to trying to replenish a decimated Starfleet the hull had been pulled back in, the designs updated, and the ship finished.

All cargo was packed in up to twenty-seven drop shuttles, each capable of ferrying just over three hundred and fifty metric tons of cargo to the surface in their maximum load configuration. Two hundred and seventy-five if they wanted the shuttles to be able to get back to orbit. One *Vega*-class ship could be loaded with a formidable quick-reaction force for fast interdictions or contingencies. On this trip Jackson would be bringing reinforcements, critical equipment, ammunition, and specialists to Juwel to hold the planet against the Darshik incursion. He understood his burden as he doubted there would be another resupply attempt if the *Star* failed.

"Captain?" Ensign Dole asked hesitantly.

"Yes, sorry, Ensign." Jackson didn't look up. "Your course plot is fine. I'm sending it back to you now."

"Yes, sir … but … I had a question, if you don't mind."

"Of course, Ensign," Jackson said.

"Sir, how will we … how do you … I mean—" Dole trailed off. Jackson looked at him and thought he understood what he wanted to ask given the young officer's age.

"You're wondering about the mission, about combat, and whether this ship and crew is ready where others have already failed," Jackson said.

"Yes, sir."

Jackson glanced around and saw everyone on the bridge now staring at him. He had to wonder when the hell he'd gotten so old. They were all just a bunch of kids. The question wasn't necessarily appropriate given the time and place, and he'd have berated any of his other crews for it, but the wide-eyed looks he received stayed his gut reaction.

"If I didn't think the *Star* and her crew were ready, I wouldn't be sitting here, Ensign," he said finally, standing to address everyone. "I'm many things, depending on the rumors you believe, but suicidal is not one of them.

"I know you have doubts, but believe me ... when it comes time for you to do your jobs, you'll put them aside. Think of those Marines and civilians on the surface of that planet, being attacked with impunity by a superior alien force. Imagine their fear and hopelessness. We can do something about that.

"We won't be alone, either. The *Star* will be flying into battle with as strong an escort as you could ever want: The Ninth Squadron will go in first and Captain Wright will clear the way to the planet so that we can launch our shuttles and then escape. Have faith in your ship, have faith in yourselves, and have faith in each other."

"Y'all better fucking listen to the captain," a harsh voice barked from the hatchway. "You know who he is and know where he's been. You do what he says and you damn well do it *when* he says it and maybe we all make it home from this mission."

"Thank you, Chief Green," Jackson said, resisting the urge to roll his eyes. Against all odds he'd managed to talk the salty master chief into delaying his retirement and coming along with him for one last cruise. The old spacer was still an imposing figure and Jackson knew that despite his penchant for casual, often shocking profanity he would be a calming presence for the untested crew.

"My pleasure, Captain," Green nodded, never uncrossing his massive arms as he surveyed the young officers. Jackson mostly believed what he was telling them, but either way they were flying the mission. The fact that the Darshik were allowing them the chance to stand and fight meant that this mission had a more significant impact than some of the hopeless last stands he'd witnessed against the Phage.

He did take comfort in the fact that Celesta Wright would be clearing his path. If nothing else he had faith in her. She wouldn't let him down.

****

"What in the hell is this!?" Celesta snarled, throwing the tile down on her desk.

"New orders, ma'am," Commander Barrett said, stoic in the face of his captain's outburst.

"No, shit, Commander!" she said acidly. "What I want to know is why we're being pulled out of formation right before the assault carrier is loaded and deployed."

"I wasn't told why, ma'am," Barrett said, fidgeting uncomfortably.

"Spill it, Commander," Celesta said with a sigh. "We're in a secure office here."

"When I saw that the Ninth was being pulled off the escort assignment I had Lieutenant Accari use his back channels to try and find out why," Barrett said. Celesta fixed him with a flat look.

"Let's not tiptoe around what our intrepid young OPS officer is doing, Mr. Barrett," she said. "He's pulling information by seemingly taking advantage of the infatuation of a particular young woman who happens to be the Chief of Staff's aide and is willing to violate her oath to curry favor with him. I do not think we should be encouraging this for more than a few reasons."

"Understood, ma'am," Barrett nodded. "But ... since the damage is done, would you like to know what he found out?" When Celesta just nodded once he went on. "You'll be getting a secondary set of orders from Admiral Pitt. The *Icarus* is being pulled off the line and given a new assignment; the Ushin have made contact and want to talk."

"The last time that happened it sparked off an interstellar war," Celesta scoffed. "So we're to escort another consular ship?"

"No, ma'am," Barrett said. "If Accari's source is accurate *we* will be the consular ship. The *Icarus* will fly the flag and carry the VIP all the way to the rendezvous. Alone."

"Well isn't that just wonderful," Celesta said through clenched teeth. "And who will the dignitary be?"

"No idea, ma'am," Barrett said. "Since there are only two ships left in the squadron and the *Icarus* is being pulled, Command has decided to re-task the mission to the 508th in Fourth Fleet. Three *Intrepid*-class destroyers."

"Very well," Celesta said, forcing a calm exterior. "Please stand down the crew until we get these new orders."

"Aye aye, ma'am."

This wasn't good news. Captain Wolfe was counting on her to make sure the *Aludra Star* could make it down to Juwel unmolested and reinforce the defending Marines and militia. Despite the matter being taken completely out of her hands, she felt like she was letting him down.

Her anger deepened as she read through the guts of the new orders and realized she wouldn't even be permitted to warn Wolfe that the *Icarus* wouldn't be there. A strict com silence order had been imposed as an operational security measure. Obviously CENTCOM was worried about potential leaks regarding such a delicate mission before they could get her ship prepped and on the way. There was no way for her to warn him that the Ninth was being pulled, nor could she reach out to the Fourth Fleet skippers to give them all the pre-mission planning her staff had already put in. She understood the reasoning for the precautions, but it was still galling.

"Bridge, this is Captain Wright," she said, waiting for the computer to chirp, indicating the intercom channel was open.

"*Go ahead, Captain.*"

"Inform Flight OPS I will require a shuttle to take Commander Barrett and myself to New Sierra Platform within the hour," Celesta said.

"*Aye aye, ma'am.*"

****

"So … cut the bullshit. What do you make of this?"

"I don't think it's a ruse, Mr. President," Franco Sala said after a moment's thought. Sala was the Director of CENTCOM Intelligence Section, formerly the Central Intelligence Service when it operated under the old Confederate charter. The reorganization brought the CIS's formidable assets under the umbrella of the new United Terran Federation's military command structure. Sala, a tall, willowy man with dark eyes and an olive complexion had been brought over to resume his old post for the sake of continuity, but President Augustus Wellington didn't trust or even particularly like the man. The former senator had to admit, however, that the sneaky bastard knew his business.

"So why, after they led our taskforce into a trap meant to wipe it out, are they coming back with hat in hand?" Wellington asked. The President was leaning back in his overstuffed office chair and looking worse for wear as his inner circle briefed him on the latest developments.

"Based on our post-mission analysis of the data from the com drone Senior Captain Wright rigged to return from that Darshik system we suspect they may have betrayed us under duress," Sala said, steepling his fingers. "When she destroyed that dormant Super Alpha in what was likely a somewhat misguided effort at revenge, we clearly saw from the Jacobson drone sensor feeds that the Darshik ships immediately turned on the Ushin ships in that system."

"Admiral, do you agree with that assessment?" Wellington asked.

"All but the part of Captain Wright's actions being *misguided,*" Fleet Admiral Marcum said from where he sat opposite Sala. "Celesta saw an opportunity to inflict serious psychological damage on the enemy and took it. I commend her initiative and without her *misguided* actions we'd not have any of the data the director used in his recent analysis."

"We're not here for a dick-measuring contest," Wellington growled. "Sala, I have no interest in cheap shots at our field commanders couched as hindsight analysis. Wright made a call under duress and cut-off from the chain of command, it's what she's there for and I agree with her snap judgement. Marcum ... control your killer instincts; we don't have a lot of time before Ambassador Cole will be here and the *Icarus* is on her way."

Ambassador Cole had been the original diplomat sent to negotiate with the Ushin. His personal ship had been destroyed in the battle over New Sierra but he'd managed to get to a lifeboat along with about half the *John Arden's* crew; he wasn't recovered for nearly a full week due to all the debris and wreckage in local space. Despite the ordeal, he'd insisted that he be allowed to continue his work with the new alien species. The President had a fairly neutral opinion of Cole, but since he had nobody better in mind for the job he allowed him to retain his position.

"Which brings up another point, Mr. President," Sala said. "Do we really feel that sending a warship sends the best message?"

"I think it sends the *perfect* message." Wellington's eyes bored into Sala's. "And not just any warship and any commander ... the *same* ship and captain that eluded their trap and bloodied their nose. The Ushin will know before negotiations even restart that we do not trust them and as far as the Terran Federation is concerned we are on wartime footing and it is they who need to convince us otherwise."

Sala just swallowed hard. "Very bold, sir," he said finally. "I assume you have a contingency plan if this provokes the Ushin and we find ourselves in a two-front war?"

"There are no contingencies in this war, Director Sala," Wellington said quietly. "It's all or nothing. We don't have the reserves to play games and I'm not giving the Ushin another opening to screw us like they did the last time. Now … let's get down to the guts of this. Cole needs to know exactly what he's being empowered to offer and what he needs to turn down flat. *That* is the reason you were summoned and you've wasted enough time before we'll have to sell this idea to whom I'm certain will be an unenthusiastic Captain Wright."

Chapter 4

"Message is authenticated, sir," the com operator said over his shoulder. "Command is verifying that a drone made it through and sent a valid update."

"Is Command saying whether they're going to disseminate the information to the forward units?" Major Baer said, resisting the urge to roll his eyes in front of his troops. CENTCOM had been trying to get com drones into the system for weeks and the Darshik had shown that they were quite adept at knocking them down before they could broadcast their payload to the planet. The fact they couldn't get resupplied and reinforced was bad enough, but the com blackout had an especially demoralizing effect. It was heartening to know that CENTCOM hadn't given up and was still at least trying to get a message to them.

"It's coming in now, sir," the operator said, surprising Baer. "It's listed for your eyes only ... here." The young enlisted man handed over a secure tile from his gear bag, the screen already flashing a green circle where Baer had to press his thumb to provide a biometric reading. After that he entered his ten-digit authentication code twice and was then rewarded with a text only message from Colonel Rucker himself, the Marine officer leading their cut-off detachment.

At 0350 GST we received a full transmission from an inbound com drone before the Darshik blockade destroyed it. CENTCOM is sending a relief fleet to stabilize the ground campaign and take back contested space within the Juwel System. We expect the first combat elements of this convoy no earlier than two weeks from receipt of this message.

I have also learned that Captains Celesta Wright and Jackson Wolfe will be commanding two of the ships being sent. I take this as a good sign that CENTCOM takes the threat here seriously and does not intend to withdraw and allow the Darshik to secure their hold on this planet.

Disseminate this information to your Marines as you see fit. This will not be an easy time waiting for relief assuming that Wright and Wolfe can make it through the blockade at all. For now we will continue to fight the enemy directly, but I want all my officers to be planning ahead in case we need to dissolve into the population and continue operations as a guerilla force. Carry on, Marines.

Col. Rucker

"Good news, sir?" Baer turned and saw Sergeant Willy Barton leaning against the wheel of one of the few armored personnel carriers that had made it to the surface and was now serving as a mobile command post.

"It's not all bad news," he said, forcing a smile. "CENTCOM got word through the blockade … they're sending a relief convoy."

"They've sent two so far, Major," Barton said. "It hasn't helped so far."

"Well now Fleet is sending their top guns," Baer said. "Captain Wolfe and Captain Wright will be leading the relief convoy."

Barton whistled, pushing off the APC's wheel. "I doubt Fleet would risk those two unless they were certain they could get through ... not for one colony planet out near the Frontier," he said. "The PR nightmare alone if both were lost is something I don't think the new Federation government can afford."

"I wasn't aware you were so politically savvy, Sergeant," Baer said. "I happen to agree with your assessment, however. Please get your squad ready ... you'll be rejoining your platoon shortly. Help is still some time away and there's still aliens to kill."

"Aye aye, sir," Barton said, his arm moving up slightly before he caught himself. While Baer doubted there were Darshik snipers hiding in the trees he was still thankful Barton had remembered not to salute him while so close to the front lines.

He watched one of his best squad leaders walk away with some sense of regret. It was important for his Marines to remain motivated and to have some sense of hope while they fought, but he feared that even if the relief convoy made it to Juwel the advance detachment would be long dead. Time was not on their side and the enemy was moving fresh troops in theater almost continually. But telling Sergeant Barton that would accomplish nothing other than to negatively impact his ability to operate in the field. Colonel Rucker had given him carte blanche with the information the com drone had brought, so for the moment he decided he would bias what he told his people in the direction of optimism.

If he were being honest with even himself he put no stock in the news that CENTCOM was dispatching two of its most infamous ship masters to free Juwel. The names were impressive, but he looked upon the reported exploits of Jackson Wolfe and Celesta Wright with a certain amount of skepticism. It was entirely possible, even likely, that the old Confederacy had inflated or fabricated these stories for morale or to deflect from an unpleasant truth. The next few weeks would tell whether these captains lived up to their vaunted legends or if another load of spacers was about to get blasted out of the sky.

****

"Where's our local expert?" Barton asked as his squad milled around the bed of the large agricultural truck they'd been riding in. They'd taken the time to make some improvements as he could see hastily welded mounting platforms for their machine guns and some light armor added using what metal they could scavenge.

"He's with Spencer getting some time on the ER," Corporal Alejandro Castillo said from where he was holding up a steel plate another PFC was tack-welding to the truck. "We figured if he was going to be rolling with us we may as well take advantage of his shooting ability."

"Thanks," Barton said with a wave, using the hand to shield his eyes as the welder blew brilliant sparks away from the point of contact. The "ER," as it was called, was the extended range version of the ST-22 standard infantry carbine. The weapon was officially designated the ST-

22ER and was designed so that it looked enough like its cousin that an enemy would have a difficult time picking out who were the designated marksmen in the squad.

As he walked towards the sound of weapons fire he reflected on how out of date the United Federation Marine Corps really was. Doctrine for their operations had been developed hundreds of years ago with an eye towards a conflict that had never taken place: humans at war with other humans. Now, with these aliens, it was all out the window. Things like not saluting officers near the front and disguising their own snipers seemed silly against such a foe, but tradition was a powerful, sometimes comforting force that they could grab onto in times like this. He was loath to admit it, but the Corps had really become little more than ceremonial and crowd-control troops over the centuries.

"Cease fire!" Barton nodded to the PFC acting as a range safety officer as the young civilian and one of his squads DMs safed their weapons and stood up.

"Emil, right?" Barton asked. "How's the training going?"

"Just a slight learning curve for the modern optics, Sergeant," the PFC said. "But he's already shooting much better than he would need to if he was qualifying on the ER."

"Excellent," Barton said. "And you're sure you want to do this? I'm not going to lie to you, Emil … this is going to be a dangerous trip."

"I'm ready, sir," Emil said, his mouth pressed into a thin line.

"I'm not an officer so don't call me sir. Sergeant, Sarge, or Barton are all acceptable," Barton said with a reassuring smile. "If you yell *sir* and it's something important I'm likely to ignore you."

"Yes, si—Sergeant," Emil caught himself.

"You three police this area and then get back to the truck," Barton said. "We'll be moving out once it's dark so it wouldn't be a bad idea to try and catch a few hours of sleep and get yourself fed while we're at the command post."

"We have a mission, Sarge?" the PFC asked.

"Yes we do, Pritchett," Barton smiled humorlessly. "Recon."

A chorus of curses and groans met this news. Recon patrols were long and put them beyond the range of any reasonable expectation of being reinforced. The bitch of it was they weren't trained specifically for recon missions, but they were all that Major Baer had to send.

****

Emil's stomach was in knots as the old truck bounced across the rutted access road. He didn't know why the hell he had volunteered to go with the Marines as a local guide when they'd asked old Finn for somebody reliable. At the time he'd wanted to make up for freezing when the enemy had made initial contact outside their small town, but now he felt like all he'd done was make another grave mistake to atone for the first.

He was no fighter. Being surrounded by professional soldiers, warriors, and listening to their casual banter and gallows humor only reinforced how utterly out of his element he really was. He could shoot, sure, but the exotic rifle that had been placed in his hands after just a cursory explanation of how it worked was more intimidating than it was comforting. The fact the private instructing him seemed to feel that he was supposed to be what they called a designated marksman made it even worse.

"Hey kid," a voice called out. He peered around and saw Sergeant Barton staring at him intently. When he caught Emil's eye he waved him over to sit next to him, gesturing for the com operator to take the bench opposite.

"You're scared," Barton said matter-of-factly once Emil had sat down. The sergeant was leaning in so that he wasn't broadcasting the conversation to the entire truck. "There's no need to try and hide that. All these jarheads talking about killing and dying are also scared, it's just their way of dealing with it."

"I'm no soldier, Sarge," Emil said. "I just don't want to—"

"This is the first war human infantry has fought since before the first starships went into space," Barton interrupted him. "That's hundreds of years … nobody on this truck has had shots fired at them in anger before this Darshik mess. I appreciate that you volunteered when nobody else stepped up, but I'm not asking you to be a hero. Just help us as you can with your knowledge of the area and the people."

"That I can do," Emil said. "I heard one of your troops say that Captain Wright was on her way to Juwel; is that true?"

"That's what I was told," Barton said neutrally.

"I suppose if anyone can beat the blockade it's her," Emil said. "I can't even imagine what it must be like … flying on a starship between the worlds."

"Mostly long and boring," Barton smiled indulgently. "There aren't any windows and there's nothing to see anyway until you get really, really close to something. The reality is that it's weeks of sitting around trying not to think about the laws of physics a ship built by the lowest bidder is breaking while you're inside of it."

Emil laughed at that. "Still," he went on, "to just see what else is out there. I was born here and thanks to this war I'll probably never get the chance to leave."

"Oh, I wouldn't say never. Things are bound to—"

Barton never got to finish his sentence as the world around them erupted into fire and Emil was thrown out of the open truck bed, landing hard enough on his back to knock the wind out of him.

When he was finally able to force a breath into his lungs he saw the truck was still rolling slowly along in the distance and was completely consumed by fire. As he stared another explosion obliterated the vehicle and blinded him for a moment while he still tried to figure out what the hell had just happened. He was surprised that he was still holding his borrowed rifle and rolled over onto his hands and knees, taking stock of himself and equally shocked to find that he seemed to be okay. He'd been flung clear and had landed in the loose soil around an irrigation outlet.

"Emil! Are you hurt?"

Emil looked up at the voice, his ears still ringing and his wits a bit scrambled. He blinked as the bloody visage of Sergeant Barton came into view. "Are you hurt?" the Marine repeated.

"I … I don't think so," he finally got out.

"Then on your feet," Barton said, looking around wildly. "We have to move. That was enemy light artillery; they know we're here. Let's go!" The sergeant dragged Emil to his feet and gave him a none-to-gentle shove towards a treeline a few hundred meters away. "Run, damn you!"

As Emil ran wildly into the night he risked a look back over his shoulder and saw enemy soldiers approaching the still-burning wreckage … lots of them. The sight caused him to put on an extra adrenaline-fueled burst of speed and he soon caught up with Barton as they raced for the dubious cover of the treeline. When they reached it Barton pulled him down and put his finger to his lips, ordering him to silence as he scanned the scene with a thermal monocular.

"Do you want the good news, or the bad news?" he whispered finally.

"Let's start with good," Emil breathed.

"We're still alive."

"That's it?"

"That's it," Barton said. "The bad news is that we appear to be the only two of our squad left alive and the enemy is well behind what we thought was the front line and in sizable numbers. We also have no com equipment and the only gear that is left is what we're carrying."

"That's a lot of bad news," Emil said.

"Yes." Barton continued to survey the area for a few more minutes. "They don't appear interested in finding anyone who may have survived. They're turning back now. I don't suppose you happen to know where we are?"

Emil looked around for a landmark but nothing looked familiar in the weak light of the moons. Fighting down growing panic he tried to reason where they might be from where they had come from. "This whole area is large, corporate farms," he said. "Mostly tended to by automated equipment so if I'm right we're kilometers from the nearest house that might be able to send a message for us."

"Shit," Barton swore. "Well, let's pick a direction and get moving. We have to let Command know the enemy is on the move."

Chapter 5

"You asked to see me, Captain?"

Celesta looked up at Ambassador Cole and just stared for a long, uncomfortable moment. Cole, a trained diplomat, simply returned her gaze with his own unreadable one.

"I just want to make sure we don't have any misunderstandings before we transition out of this system, Mr. Ambassador," she said finally. "To that end I will be a bit blunt: This is not a mission I volunteered for nor do I particularly agree with its execution."

"In what way, Captain?" Cole asked politely. "May I sit?"

Celesta gestured to the chairs in front of her desk and nodded. "I think sending a single ship is foolish," she continued. "I think sending a warship might send the wrong message and I think sending the *Icarus* in particular is an overt provocation. I feel that the Diplomatic Corps would have been wiser to send a proper consular ship with a military escort if that was deemed necessary."

Cole looked ready to fire back and then stopped himself for a beat, taking in and releasing a deep breath. "While my normal response to a Fleet officer trying to dictate diplomatic strategy would be to tell you to follow your orders and stick to what you're qualified for, I do recognize that you're unique in your field, Captain," he said slowly. "You have more direct contact with alien species than most in government and your instincts have proven to be right more times than not, but I believe there's a flaw in your logic.

"We're not trying to win over the Ushin. We're going as a favor to let them try to convince us why we shouldn't view them as a direct enemy to humanity and act accordingly. At least, that's what we'll be making them think. The fact they reached back out to us after deliberately leading our taskforce into a trap has to mean something significant. I have my own theories, but we'll need to talk to them again to know for certain, and I'm the one who specifically requested the ship and captain that successfully attacked that Darshik system ... I think it sends precisely the right message."

"We may have to agree to disagree," Celesta said.

"Fair enough, but I think we're actually talking about something quite different," Cole said. "I know that your ship was pulled off the mission heading to the Juwel System, a mission that has your former mentor flying a glorified freighter into the teeth of an enemy blockade. In your position I would also likely view this new assignment with a certain lack of enthusiasm."

"I made no secret of my displeasure at the Ninth being pulled from the relief convoy," Celesta said calmly. "However, that has nothing to do with why I wanted to speak with you prior to departure. I just want you to understand that my first responsibility is to my ship and crew. Your mission may be the objective, but you do not command the *Icarus* and I won't put her in harm's way without good reason."

"I understand the chain of command on a ship underway," Cole said with an indulgent smile that made Celesta bristle. "I also am well-aware that this is a Fleet ship, not a diplomatic courier. You'll get no direct interference from me."

"And you have no set of signed orders on you that would allow you to legally assume command of this ship should I make any decisions you disagree with?" Celesta dug, knowing the ambassador had come out of a meeting with CENTCOM top brass before her shuttle had arrived at New Sierra Platform for her briefing.

Cole visibly squirmed. "There may have been some discussions regarding that, Captain, but I can assure you that I have no intention of trying such a foolish stunt," he said firmly. "We're on the same team ... if you truly feel the risk is too great in a given situation I have to trust you just as I hope that you'll trust me when I say that some risks might be necessary for the greater good." He took a deep breath before continuing. "I appreciate your position and your loyalty, Captain Wright ... but believe me when I tell you this is a mission vital to the survival of the Federation. If there's even a slim chance that relations can be patched with the Ushin to the point of extracting aid, even if it's only in the form of information, we have to take it."

"I think that just about covers things then, Mr. Ambassador," Celesta said with a nod. "As I said: I just want to make sure we fully understand each other before this mission begins."

"I think we do, Captain." Cole stood up and moved to leave. "I will stay out of the way while we make our way back out to the meeting point. I ... think that would be best for both of us."

Before she could answer he'd walked out of the office and closed the hatch behind him.

"That could have gone better," Celesta said to the ceiling. She'd called the ambassador to her office with the intent of firmly establishing her absolute authority as captain of the *Icarus* and to ensure he knew how displeased she was that her ship was pulled off the line for a mission that didn't require a destroyer. Instead, she felt Cole had managed to get the better of her during the exchange. He'd baited her into overextending and in hindsight she realized how childish she'd looked. Her personal desires aside there was one thing Admiral Marcum had said to her that kept ringing through her head.

"I know she's your first command, Celesta, but that ship belongs to the Terran Federation ..."

The *Icarus* was the property of the people of the United Terran Federation and their elected leadership had decided that the ship was needed in a place other than where she wanted to fly her. She'd have to suck it up, swallow the bitter disappointment of not being able to fly with Captain Wolfe again, and get down to the business at hand.

"Bridge, Captain," she called out.

"*Go ahead, Captain,*" Commander Barrett's voice came back immediately.

"Mr. Barrett … prepare the *Icarus* for departure," she said crisply. "I want to be underway within the hour and steaming for our jump point."

"*Preparing the Icarus for departure, aye,*" Barrett said. "*She'll be ready for movement by the time you get to the bridge, Captain.*"

"Very good, Commander." Celesta stood and straightened her uniform before marching out of her office, nodding at the Marine sentry her detachment commander automatically assigned to her when they were carrying passengers. As she walked up the passageway to the bridge she could feel the deck vibrate softly as power was fed to the propulsion systems in preparation for moving the destroyer out of high orbit over New Sierra. With any luck she would be able to fly out to the meeting point, Cole would get his work done quickly, and she could steam full bore back to Juwel.

****

"Captain Wolfe, what you're suggesting is—"

"Excuse me, Commander," Jackson interrupted the acting CO of the destroyer *Resolute* over the video conference link, "but I wasn't suggesting anything. I am informing you of the maneuver the *Aludra Star* will perform to enter the Juwel System, and as a courtesy to you I am strongly recommending you do the same."

"What I believe Commander Bevin was going to say, with all due respect, Senior Captain, is that the course you've shared with us is not a commonly accepted maneuver," Captain Sanders aboard the *Racer* said smoothly. "We're all quite familiar with your success in using non-authorized jump points, but even you have typically transitioned *further* from a system's primary star, not closer."

"This is true," Jackson nodded. "However, this situation requires a different tactic. Jumping in far outside the system would be a useless gesture, even if we tried to adjust to come in around the known jump points. The light from our transition would beat us by many hours to the picket ships, we would have to burn our engines hard for much longer to make it to Juwel in time, and we'd have to run silent so the enemy ships would have the advantage of surprise when deploying to meet us.

"Believe me, the usual method of transitioning short and sneaking the rest of the way in is simply unworkable due to time constraints and the fact the enemy is already looking for us. We're going to get one more shot to push the Darshik back out of the Juwel System … that means the *Star* has to make it to the planet *and* your ships need to completely eliminate the blockade."

The debate had been going on for the better part of an hour and Jackson knew he was no closer to convincing the skittish destroyer captains that drastic and decisive action was needed to successfully execute their mission than when he started. Checking the time on the wall display he relaxed and let the drama continue to play out. The *Star* was being loaded and her drop shuttles were still in the process of being inspected and loaded into the launch bays by Flight OPS.

One of the main problems was that despite being the ranking officer in the formation it was made clear by CENTCOM that he was not in overall command of the mission. It wasn't anything personal; traditionally overall responsibility was given to the senior officer serving aboard a ship of the line, not a combat cargo hauler like the *Star*. There were some practical reasons for this as well as it wouldn't make much sense for Jackson to be given tactical authority over the destroyer squadron when his ship's mission was to evade the enemy and deploy her shuttles as close to the planet as he could get.

"Captain Wolfe, while I appreciate your experience and enthusiasm, I'm afraid I just can't authorize this type of risk-taking," Senior Captain Edward Rawls said, exerting control over the informal meeting. Rawls was the overall mission commander despite the fact Wolfe had more time in grade and technically outranked him. Jackson knew of Rawls by reputation and was underwhelmed. A history of timidity and hiding behind procedure to avoid making the tough decisions were a couple of the reasons he had a poor opinion of the man's ability to command.

"Our ships will make the approach to the Juwel System as prescribed by CENTCOM approved navigational data," Rawls continued. "I would encourage you to fly in behind our ships and allow us to provide a screen per Fourth Fleet tactical doctrine so your assault carrier has a better chance of making it all the way to Juwel with her cargo."

Jackson wanted to point out that two larger formations had already smashed themselves against the Darshik blockade. By transitioning in right where they were expected the 508th destroyers would actually be giving away the presence of a Terran taskforce and deny him the opportunity to sneak down into the system unnoticed. He also wanted to tell the man that his blind adherence to procedure was likely going to get a lot of good spacers killed, a resource the Federation couldn't afford to waste needlessly. In the end he said neither.

"Command prerogative is yours, of course," he said, failing to keep the resignation out of his voice. "If you're unwilling to consider my plan then I would suggest adjusting your course and transitioning in short, but not so short that you have days of travel before you hit their lines. They'll be waiting for you."

"Thank you for your … concern, Captain Wolfe," Rawls said with a barely visible sneer. "I think we'll manage just fine. We're on schedule for an on-time departure and will begin pushing up out of orbit within the hour."

"We're also on schedule," Jackson said. "Drop shuttles are being inspected and prepped now; I expect to be underway within the hour as well."

"Very good," Rawls said. "If there's nothing else? Dismissed then … *Relentless* out."

Jackson reached over and terminated his channel link without signing off or even acknowledging the remaining commanders. Rawls's stubbornness was almost certain to get one or both of them killed. He stood and walked out of the cramped office, pausing to readjust his prosthetic leg. There was a series of hard, booming thumps that reverberated through the hull that let him know Flight OPS was loading the drop shuttles into the launch cradles.

The shuttles would fold their wings up and be pulled into the cradle where the crews would manually hook up the hard points. The flight crews for the shuttles would be arriving shortly as the port crews used tugs to maneuver the fueled and prepped drop shuttles out to the assault carrier. Once Flight OPS signed off on the loading and the pilots had gone down to do their final inspection he would be clear to get underway. He was anxious to try and beat the Fourth Fleet destroyers out of the system. They were significantly faster than the *Star* and he hoped that if he stuck to his original plan their arrival might still work as the diversion he would need to deploy his shuttles and try to bug out of the Juwel System without engaging the more capable enemy ships.

"Captain," the second watch OPS officer nodded to Jackson as he walked in. "Flight OPS is reporting that three shuttles are loaded and secured and they don't foresee any issues with the others."

"Thanks," Jackson said distractedly. "Tell them I want to be lighting engines the moment we're cleared to begin maneuvering. The shuttle pilots can check their rides as we fly out to the jump point."

"Aye, sir," the lieutenant said, disapproval etched on her face as she relayed his orders. He was surrounded by people who seemed almost religiously opposed to deviating from standard procedure. Normally the pilots would leisurely go through the shuttles, drinking coffee and joking with each other. The first time Jackson had observed the procedure he became convinced the pilots actually dragged out their checks on purpose as a sort of game, knowing that the ship wouldn't fire engines and leave orbit until they were satisfied.

He almost wished he could indulge them since that would mean they were on a relaxed schedule and not flying into the teeth of an enemy blockade that had so far proved to be damn near impenetrable. Jackson knew that some of the officers that had flown on assault carriers their entire career weren't all that enthusiastic about a destroyerman crashing the party and shaking up the way things had been done for generations. The readiness drills and combat exercises he ordered were met with grumbles and complaining, but the crew had started to show signs they were shaking off the lethargy he'd felt when he reported aboard the *Star*. Against their will, they were becoming a battle-ready crew. Even though they were much improved, Jackson was skeptical they were up to the task ahead of them. The Juwel mission would not be easy or over quickly.

For the thousandth time he wanted to find out who had pulled the Ninth off the missions and strangle the life from them. He'd be a lot more confident if Celesta Wright was commanding the *Icarus* in ahead of him than he was with Ed Rawls's squadron of *Intrepid*-class ships.

Chapter 6

"Coming onto final course, Captain," the OPS officer called out. The *Aludra Star* was steaming up the well away from the planet New Sierra, her engines running at full power. Unlike her destroyer escorts that were able to pull away from the planet quickly and make for their jump point, the heavily loaded assault carrier had to lumber around the planet through a series of transfer orbits before achieving enough velocity to break away and head into the outer system.

The carrier had a unique configuration in that while it only flew normally on two main magneto-plasma drive engines the ship was fitted with four MPDs. Both nacelles that flanked the main hull had two engines each in a stacked configuration. In fact, when Jackson had been researching his new command he'd learned that the *Vega*-class had originally been designed with four engines in mind, but somewhere during the unusual way in which the ship had been conceived, mothballed, and then hastily finished there'd been a serious miscommunication; the cooling systems and powerplant were unable to power all four engines at the same time, at least not for very long. Instead of redesigning and fabricating new parts for the ship Tsuyo's shipbuilders had left the two engines and renamed them as "spares," turning a serious mistake into a "feature."

The hell of it was that with all four engines the carrier would have a better acceleration profile than his first *Raptor*-class destroyer did and would have held her own even with the more modern *Starwolf*-class ships. The

Intrepid-class destroyers escorting him, an updated derivative design of the old *Raptor*-class, would have been left behind when they pushed for the jump point, not the other way around. There was an obvious tactical advantage to having the four engines but the designers and engineers made sure to put enough safeguards in so that an enterprising or panicked captain couldn't just fire up the other two and destroy the powerplant. As it stood the only way the auxiliary engines could be fired up was if the primary MPD in that nacelle failed ... of course when an MPD failed it was equally likely to take out the one sitting three meters away as not so the point was moot.

"Captain, Flight OPS reports that all drop shuttles are inspected and signed off on by their crews," Ensign Dole said. The first watch OPS officer was efficient, but showed a glaring lack of ambition and ingenuity. The fact he was still an ensign at all spoke volumes.

"Very good," Jackson said. "Inform Commander Chambliss that he is clear to do his own final inspection of the gangways, umbilicals, and hardmounts. Once he's signed off on those you can clear him to close the drop hatches."

"Aye, sir," Dole said and pulled his headset back up.

"Coms!"

"Yes, sir!" Lieutenant Epsen said, startled.

"Please have the Marine detachment commander report to the bridge personally," Jackson said. "I'd like to talk with him before we hit the jump point."

"Yes, sir."

The next few hours were a flurry of activity and at one point there was even a line outside the hatchway as officers queued up to see the captain on the cramped bridge. Chief Green's deep, harsh voice could be heard in the passageway telling people if they hadn't been summoned or it wasn't something vital to ship's operation to take a hike until they transitioned into warp.

Jackson was in the middle of discussing the quartering arrangements with the relief Marine detachment commander when three sharp blasts from klaxon alarms echoed through the ship.

"Drop hatches closing!" Ensign Dole's voice echoed on a slight delay over the intercom as the OPS officer cleared the areas one more time before commanding the computer to close the ship up. A few seconds later booming reverberations could be felt through the ship as the massive drop hatches swung closed and locked, the *Star*'s hull ringing like a bell.

"All hatches confirmed closed and locked, Captain," Dole said after a moment. "The *Star* is cleaned up and cleared for acceleration."

"Excellent," Jackson said. "Helm, bring the *Star* to transition velocity plus five, all ahead full."

"All engines ahead full, aye!" the helmsman said. "On course for jump point alpha, target velocity transition plus five." Jackson routinely liked to transition at five percent past the prescribed transition velocity from his days commanding destroyers. Even though the regulation had a cushion built into it he preferred to carry a little extra speed coming out the other side to be able to maneuver immediately before the mains were reengaged.

Jackson shook his head with bemusement as the *Star* rumbled and groaned under full acceleration. She sounded like she was coming apart but the acceleration numbers were a paltry forty-five g's. With a target velocity of just over .08c for transition it would take the ship fifty-eight hours to hit the jump point. He could bump his speed up, but with what he was now planning to do, thanks in no small part to Captain Rawls's incalcitrance, it wouldn't matter if they arrived late to the party. Actually, it would probably be preferable.

"Steady as she goes," he said, standing and grabbing his coffee mug. "Ensign, you have the bridge until Commander Simmons comes on duty."

"I have the bridge, aye," Dole said, then hesitated. "When is the XO due to come on watch, sir?"

Jackson made another mental checkbox in the "negative" column regarding his OPS officer. Anybody too timid to want to be in charge of a starship within a secure Terran system while it was just flying leisurely to a jump point just didn't have the mettle to command. "He'll be up shortly," Jackson said. "He's down briefing the drop shuttle flight crews."

"Yes, sir."

Jackson sighed mentally as he walked off the bridge. Back when he was an ensign he'd done anything and everything he could just for a chance at the big chair. He didn't hold it against Dole that he had no such aspirations; some people were just naturally followers. The problem arose in that on a warship there was no guarantee that any officer serving on the bridge wouldn't be called upon to take control of the ship in an emergency or combat situation. He'd watch his too old, too timid ensign carefully on the trip out and then make the final call before they hit the Juwel System as to whether he needed to be replaced or not.

****

"Secure from warp flight, bring the RDS online," Celesta said pensively.

"Retracting warp emitters now, Captain," Accari said. "RDS coming online, fifteen seconds until we're clear to maneuver."

"Very good," Celesta replied. "Tactical?"

"Passive scans in progress now, ma'am," Lieutenant Commander Adler said. "No signals were received when we transitioned in."

The *Icarus* had just completed the extended warp flight from the DeLonges System, home of the New Sierra Platform and the new capital system of the United Terran Federation, to the meeting place that had been dictated by the Ushin. Celesta had pushed the destroyer to complete the trip in a single leg in order to hopefully get there ahead of the alien delegation. She had a passing familiarity with the planet they'd chosen as she had been there once before; it was the planet discovered by the Tsuyo deep space probes that had been their original meeting place, now simply designated UW01 and pronounced by everyone in the Fleet as Ooo-won.

Her familiarity with navigating to the planet aside, she'd argued vehemently that CENTCOM change the venue to someplace either neutral or a system where they held a distinct advantage. She'd been curtly told that the diplomatic details were none of her concern and her only job was to get the *Icarus* to where it was supposed to be, when it was supposed to be there. Even though she'd ground her teeth and followed her orders she couldn't shake the feeling they were flying into yet another trap.

"RDS is up, ma'am," Accari broke into her thoughts. "Engineering has cleared the *Icarus* to maneuver. Warp drive emitters are stowed and the hatches are secured."

"Thank you, Lieutenant," Celesta stood up. "Nav! Plot us a decaying heliocentric course down into the system. I want to take advantage of the terrain so follow the pull of any planets or natural satellites in our path; the key is to try and appear as uninteresting as possible. OPS, tell CIC I want the towed array deployed once we're underway. We're remaining passive until I say otherwise." After the lessons learned during the previous war the CIC on Terran warships had come into its own; it was now a true nerve center for the ship's combat operations and not just a place to train up young officers or stash troublemakers.

"CIC confirms the towed array is ready for immediate deployment, ma'am," Accari said.

"Initial course is plotted and input, Captain," the specialist at Nav reported. "We don't have a complete workup on this system so I'll be making real-time adjustments as data becomes available."

"Very well," Celesta said, pacing the bridge. "Helm! You're clear to engage the RDS pod and come onto your first course. Ahead one-half."

"Engines ahead one-half, aye," the helmsman said, pushing the throttles up.

There was no sensation of movement or even a rumble of deck plates to tell her the *Icarus* was moving, just the acceleration and relative velocity numbers on the main display climbing told her the helmsman's commands had been executed. The new generation of reactionless drive system (RDS) that had been fitted to the *Icarus* after the prototype unit had been destroyed by a Darshik energy lance gave her little to complain about. The first unit had been unreliable, somewhat dangerous, and implemented far before it was ready to be put on an operational vessel.

The Gen III machinery, however, was an order of magnitude better. It had been properly integrated into her ship's power management system and attitude control computers so seamlessly that the drive's gravity fields worked in concert with their artificial gravity and didn't blow power junctions out at the slightest provocation. It was so reliable in testing, in fact, that Celesta had abandoned her standing order of keeping the MPD main engines primed and ready for instant engagement. Unless they were flying into imminent battle she ordered her engineers to keep the engines pre-heated but the plasma chambers were empty to keep the power draw to a minimum and reduce their thermal signature from the occasional pressure relief venting. By drastically reducing the thermal signature of her ship Celesta was able to become just a hole in space, drifting silently and listening.

"Any word from our contact, ma'am?" Commander Barrett asked as he walked onto the bridge. Celesta looked down and saw that it was thirty minutes prior to the start of second watch; she'd been on the bridge monitoring the passive sensor returns for over seven hours.

"None, XO," she stifled a yawn and relaxed her shoulders. "We're still some days early so I don't expect to receive a signal anytime soon. Let's go ahead and keep the ship on normal watch schedules and maintain a heightened state of alert. Has there been anything I need to know regarding our VIP?"

Barrett blinked at that. "Ambassador Cole? No, ma'am," he said. "He's been staying in his quarters other than to take meals in the officer's mess or occasionally go to the command deck lounge to read. Am I supposed to have Security keeping an eye on him?"

"No, no," Celesta said quickly. "He's a guest and has given no reason for distrust. I was just curious if he was interacting with the crew or not. Sometimes things slip out in the course of conversation."

"Ah," Barrett said. "No ... as I said, he's been keeping to himself. Probably by design now that I look at it from that point of view."

"You have the bridge, XO." Celesta grabbed her coffee mug and tile. "Don't hesitate to call if you pick up anything."

"I have the bridge, aye," Barrett said. "Have a good evening, Captain."

****

The *Icarus* slowly spiraled into the system, not actually named yet but given the reference designator Lima-211 by Navcom. They'd picked up nothing of interest for days. The ship's passive sensors coupled with the much more sensitive equipment aboard the towed array built an impressively detailed model of the Lima-211 System, but there was nothing other than the expected planets, asteroids, moons, and a single lonely comet in addition to the average G-type main sequence star.

"CIC is sending up an exception report, sir," the second watch OPS officer said. "This is a preliminary; they're still chewing through the raw data."

"Send it over to me as soon as you get it," Barrett said. "We'll look at it at the same time and then compare notes."

"Aye, sir."

An exception report was simply a formal write-up of a sensor anomaly that neither the computers nor the operators could identify but did not think to be threatening. Most exception reports were glanced at, filed away, and then ignored. But Barrett was bored and the review would at least be something to stimulate his mind while they waited for their Ushin contact.

"Coming to your terminal now, Commander."

"Thank you, Ensign," Barrett said absently as he accessed the file.

Barrett began reading the report summary and saw that the bulk of it pertained to a visual spectrum anomaly that had appeared briefly in the outer system. It was a non-uniform burst that dissipated quickly and was nineteen degrees port-aft of the *Icarus* at an estimated distance of three-point-eight billion kilometers when it was recorded, putting it more or less on the opposite side of the system. CIC was in the process of correlating any other spectral data to the event but their initial conclusions didn't include whether or not the flash was associated with any electromagnetic radiation or gravimetric distortion. Given how close to the primary star their line of sight to the occurrence crossed he expected it would be some time before they could dig out and isolate any relevant data.

"Do you think it could be the Ushin delegation arriving?" Barrett wondered aloud.

"Keep reading, sir," the OPS officer said. Barrett scrolled through and found what his officer was referring to: *Anomaly is inconsistent with the transition flash of any known class of starship including those operated by the Ushin or the Darshik.*

"So much for that theory," Barrett muttered as he kept reading. He saw that the techs down in CIC also calculated that the intensity of the anomaly was far too weak to be a transition flash with one caveat: It was close to what they would expect to see for a transitioning Broadhead-class ship.

The small, stealthy, long-range reconnaissance ships were ultra-rare and even their existence was classified. Barrett knew of one person who was currently operating one of the small vessels and it just so happened that he had a connection to the captain, but he didn't think CENTCOM would bother sending Agent Pike this far out of

Terran space just to keep an eye on them when the *Icarus* was carrying ten point-to-point com drones for the mission.

By the end of the lengthy report all he could conclude was that the CIC had no idea what the flash was and they weren't at all confident that even given further data they would figure it out. But, for the sake of something to do, they'd keep trying.

It was some five hours later when CIC had something else to report that made Barrett dismiss the exception report from his mind completely.

"Verified transition flash," the tactical officer said. "Ushin vessel ... cruiser-class. Single event detected."

"So it looks like they honored their side of the deal and came with one ship as well," Barrett said. "Coms! Inform the captain that we have initial confirmation that the Ushin delegation has arrived in-system."

"Aye, sir," the coms officer said, fumbling with her headset to send the message.

"Report!" Celesta Wright demanded as she stormed onto the bridge. Barrett was a little taken aback by her demeanor and it must have showed.

"Sorry, XO," she said more calmly. "Too much coffee this morning. What do we have?"

"Single cruiser-class vessel, transition flash consistent with Ushin make and right on schedule according to the timetable they provided us," Barrett said while vacating the big chair and logging in to the terminal at his own station.

"Coms! Please have our VIP escorted to the bridge," she said before turning back to Barrett. "We don't know if they'll try to send any radio communications first before we all meet over that planet." Barrett just nodded.

"Permission to come on the bridge, Captain," an impeccably dressed Ambassador Cole said respectfully from the hatchway not even five minutes later, trailed by his Marine escort. Barrett appreciated the show of respect for his captain from the civilian official. His estimation of the man ticked up a notch from that simple act, although the cynic in him had to admit that as a trained diplomat it could have been a calculated move by Cole to elicit just that sort of reaction from the bridge crew.

"Granted, Mr. Ambassador," Celesta said. "We have initial confirmation that the Ushin delegation has arrived on time and alone, or at least that *some* Ushin cruiser is here with us. Recommendations?"

Cole froze for a moment, clearly not expecting that last part. "I believe caution is in order, Captain Wright," he said after a moment. "As you say, we only know that a ship has arrived, not necessarily the ship we're waiting for. Perhaps it would be prudent to wait and see if they attempt to contact us first before exposing the *Icarus*. I of course defer to you in all matters regarding this phase of the mission, however."

"You and I happen to be in complete agreement this time, Ambassador," Celesta said and gestured to a seat that was to the left of the command chair and slightly behind the OPS station. Cole nodded and sat down in the seat, looking relaxed and confident.

"Mr. Accari, please ensure that we're maintaining strict emission security protocols including visible wavelength light emissions," Barrett said. "Coms, have CIC begin sending up predictive courses for the ship assuming that they're pushing towards the planet."

"Aye, sir."

"What are your thoughts, XO?" Celesta asked.

"Given our current course and speed we'll likely intersect their flightpath before we're inside the orbit of the sixth planet," Barrett said, pointing to the two-dimensional map of the star system that was on the main display. "More specifically, we'll be crossing where they've already been if they fly the nominal approach to the planet given what we know about their ships' performance."

"How does this help us?" Celesta prodded, sounding a tad impatient.

"The Ushin use plasma thrust main drives," Barrett continued. "If we increase velocity we can swing around and come in behind them close enough for our passive sensors to pick up their exhaust trail. If we can pick their ship out of the clutter we can begin to actively track them. This is all assuming that we've not heard from them beforehand … if they begin broadcasting a greeting then all of this goes out the airlock."

Barrett paused as his captain tapped at her chin with a forefinger, staring at the tactical layouts on the main display, her eyes narrowed slightly.

"While I think it could be construed as mildly aggressive to sneak around and position a destroyer behind their cruiser on a diplomatic mission, I also think they deserve no less," she said finally. "Ambassador?"

"As I said, Captain: I am merely an observer at this stage," Cole said though he looked to be in some distress at the idea of rolling in behind the other ship without announcing their presence.

"Nav! Calculate the velocity increase needed to execute Commander Barrett's plan," Celesta ordered. "I don't want any drastic changes in acceleration, slow and steady."

"Aye aye, ma'am," the specialist said. "I've been running the numbers already while the XO was talking … new acceleration profile going to the helm now."

"Execute at your discretion, helmsman," Celesta sat in her seat and leaned back.

"Engines ahead one-third, aye." The helmsman pushed the throttles up. "Increasing relative velocity by twenty-eight percent, no change in course."

Barrett was happy that Captain Wright had decided to follow his suggestion, but he was also painfully aware that it was now a matter of record in the ship's log that he'd been the one to recommend the change to their plan. Any failure would now lead right back to him. What surprised him was that he wasn't nervous or scared of the consequences, but rather—what was it?—exhilarated? Maybe that was the best way to describe what he was feeling as, for a brief moment, he wasn't a background player in such an important operation. He started to understand what it was Captain Wolfe had tried to tell him those years ago when he was serving on the *Blue Jacket* as a tactical officer and had hesitated at a critical moment. Wolfe had told him that command wasn't for everyone, and there was no shame in that. Now, for the first time in his career, Michael Barrett began to seriously consider that he might have a ship of his own someday soon.

Chapter 7

"What road is this?"

"It might be Westfall Bypass Twenty-One, or it could be the James Weber Highway," Emil said uncertainly. "I can't be sure how far south we've come in the dark." Sergeant Barton tried to contain his irritation with the young civilian as he scanned the area with a thermal sight.

"You're not much of a local area expert," he said flatly.

"I ... don't get around much," Emil said, his voice a mixture of embarrassment and defensiveness. "Didn't you guys have current maps of Juwel provided when you land?"

"Sure do," Barton said. "They were loaded on the tile that was in my pack when our truck was blown up, but point to you ... I should have loaded the local area onto my personal comlink before the patrol left. Can't send a message since it can't access the Mil-Net, but it still works as a mini tile."

The pair had been on the run since they escaped their vehicle being hit with what appeared to be a short-range mortar strike, but they hadn't escaped unnoticed. The Darshik soldiers had descended onto the wreck so quickly that Barton knew they'd been surveying the road before his patrol happened down it. They'd been cutting across fields and down small, unmarked roads in the agricultural area but so far had been unable to completely shake the three Darshik troops that had been tracking them.

He wasn't willing to let them come within range of Emil's sniper rifle since the kid wasn't a trained soldier and they were outnumbered. It would be better to take their chances at escaping than to try and make a stand given that the Darshik likely could call in either reinforcements or a fire mission before they could kill them all. What he found more than a little curious was the effort the enemy was putting into running down two stragglers. So far during the Juwel campaign they'd showed no interest in individual Marines or militia; all their efforts had been focused on controlling major logistical arteries and keeping the populations of major urban centers in their cities.

"How's it look?" Emil asked nervously.

"Looks clear," Barton said, biting back on the retort that if he needed Emil to know something, he'd tell him. The kid was terrified and, honestly, so was he. He wasn't NOVA or Marine SpecOps, he was a staff sergeant in 2nd Marine Expeditionary Battalion and being stranded behind enemy lines alone wasn't something he'd trained for. But he swallowed down his fear and focused on the task at hand: getting back to HQ or finding a way to report in that the enemy was much closer to the rear than anyone had thought. The image of Darshik troops springing up in their hastily built forward operating base and slaughtering his friends and comrades drove him on.

"There's a small homestead about one and half kilometers across that highway," he went on. "It's dark and I'm not seeing any thermal signatures, so I doubt anyone is there, but maybe the grid power is still up and there's a way to send a message over your local com system."

Despite the best efforts of the old Terran Confederation there were no set standards for civilian com protocols, at least none that were adhered to. The frequency, modulation, and basic infrastructure usually varied significantly from planet to planet. Barton had a comlink that worked great when on a CENTCOM facility or a planet with a heavy Fleet presence, but on a planet like Juwel all it did was show the spinning antenna icon telling him that it couldn't acquire a signal. He knew from his intel briefs that the planet still utilized a lot of ground-based coms with extensive fiber optic networks even all the way out to isolated farms like the one he was staring at through his scope.

"Does it have its own water tower?" Emil asked suddenly.

"What the hell is a water tower?" Barton asked.

"It's a water tank up on pylons," Emil said. "Should be about twice the height of the barn."

"Why—never mind. Stand by," Barton said as he flicked the zoom switch on his underpowered optics. He scanned around a bit and saw something that was unmistakably what his young charge was talking about: a giant water tank up in the air for some reason. The sergeant was a city boy from Columbiana so he had to assume the bizarre apparatus had something to do with rural agriculture.

"I've got eyes on your tower," he said. "Why is this important?"

"I know what farm that is," Emil said. "It's a commune actually. Anyway … that's James Weber Highway in front of us."

"Well done," Barton nodded appreciatively. "Should we bother trying to see if there's anything there we can use?"

"They'll have food and water," Emil said quietly. "But I'm not sure about anything else. They're a strange bunch, keep mostly to themselves."

"Okay, let's move," Barton said with one more look around through the thermal sight. "I'm not picking up any movement and we haven't seen those Darshik trackers for a bit. It's going to be dawn soon so we need to get our asses in gear."

They moved quickly from their place of concealment and jogged up to the paved, six-lane highway. There was something eerie about walking across the major roadway in the dead silence with no vehicles to be heard or seen like some sort of post-apocalyptic hell. Once they'd crossed the highway Barton gave up any pretense of stealth and broke into a light jog, anxious to get to the farm and check it for com equipment and find a place to sit for a moment and collect his thoughts.

The "farm" ended up being a sort of compound that was fenced off and secured with a heavy gate that swung freely on its hinges, evidence the previous occupants had left in a hurry. What had Emil called it? A commune, that was it … although from some of the strange sculptures he was seeing in the gravel common area it was more likely a religious cult. Hopefully they weren't the type that didn't believe in communication with the outside world.

As Barton was walking across the open area, his boots softly crunching the gravel, he heard a metallic click and froze. He scanned the area and cursed the loss of his night vision optics for the tenth time since the attack on his patrol. The small thermal monocular was decent but of little use for wide field of view situations. The noise had been distinctive and very familiar so he went out on a limb and assumed it wasn't part of an elaborate Darshik ambush.

"We're human," he called out softly. "Hold your fire … we're with the Marine force trying to repel—"

"Sergeant Barton?" a voice called out.

"Yeah, it's me, Castillo," Barton said as the tension drained from his body. Being in someone's sights was always unpleasant and his hands shook slightly from the sudden adrenaline dump. A murky silhouette separated itself from one of the smaller buildings and started towards him, soon resolving into the smiling form of Corporal Alejandro Castillo, his ST-22 carbine slung over his shoulder.

"It's good to see you, Sarge," he said quietly. "Damn good."

"You too, Corporal," Barton whispered as he continued to look around. "Did you get a chance to recon this place?"

"Not much here," Castillo said as Emil walked up to the pair. The kid had taken it upon himself to walk around the backs of the buildings on the west side of the compound to clear them. The initiative had impressed Barton so he hadn't bothered to stop him from putting himself into unnecessary danger. This was Emil's planet and he had every right to take up arms and defend it, not just follow the Marines around like a lost puppy.

"Whoever lived here stripped the place bare when they evac'd," Castillo continued. "Found some dried rations and some clothes but nothing useful. I've only had time to check these two buildings, though." Barton followed Castillo's pointed finger to the two larger buildings near the back of the lot.

"What do you think, Emil?" he asked. "Is it worth searching the whole place?"

"If Corporal Castillo didn't find anything in either of the main dorms then I doubt we'll have much luck in the other buildings," Emil said. "I didn't have much interaction with these people but any communication equipment they might have would have been in there. The other buildings are storage and a couple storefronts to sell the crap they made in that barn over there. If they ran I would almost guarantee that they took any mobile com with them."

"Fuck," Barton swore softly, beginning to get antsy the longer they stood still. The Darshik troops were likely still trying to track them and had proved to be disturbingly good at it. "What are the chances they have a vehicle?"

"I'd imagine they took them when they left," Castillo said.

"Doesn't hurt to check." Emil shrugged, turned and walked towards the barn he'd indicated before. The two

Marines followed closely behind him, each covering a hemisphere with their rifles. Barton wanted to get moving, quickly, and try to warn HQ that the Darshik were operating well behind the lines and to be ready. The fact they couldn't get in touch with them somehow showed a glaring oversight in their kit, antiquated as it was. If not given full com ability then each member of a patrol should at least have an emergency beacon or something that would alert Command that all was not well with their forward units.

They found one of the smaller doors unlocked after unsuccessfully pulling on the larger, main door and slipped inside. It was near pitch black so Barton pulled his small tactical light and flicked on the switch.

"Damnit!" Castillo yelled. "Give me a warning next time, you almost fried my retinas!"

"I take it you still have your night vision optics?" Barton asked as he flicked the light off.

"Yeah, for all the fucking good they're doing me now," Castillo snapped. "All I see is purple spots."

"Sorry," Barton said. "Light coming back on." He played the beam over the unfamiliar equipment and work benches in the barn, pausing on sets of heavy tread marks in the dirt that indicated at least two large vehicles had rolled out of the building recently.

"Sergeant, over here," Emil's voice drifted over. When the two Marines reached him, he gestured to a pair of four-wheeled recreational off-road vehicles that were covered in what looked to be years of dust and grime.

"They're older than dirt, but this one still has half a charge and I think I can get that back-up generator over there running"—he pointed with his left hand to what looked like just another pile of junk—"and get the other one charged."

"How fast are these?" Castillo asked.

"Maybe seventy KPH over flat ground or a road." Emil shrugged. "Probably less since one will be carrying two people. That and they're not really that stable when running wide open. But a single charge for the batteries, assuming they're not degraded, will easily get us back to your HQ."

"How soon before you can determine if these are salvageable or not?" Barton asked.

"In twenty minutes I'll know if I can get the generator going," Emil said. "Say another ten after that before we know if these can take a charge."

"Get to it," Barton said. "If we can get these running it'll be worth the delay. Corporal Castillo and I will be outside standing watch; just give a quiet call if you need any help."

Emil nodded and peeled off his jacket, diving into the mess around the back-up generator that looked like it hadn't been touched in quite some time.

****

"We have them, Captain!"

"Calm yourself, Mr. Accari," Celesta said. "What do you have?"

"CIC confirms light anomaly off our port bow is indeed an Ushin cruiser-class ship," Accari said, looking chagrined at his outburst. "We're quartering into them at a range of approximately sixty-two million kilometers, twelve degrees of declination."

"Thank you, OPS," Celesta said. "Tactical! Begin tracking of confirmed Ushin bogey, maintain passive sensor posture but begin building a firing solution for the Shrikes so we're not caught flat-footed."

"Aye, ma'am," Adler said crisply.

The bridge was quiet as her crew went about their tasks and she was left to think about how she wanted to handle things now that they'd made contact. The Ushin, in her mind, were no different than the Darshik: an enemy of humanity, at least in deed if not declaration. But, she'd been sent as a diplomatic envoy so what was the protocol when approaching a ship belonging to a species that had tried to lead most of their fleet into an ambush?

She quickly put all considerations of the political ramifications of any course of action she might choose out of her mind. While her mission was to deliver the ambassador to the meeting point safely, her primary responsibility was still the safety of her ship and crew. There was nothing she'd been told so far from CENTCOM that made her any more inclined to trust the Ushin than she had when they'd led them into a Darshik trap.

"Nav, course correction; I want the *Icarus* to be on a pursuit course of the Ushin target," Celesta ordered.

"Using the least amount of acceleration possible I also want to close the range to ten million kilometers by the time they begin their course change to push for the planet." The planet they planned to meet over once again was on the far side of the system so the Ushin, with their plasma thrust engines, would have to respect the gravitational pull of the primary star more than she would with the *Icarus's* improved reactionless drive. Given what she'd seen of them so far she felt confident that they would fly on an arcing course that would allow them to intercept the planet's orbit and then chase it without requiring any extensive engine burns for a drastic course change.

"Course calculated and entered, ma'am," the chief called out from his position next to the young specialist at the nav station as he pointed to something on the display.

"Helm, you're clear to execute new course," Celesta said. "Tactical! Assume a defensive posture … I want our weapons primed for rapid deployment and a constantly updated firing solution for the Shrikes running. OPS, tell CIC they're now chiefly responsible for our sphere of awareness. Retract the towed array but continue monitoring with the passives, all frequencies, all directions."

"Aye, ma'am," Adler and Accari parroted each other.

"I'm not going to do anything provocative, Mr. Ambassador, but I refuse to be caught with my guard down so far from home." Celesta leaned in to where Cole was sitting. "I have no intention or desire to pick a fight with the Ushin cruiser."

"I have complete faith in your ability to execute our mission and ensure the ship makes it back to Terran space safely, Captain Wright," Cole said just at the perfect volume level to ensure the crew heard it but still appear that he was trying to have a private conversation. "It's why I specifically requested the *Icarus* for such a vital mission."

Celesta just grunted and leaned back into her seat. She knew for a fact it was Admiral Pitt that had pulled the *Icarus* off the line at the request of Admiral Marcum and with the approval of President Wellington, not to mention against her strident protests, and the ambassador had little to do with the decision. Marcum *was* trying to provoke rash action from the Ushin or at least throw them off balance during the negotiations by arriving in a ship they'd surely recognize from the previous engagements.

While she'd not been around too many actual ambassadors Cole seemed to fit the mold she'd constructed in her mind given her brief interactions with the old Confederacy's diplomatic corps. He was always on, always performing and maintaining character. The little throwaway comment meant to bolster the morale of her crew seemed to be something he did instinctually.

"Coms, please call the XO to the bridge. OPS, begin turnover to second watch," she said, ignoring the ambassador's comment. "We're going to compress the watch schedule so that first is back at station and settled before we'll likely see any further action from the … objective." She avoided using the word target in front of the ambassador, but it was still how she viewed the cruiser ahead of them.

****

Celesta's limited rack time was interrupted well before she intended to get up by the intercom in her stateroom and her personal comlink chirping out an alert. It only took a second for her brain to fully engage after being roused from a deep sleep and she silenced her comlink as she swung her legs over to the floor.

"This is Wright," she said loudly.

"*Captain, the Ushin cruiser has begun broadcasting a greeting,*" Commander Barrett's voice came over the intercom. "*They're still two and a half hours from their first projected course change given no change in velocity.*"

"How long until we're actually supposed to be here in this system?" Celesta asked, struggling to do the math in her still-fuzzy head.

"*About thirty-two hours, ma'am.*"

"Send no reply," she said, standing up and stretching. "Continue to pursue and monitor the cruiser and have CIC begin breaking down the broadcast to see if it's as innocuous as a simple greeting or if there's something piggybacking on the carrier. I'll be up in a few minutes. Wright out."

Less than ten minutes later Celesta stormed onto the bridge. "Let me hear it," she said sharply. "Go ahead and get the first watch bridge crew up here while we're at it."

"Coms, call up first watch," Barrett said while prodding the second watch OPS officer to begin the playback.

"*We convey our greetings to the emissaries of the powerful Terran Empire*," the message started out in a monotone, droning voice that was obviously artificially generated. "*We regret all misunderstandings and wish to open negotiations again. Eagerly we await your response.*"

"That's it, ma'am," Barrett said. "It pauses for twenty point two-two seconds and then repeats. They're still broadcasting it and CIC is looking for any repetitive patterns that appear incongruous with the message loop since the carrier frequency is being continuously pumped out."

"Get Ambassador Cole up here too," Celesta said, frowning. "He needs to hear this as soon as possible. In the meantime, maintain our posture; no return transmission of any kind. Nav! Update our acceleration profile; I don't want to close on the cruiser any more than we already are. Maintain our interval as best you can given the data from the passive array. OPS, give her a hand with an updated estimate from the tactical computers."

"Aye aye, Captain," the ensign at OPS said.

The ambassador arrived mere minutes later, impeccably dressed and groomed and looking fresh as ever despite having just gone to his quarters four hours prior. Celesta was duly impressed and that must have been telegraphed in her expression when Cole walked up to where they were huddled around the OPS station even as bleary-eyed first watch crew began filtering in.

"Despite being an insufferable diplomat, Captain, at one point I actually worked for a living," he said with a genuine, self-deprecating chuckle. "Once upon a time I served as an enlisted spacer on a Fourth Fleet frigate ... the old habits die hard. I can be dressed and out the hatch in less than two minutes given the proper motivation."

"I see," Celesta said neutrally, once again revising her opinion of her VIP passenger up a tick. "Well, Mr. Ambassador, it seems your Ushin friends have decided to try and make contact first. Play the message, Ensign."

Cole listened to the message in its entirety four times, his frown deepening each time it repeated. "And there were no other messages? No text embedded in the transmission?" he asked, obviously unhappy.

"Not that CIC has been able to mine out of the signal yet." Celesta shook her head. "You seem ... displeased. Were you expecting more in the initial contact attempt?"

"Since the specific content and raw data of the aliens' communication attempts are highly classified allow me to enlighten you, as I'm sure you've not been privy to it," Cole said. "Before I do, please understand that I'm not actually authorized to tell you any of this. But ... we're out here, and CENTCOM and the Federation are not. I think it might be prudent, under the circumstances, if you had all the pertinent information so that we can approach this problem together."

"Understood," Celesta nodded. "Nothing you say here goes past this bridge. Everybody got that?" A chorus of affirmatives and head nods within earshot of the captain followed.

"Very well," Cole sighed. "This message has me suspicious in that the Ushin don't even speak like this in real time. Their grasp of our language is much more firm and nuanced; this sounds like some of the very early attempts when the translation matrix was undeveloped. Why? Why the sudden reversion to the poor grammar and improper syntax?"

"How big of a difference are we talking about?" Commander Barrett asked.

"My last conversation with an Ushin representative was during the battle in the DeLonges System when they offered us over two dozen planets in exchange for military intervention on their behalf," Cole explained. "Their emissary spoke flawless Standard with a definite New American accent, which makes sense given that it was a Fourth Fleet exploration vessel that Tsuyo contracted to come out here when first contact was made. This message is reminiscent of those first clumsy attempts at two-way communication."

"And you feel there's no logical explanation for this?" Barrett asked.

"None that I can see," Cole said. "Granted I don't have much insight into Ushin culture so I can't say for sure how compartmentalized they are with regards to sharing information amongst themselves, but to think there were two distinct groups talking to humans that didn't have the same data available flies in the face of what I was told during the last meeting."

"I would say that makes an obvious answer pop out," Celesta said. "We haven't been dealing with the same group of Ushin every time. Either that or there's a faction operating outside the authority of their government."

"Or the battle over DeLonges was a setup and the Ushin ships and delegation were actually Darshik," Accari said absently before looking around. "Pardon my interruption, Captain."

"That's okay, Lieutenant," Celesta waved him off. "Your theory is as valid as the others. The reality is that we have no idea—"

"Captain!" a shout made everyone jump. "The Ushin ship just exploded!"

"Cause?" Celesta barked, striding quickly back to her seat.

"Unknown," Lieutenant Commander Adler said.

"CIC is analyzing the sensor logs now," Accari said.

Celesta's eyes narrowed as she quickly ran through options in her mind. She felt in her gut that the Ushin ship wasn't destroyed by any internal malfunction: it was hit with a ship-to-ship weapon by another ship they weren't aware of. Assuming that, did that enemy ship know where they were? The *Icarus* was flying silent, but blind without active sensors and she knew from hard-won experience that the Darshik could sneak up behind them without the passives detecting them.

"Did we detect anything anomalous prior to the Ushin ship being destroyed?" she asked.

"No, ma'am. Nothing that—"

"The exception report," Barrett interrupted Lieutenant Commander Adler. "Captain, we had a recorded visible light anomaly that at the time was inconsistent with the transition flash of any ship in our database. Given events I have to consider that there is an enemy ship in the system that we're unaware of."

"Shit," Celesta swore in an uncharacteristically outward display of frustration. "Tactical, full active sensors and bring all weapons online. OPS, sound general quarters, set condition 1SS."

"Active sensors coming up," Adler said as Accari's voice echoed through the ship, calling her crew to prepare for imminent combat action. "The transmitters were cold so there will be a slight delay."

"Understood," Celesta said. "Just get me a clear picture of what's around us as fast as you can and be ready to shoot at any target I—"

"Contact!" Adler cried. "It's close and coming fast, coming at us off the port bow! Auto defense is engaging!" There was no time for any orders from Celesta as the *Icarus's* tactical computers took over and began firing the forward, port laser batteries at the incoming ship before she could even have her tactical officer give her an exact range to target or its speed and bearing. The moment seemed to stretch on for eternity, the muted whine of the *Icarus* firing her laser batteries preceding the horrendous crash that sent alarms blaring on the bridge and alerts scrolling across the main display.

"Glancing blow by a Darshik plasma lance!" Accari shouted. "Hull breeches in three forward compartments, pressure hatches engaged."

"Enemy ship has veered off sharply and is disengaging!" Adler yelled to be heard over the alarms. "Moderate damage to their port flank by our lasers."

"Helm! Come about to pursue!" Celesta said, her fists clenched. She was furious that yet another operation she'd been in command of had so quickly devolved into an absolute cluster fuck including her ship being damaged again.

"Transition flash detected," Accari said. "Close too … Tactical, confirm that target no longer appears on sensors."

"Confirmed," Adler said. "Unknown ship executed a warp transition deep within the system."

"Unknown?" Celesta scoffed. "We can't even confirm that was a Darshik ship?"

"Tactics and weapons were similar, ma'am, but the ship matched no known configuration and the measured power output was an order of magnitude higher than any of the cruisers. We weren't able to get a valid reading on engine output for some reason." Accari went down the list CIC had sent up of the initial analysis of the engagement. "There's no conclusive—"

"That will be all, Lieutenant," Celesta cut him off. "Damage control report, if you please."

"Outer hull breaches in compartments 9F, 9H, and 11H." Accari turned to his other display. "Emergency pressure hatches closed and are holding, zero casualties, zero injuries. The affected systems are forward spectrometer array number one, secondary particle analysis collector, and the primary Link transceiver stack. No estimates for repairs as of yet."

"All systems we can do without for the moment," Celesta said. "Tell the backshops I want everyone to stay put. We'll deal with that when we're not expecting another attack at any moment. Helm, all ahead flank. Let's not present an easy target."

"Engines ahead flank, aye."

"OPS, have a Jacobson drone prepped," Celesta said, almost as an afterthought. "Full sensor package. I want to drop it and let it scan the wreckage of the Ushin ship while we press on. Nav, adjust our course to flatten back out and maintain our orbit in relation to the primary star; I no longer want to approach the target planet. Helm, come onto new course when you get it, no change in engine output."

"Aye aye, Captain."

It was another tense three hours before Celesta began to think that the Darshik ship had taken the chance to extend and escape rather than try another of their intrasystem "hops" and take another pass at them. It was a tactic that Terran ships were incapable of duplicating and the ability to jump around within a star system had been used against her before quite effectively when the Darshik first appeared in the Xi'an System. She wanted to stop and dig into the data from the engagement but she couldn't risk breaking her attention for the time it would take to begin poring over the CIC data dump.

The adrenaline of combat and the strain of waiting for a second attack were taking its toll, and she almost felt lightheaded as she watched the main display constantly shift as the tactical computer categorized and labeled radar returns while the *Icarus* roared around her orbit at full power. She looked over at the master status and saw the RDS had already pushed the destroyer to nearly seventy-five percent of her maximum sub-luminal speed. There was no way in hell the enemy ship would be able to move in with their energy lance unless they were already closing from behind.

"Helm, zero thrust … steady as she goes," she ordered quietly.

"Engines to zero thrust, aye," the helmsman said. "Maintaining current course and speed."

"OPS, tell Engineering that they're clear to begin coordinating damage control parties," Celesta said. "Tell Commander Graham that I want hull integrity at one hundred percent and tested before any of the technicians are allowed in to begin checking their equipment."

"Aye, ma'am," Accari said.

Slowly the crew began to uncoil as their velocity and fully active sensor array made it virtually impossible for the unknown ship to simply appear again and take a swipe at them. Celesta had relieved Barrett and told him to grab some food and rest. As he walked off the bridge the look he gave her said he understood that she was very much displeased that an exception report had been glossed over while the ship was in such a dangerous position. She would talk to him about it after her temper had returned to a low simmer. It wouldn't do any good to just unload on him at the moment, and since Commander Barrett was not a sloppy or incompetent officer she had to assume that any action, or in this case inaction, on his part was due to her flawed leadership.

Things were balanced on a razor's edge now, even more so than when they faced the Phage. That particular enemy was easy to figure out at least. These Darshik had motivations that made little sense and the Ushin were an even bigger mystery. There was no telling whose side they were actually on and at no time since they'd begun their association with the alien species had anything remotely positive for humanity come out of it.

"What do you feel our most prudent course of action should be, Captain?" Ambassador Cole said from her left. She'd almost forgotten the man was sitting there as quiet as he'd been.

"As soon as we wrap up our analysis of the Ushin wreckage, recover our drone, and Commander Graham clears the ship for warp flight we'll push back for Terran space," Celesta said. "I don't feel there's anything more to be gained by staying here unless you have anything else you'd like to share?"

"No, ma'am," Cole said. "Without an Ushin delegation to talk to I'm simply a passenger. In fact, I should probably get out of the way. I will be in my quarters if I'm needed." With that he stood gracefully and strode off the bridge. She watched his departing back for a moment before pushing all thoughts of him from her mind and moving her display around so she could actively monitor the damage control crews as they dealt with the breaches in the forward compartments.

For some strange reason her thoughts flitted to Jackson Wolfe and the *Aludra Star*, a sturdy but underpowered ship that her former mentor was about to take into the teeth of the Darshik blockade of the Juwel System. For a moment she considered taking the *Icarus* there since her mission was now null and void given the absence of an Ushin party to negotiate with. On a whim she opened a new window on her display and began running the calculations as to whether the *Icarus* was even outfitted to make the trip or not. A destroyer didn't have especially long legs and they were already pushing into her safety margin with this now-pointless trip.

Chapter 8

The *Aludra Star* was drifting powerless in interstellar space, but by design and not by any sort of calamity. Captain Wolfe was taking the extra time to perfectly calibrate his navigation systems and get as precise a location as possible before executing their next and final warp flight into the Juwel System.

"I must stress again, sir, how uncomfortable I am with this course of action," Commander Simmons said for at least the fifth time since the briefing had begun. "To call this *unorthodox* would be to gloss over the extreme danger you're putting the ship and crew in."

"I'm not unsympathetic to your concerns, XO," Jackson said patiently, "but you've seen the data the same as I have. There is simply no feasible way to get to Juwel by hitting one of the normal jump points or even something as transparent as vectoring off and transitioning in somewhere else along the outer system. The Darshik blockade is too tight and their ships are too fast. Even if we could outrun them to the planet, which we can't, we wouldn't be able to decelerate fast enough to safely deploy the drop shuttles."

"I understand the challenges, sir, but I must still—"

"Stop," Jackson said. "Just … stop. This is not a negotiation, Simmons. This is the plan of action I have decided upon. I have weighed all of our options and, honestly, all of them tend to fall under the category of suicide run to varying degrees. At least this one gives us a chance to complete our mission." He sighed before continuing, uninterested in convincing his recalcitrant executive officer but still trying to make sure the rest of his command crew understood the stakes.

"The only way to guarantee our survival is to either not attempt to fly into the Juwel System at all, fly through so fast that we transition out the other side without deploying the shuttles, or deploying the shuttles at such a velocity that nothing reaches the surface intact including our Marines."

"We didn't come all this way to not even try," Commander Chambliss said. "Especially just so we can save our own skin." Chambliss was the Flight OPS department head and as a full commander regularly pushed back against Simmons. Jackson had decided to let it go for now and see how it shook out. He didn't have an especially high opinion of his XO so far, unfortunately that being a near-constant theme in his career, but he had no way to realistically replace him. He'd been shoved into the unfamiliar class of ship and given a mission nobody in their right mind would volunteer for … also a recurring theme in his years of service.

"The operation as I've outlined it moves forward," Jackson said. "End of discussion. If you're as concerned about the survival of the *Star* as you appear to be I would hope that motivates you to make sure our systems are dialed in as tight as they possibly can be. I can't overstate the precision needed to successfully pull this off. Dismissed. Lieutenant Commander Sharpe, you stay, please."

All his other officers filed out of the cramped conference room, Simmons muttering under his breath, while his chief engineer remained in his seat. Despite the fact that most of the critical details of Jackson's plan fell squarely in his lap the quiet officer had decided not to speak up during the meeting or offer an opinion one way or another. That both intrigued and worried Jackson.

"So ... what's your honest opinion of the plan?" Jackson said without preamble as the hatch clanged shut. "No sugar coating."

"I'll need your command codes, sir," Sharpe said.

Jackson just blinked twice, wondering if he missed something. "Excuse me?"

"Your command codes, the highest level you were given for the *Star* before we left the platform," Sharpe repeated. "I need them to make your plan work, sir."

"You'll need to explain," Jackson said, leaning back. "Why do you need any command codes I may or may not have?"

"We're going to need to bypass several safety interlocks to pull this off," Sharpe said, leaning forward. His demeanor could be described as ... enthusiastic? Now Jackson really was worried.

"The problem is that by the time we transition in, get our bearing, fire the mains, begin to navigate"—Sharpe splayed his hands wide and leaned back in his seat—"we'll be hundreds of thousands of kilometers off-target with no way to remedy it. We'll have to come around which means fighting through the Darshik fleet anyway, something we're doing all this to avoid."

"So what's the solution?" Jackson asked.

"Before we transition in I want to bring the mains online," Sharpe said. "While we're still in warp."

Jackson sucked in a breath at that. "Have you been drinking, Sharpe?"

"No, sir," Sharpe waved him off. "I know the standard fleet doctrine on this that's beaten into our heads in the first year of the Academy. The powerful EM fields generated by the mains will disrupt the warp drive emitters and cause a distortion variance that will spread your molecules over several light years … that's all bullshit.

"That was true with the first-generation warp drives and the old, unshielded MPDs. The Gen IV warp drives can easily compensate for any interference from the mains, not to mention the new MPD pods are all shielded and use more efficient, directional field emitters. It was a function of hiding their signature to enemy sensors but the result is that the mains really don't put out that much radiated RF anymore. But the policy of full MPD shut-down during warp flight operations is so ingrained that it's institutional."

"Moving past that for a moment—and I'll want to see your raw numbers on what you just said—why do you want to fire the mains before transition?" Jackson asked, beginning to get a headache and worrying that his chief engineer might either be semi-insane or have a chemical dependency problem.

"Getting back to my first point, I want the mains to fire at full reverse the moment the sensors determine we're back in real-space," Sharpe said. "Even before we have a position fix or if local space is clear of enemy ships. I want to bleed off our transition velocity as quickly as possible … it's really quite essential for your plan to have a chance, sir."

Jackson leaned back and thought about what the officer was telling him. Sharpe's plan made sense on a few levels. He would have to bleed off relative velocity as quickly as he could and there was no harm in firing the engines at full reverse before they even knew where they were. The engines wouldn't actually push them backwards into anything, just slow the ship along a flightpath they were already on.

The more he thought it over the more impressed he was with the youngish-looking lieutenant commander in front of him. Instead of spending his time in the meeting complaining about how dangerous the mission was, he had been working out all the technical details in his head. Not only that, but he'd been thinking in terms of overall strategy as it related to the operation of the *Star*. He'd only known one other engineer that was even aware that starships weren't built just so they would have something to work on.

Jackson pushed aside the momentary jolt of pain at the memory of his old friend, Daya Singh, and looked at Sharpe with a new appreciation. When he'd first assumed command the chief engineer had struck him as efficient but not necessarily inspiring. His mousy appearance might have had a lot to do with that, Jackson admitted to himself with no small amount of shame given his own uphill struggle in Starfleet.

"Come to my office at the end of first watch, Lieutenant Commander, and we'll see about what authorization codes I might have that you could use," Jackson said.

"Yes, sir. Thank you, sir." Sharpe smiled and stood.

Jackson called out to him just as he was about to walk through the hatch. "And Sharpe ... excellent work," he nodded to the engineer. "I like officers who find paths around problems regardless of Fleet tradition and dogma. Keep me apprised of your progress."

"Of course, Captain," Sharpe said with an embarrassed smile and disappeared into the corridor. Jackson could only help but smile to himself at the engineer's enthusiasm for such a reckless plan.

"Ah, shit," he said, leaning back in the seat again. "Hopefully I don't destroy this ship too."

****

"That's the third group," Corporal Castillo said, lowering his optics. "And we're losing the night."

"We're assuming the darkness has been an advantage," Barton snorted. "So far these patrols haven't seemed to mind it."

"These are too big to be patrols, Sarge." Castillo shook his head. "Each party has had fifty to seventy-five soldiers and they were carrying some heavy weaponry. These guys are either being sent out to harass our lines or they're a distraction to keep our meager forces tied up."

"Imagine if we had any orbital reconnaissance or even long-range drones?" Barton griped again. "Not being able to see what the enemy is doing over the horizon is a strange feeling."

"Hasn't the militia provided you with civilian aircraft and pilots?" Emil asked, still observing the enemy troops through the powerful optics on his sniper rifle.

"The Darshik shoot them down faster than we can find volunteer pilots," Castillo said. "None of the aircraft we found around Westfall or the surrounding towns were much more than light transport or recreational craft. Not stealthy and not fast."

"Yeah," Emil agreed. "Most of what comes to Westfall is on the mag-lev trains. The capital has a big airport but most of those flights connect up north or to the eastern hemisphere."

"Your capital, Neuberlin, it's how far from Westfall?" Barton asked, frowning.

"Oh … maybe six hundred and fifty kilometers south of Westfall, maybe closer to six-seventy from here," Emil said after a moment of thought. "Why?"

"I'm just thinking aloud," Barton said. "But so far we've been pushed back by the Darshik, completely defensive at every engagement, but they've yet to come at us with the overwhelming numbers we know they have and crushed us. Why?"

"Why bother?" Castillo asked. "They have us pinned down so they don't need to commit the forces to try and overrun us. They have to know that even though they'll likely win the battle it sure as fuck won't be free. Maybe they find the potential losses unacceptable."

"Maybe," Barton said doubtfully. "Emil, what would be the quickest way to get a large number of troops into Neuberlin if you wanted to bypass Westfall and the Marines deployed there?"

"Short of dropping them into the airport I mentioned? The Transcontinental Link is east of here. It skirts around Westfall and all the farms in the area and goes straight into Neuberlin before continuing on," Emil said.

"I can see the wheels turning," Castillo said. "But Command is monitoring the militia emplacements around Neuberlin not to mention the bulk of our original force is garrisoned in the city itself protecting the government. I can't believe that the Darshik main force would be able to bypass Westfall to move on the capital without someone seeing them and raising the alarm."

"I can't see any other reason for them to keep fielding all these small skirmish units to hit and run down along our defensive perimeter," Barton said. "They could take Westfall whenever they want if they feel like committing the forces to it. They're in the same boat we are with their forward units lacking the logistical support and any heavy firepower, but they landed more troops than we did almost three to one. What if they're trying to tie us up here so they can capture the capital intact? They'd gain control of the planet's seat of power and one of the largest airports to begin bringing down more troops and equipment to hold it. It makes sense if you're trying to subdue and control the planet."

"I don't know," Castillo said. "You're thinking we should head all the way to this road the kid was talking about and look?"

Barton shook his head. "No," he said. "With just three of us on two off-road bikes it would be a waste of time. We can't search enough of it or get the information back to Command in time to be of any use. Let's keep pushing back to the forward base and report in like we're supposed to."

"That's good to hear," Castillo nodded. "We don't need to be making decisions based on wild theories, no solid intel, and no communications."

"Let's get at it then." Barton walked back over to his vehicle and climbed up onto it. "That patrol is well enough out of range now. No matter if my theory is right or not, we need to get back and report the increase in enemy contact surrounding our position."

As they pulled away to the quiet hum of electric motors and chunky-treaded off-road tires grabbing at loose gravel Barton thought about what the Darshik goal might be for Juwel. Despite the dramatic shock of landers descending from orbit and alien troops crawling across the landscape the Darshik had yet to fully commit to either kicking humans off the planet or eliminate any military resistance and impose full control over the populace.

To the sergeant's knowledge there had been no attempts at communication or demands presented so it was difficult to devise a defensive strategy when you had no idea what it was your enemy was after. Although they were being reinforced regularly, unlike the Marines, the

Darshik hadn't brought many aircraft or larger ground warfare machinery with them. They had employed very limited orbital bombardment to soften a few positions but so far the Marines had been able to meet them head on and keep the small toehold they had on the planet.

Putting aside the more high-level questions about what the Darshik hoped to accomplish with their half-assed invasion of a Terran star system, what was their immediate strategic goal? The town of Westfall had never made any sense, but if they had been trying to simply contain the Marines the entire time while the main force bypassed them and moved on the planet's capital then there was a certain logic to it. For the millionth time since their hasty deployment he wished their support equipment had safely made landfall.

****

"You hear that?" Castillo asked. "Sounds like some of ours."

"Yeah, let's move," Barton said and squeezed the accelerator, causing Emil to grab at his jacket from the sudden burst of speed. The relatively quiet electric ATVs allowed them to catch the sound of distant weapons fire, and a lot of it. There was the faint but discernible buzz of the Darshik weapons as well as the louder chatter of Terran rifles.

"It would be our luck to run into one of our own patrols that likely has a working radio, but then they're also engaged in a gunfight with the enemy and we have no idea which direction we're approaching from," Castillo shouted from his own vehicle.

"I'd rather not approach the enemy from behind and have our own people shooting at us," Barton shouted back, "but we don't have any other options. Let's just be careful."

As it turned out, luck was on their side. As they crested the next rise they saw a hasty defensive formation of vehicles, both CENTCOM issue and commandeered civilian trucks, with two full squads of Marines firing the opposite direction of their approach. Barton slowed to a crawl and then lifted both his hands, taking them off the controls momentarily when two of the Marines watching the road noticed them. After just a cursory look one of the Marines waved the ATVs forward frantically.

"Get up here! They're flanking us!" the one waving shouted and pointed to the north of the position. "Cover that rise while we call in for support!"

Barton, Castillo, and their young civilian charge rolled to a sudden stop and jumped off their vehicles, each unlimbering his weapon and moving to cover the direction the Marine had indicated.

"Emil, you're cleared to engage any enemy you see come over that hill," Barton said as he set up behind one of the heavy civilian trucks while turning to Castillo. "I guess that's one advantage to fighting aliens: We can easily identify friendlies." The corporal's response was drowned out by the roar of Emil's sniper rifle.

"Nice shot!" Castillo called out, sighting down through his optics. Barton pulled his own rifle up and saw that Emil had nailed a Darshik soldier coming up over the hill, taking it in the head before it even had its shoulders clear of the rise. He could see more forming up behind that one and squeezed off a few rounds in their direction despite knowing how far out of his effective range they were.

Emil was able to hold the flanking troops at bay long enough for the Marines they'd met up with to clear out the Darshik patrol ahead of them and push out with a small fire team to perform their own flanking maneuver. Soon the last pocket of enemy troops had nowhere to stay under cover and broke over the hill, running full bore towards Barton's position to escape the humans that had snuck around to their left side through a dry drainage ditch.

"Weapons free!" a lieutenant called from just behind and to the right of Barton. "Watch the cross fire!" All the remaining Marines opened up on the mad rush of Darshik and, despite their best efforts to return fire, the result was all but inevitable. All the enemy lay on the ground unmoving while the only Terran casualty was the ATV that Castillo had been riding. The tires, an antiquated inflatable rubber type, had been ignited by enemy weapons fire and the whole vehicle was now cheerfully burning as the Marines and few civilians took stock of themselves after the fight.

"Who're you, Marine?" the lieutenant asked, walking up as some of his men began burning the alien bodies.

"Sergeant Barton, sir," Barton said. "2nd Platoon."

"That's what I thought," the lieutenant nodded absently. "We were told to keep an eye out for any stragglers from your patrol. They found where you were ambushed but the aliens burned the vehicles so it wasn't possible to get an accurate body count. Anything to report?"

Barton quickly recapped being ambushed far behind what was considered their outermost line, being pursued by Darshik patrols, and even their theory that the aliens might be trying to hold them near Westfall as a ruse.

"Command suspects the same thing," the LT confirmed. "That's what we're out here trying to confirm. So far none of our patrols have been able to account for even a tenth of the enemy's suspected strength while we remain bottled up near Westfall. So ... where the fuck did they all go? We know they didn't leave the planet so there has to be something we're missing."

"Has Command sent scouts to check the Transcontinental Link?" Barton asked. "My local expert says that it's a major artery that's a direct shot to the capital."

"You can come with me when I make my report to the major. You know the drill, Sergeant ... we're told just enough to be a danger to ourselves," the LT said before raising his voice. "Let's get our asses in gear! I want to be Oscar Mike in two minutes! That means two, not two and half! Move it!"

The three survivors of 2nd Platoon's ill-fated patrol were given field rations and a seat in the back of the military transport. They tore through the food like men who hadn't eaten in days, which was very close to the case, and were all soon asleep, rocking gently in the seats as the vehicle bounced down the access road towards the base.

Chapter 9

"Stand by," Ensign Dole said tensely. "Transition in less than sixty seconds."

"All crew in your restraints … *now!*" Jackson barked over the shipwide channel. The sounds of buckles being snapped could be heard over the soft chimes of terminals and the hiss of the environmental vents. He forewent chewing his OPS officer out for the lack of a timely warning and instead chastised himself for not having the damn countdown to such a delicate maneuver in huge numbers on the main display.

"Three … two … one … trans—" the rest of Dole's words were cut off as everyone was slammed into their restraints. Alarms began blaring and Jackson could barely make out the roar of the main engines in full reverse as his breath was forced out of his body and his vision tunneled down to a speck.

Incredibly, the sound and force on his chest increased over the next few seconds and loud, sharp bangs could be heard and felt through the deck plates. After what felt like an eternity the pressure was abruptly gone as the artificial gravity system was able to reassert its dominion over inertia and nullify the crushing deceleration.

"Report!" Jackson rasped.

"Trying to get a position fix now, sir!" Dole said, his eyes bright red from the blood vessels that had burst during the violent maneuver. "Immediate area is clear, damage reports coming in but nothing significant and no casualties."

"Tactical, are the passive sensors up?" Jackson asked, still breathing hard and shaking from the beating he'd taken.

"Passives are up and recording, Captain," Commander Simmons reported from the tactical station where he'd been serving during combat operations. "The computer is still classifying everything but we have nothing close enough to be of concern. Shall I bring our weapons online?"

"Go ahead," Jackson said, countermanding his earlier order to keep the ship completely dark. "If we're where we're supposed to be I doubt the transition flash went unnoticed."

"Position confirmed, sir," Dole said. "We missed by eighty-two thousand kilometers, but we're well within the orbit of the fourth planet of the Juwel System. The planet itself is fifty-one-point-eight million kilometers ahead of us; sending course and bearing to the helm now."

"Excellent work everyone!" Jackson said loudly, startling a few of the bridge crew. "Helm, engage on your new course, all ahead full."

"All engines ahead full, aye," the helmsman said. The *Star* groaned and shuddered a bit as the thrust suddenly changed directions and began accelerating her along their current flightpath.

"Coms! Inform Flight OPS to begin launch prep," Jackson said. "We'll be coming in hot. OPS, any transmissions from the surface?"

"Sensors are picking up sporadic low-power transmissions, sir," Simmons answered instead. "No coms directed towards orbit that the computer can pick out and no beacons from the Marine expeditionary force that was deployed."

"We'll be operating under the assumption that they're not actively broadcasting Link or beacons to remain elusive to the Darshik forces that are undoubtedly down there," Jackson said. "We'll broadcast a challenge once we're within five hours of launching our drop shuttles."

"Why so far out, sir?" Dole asked.

"Because the ground commander may have a specific place where our shuttles need to go or, more importantly, where they absolutely should *not* go," Jackson said. "The cushion will give us time to make any course and speed adjustments necessary for Commander Chambliss to safely get the shuttles out of the launch bays and on their way."

"Commander Chambliss says the shuttles all checked out fine but the launch system is kicking out faults after our decel maneuver, Captain," Lieutenant Epsen reported from the com station. "Lieutenant Commander Sharpe is sending crews now to investigate."

"What are the nature of the faults?" Jackson asked.

"Launch bay door controller won't respond and twelve of the cradle actuators are reporting malfunctions," Epsen said. "Commander Chambliss said that he'll inform us ASAP if these are true faults or if the affected systems can be reset, sir."

"Lieutenant, I want you to actively stay on top of that and keep me apprised," Jackson said. "OPS and Tactical will be too busy and I don't expect we'll have much outside com traffic to deal with in the near-future."

"Aye, sir," Epsen said. "Tying into the maintenance net now."

Jackson appreciated that the young officer just did as he was asked without balking, unlike Ensign Dole whose favorite sayings were all just slightly different variations of, "But that's not really my job." The truth was that the *Aludra Star* was short of seasoned officers and he was leaning heavily on his veterans. His XO was serving as the tactical officer during critical operations since the lieutenant assigned to the ship, while enthusiastic, had so little experience at the station that Jackson had no choice but to bench him. He made a mental note to put an entry into the lieutenant's service jacket explicitly explaining that the replacement had not been due to lack of performance or any mistakes made. It'd be a shame to stunt the young man's career advancement due to the idiots at CENTCOM putting someone so green on a combat ship as the primary tactical operator.

"Enemy contacts," Simmons said calmly. "Sensors are picking up three distinct active sensor transmissions, all categorized as being from a Darshik cruiser, same class of ship that attacked the DeLonges System. Range puts them in the area of the DeLonges and Columbiana jump points."

"Begin active tracks," Jackson said. "That'll be layer one of their blockade. There should be at least two more ships as floaters further down in the system and I would expect at least one cruiser in orbit around Juwel itself to provide support for the ground forces and as a contingency in case any Terran ship was crazy enough to jump in so close to the primary star."

"Like us, sir?" Simmons said, his mouth turning up slightly at the corner in a lopsided smile.

"We're not crazy, Commander," Jackson corrected him. "We're just damned good."

"Yes, sir!" Simmons agreed enthusiastically. Jackson wasn't lying, exactly, but the part of the equation he'd left out of his motivational platitude was that they'd been at least twice as lucky as "damned good." There was no way to plan for the fact that there hadn't been any enemy ships in the area to take advantage of the momentary disorientation after a transition.

He knew there was no way the Darshik were going to give him unfettered access to the planet. They either had a ship or two down there already or their faster cruisers would break off and harass them the entire way, making it much more difficult to perform their decel and orbital insertion to safely launch the drop shuttles. Even though he would never tell the crew, getting safely into the system wasn't likely to be their biggest challenge and he still put the odds of successfully deploying the shuttles to the surface at fifty-fifty. He didn't calculate the odds of the *Star* making it out of the system alive quite so favorably.

"OPS, go ahead and retract the warp emitters and close the hatches," Jackson said after another few seconds of watching the main threat board populate. "Let's clean her up and be ready for anything that may pop out around the sunward side of the planet."

"Aye, sir."

The Darshik and humanity, although employing different methodology, seemed to be operating on the same relative plane of technological advancement. This meant that a lot of their tactics were necessarily similar since their ships had many of the same limitations. The Darshik could accurately execute short intrasystem warp hops, but they seemed to have no answer for Terran missiles or kinetic weapons that could hit them beyond the range of their plasma lance. Their ships had comparable speed and maneuverability but seemed to lag in sensor capability based on the more basic radar signals they'd received.

Unlike when he fought the Phage, having an enemy with similar technological limitations allowed Jackson to devise tactics with a higher degree of confidence. For example: He was certain there was at least one ship hiding behind Juwel. Any ship approaching the contested planet would likely come in from the outer system and no matter which side they came in at they would have to maneuver around and come down the well towards the primary star. The interference from the star made it easy for a ship to stay quiet and hidden on the far side of a planet, allowing one or two ships to cover their ground forces and give a nasty surprise to anyone that made it past the picket ships hanging out in the outer system.

"Hmm," Jackson mumbled, tapping his chin with his forefinger as he thought about it. The *Star* didn't have a lot of weapons to spare just to satisfy one of his whims, but the more he thought about it the more confident he became that he was right about his hunch.

"Captain?" Commander Simmons asked.

"XO, prep two Shrikes for launch," Jackson said. "I want them to spit out of the tubes on the launch booster only, don't fire the first stage yet. Keep the remote link open to both and keep sending them real-time targeting updates; I will give you the target package momentarily."

"Aye aye, sir," Simmons said without hesitation. "Two Shrikes ready to fire from tubes two and three. Standing by for initial targeting data."

"*He's completely confused but he isn't holding things up with needless questions,*" Jackson thought appreciatively as he worked through the rest of his strategy.

"Helm, zero thrust," he ordered. "Tactical, launch both Shrikes with unassociated targeting … have them hold course towards the horizon of Juwel, no active sensors from either weapon."

"Left or right horizon, sir?" Simmons asked.

"Right relative to our position," Jackson said after a moment of thought.

"Shrike targeting updated … launching," Simmons said. "Both missiles have cleared the tubes, tubes two and three reloading."

"Helm, all reverse one-quarter," Jackson ordered. "Just begin gently braking her and bear … half a degree to starboard off current course."

"All engines reverse one-quarter, aye!" the helmsman said. "Coming to starboard zero point five degrees."

"If I may, Captain, why have we set two of our missiles adrift into the flight path our drop shuttles will be taking?" Simmons asked. Jackson, having had a career defined by open disrespect and second-guessing by subordinates, swallowed down his indignation and biting retort as he saw that Simmons was earnestly asking.

"When we begin our deceleration maneuver prior to launch we'll be vulnerable," Jackson said. "The *Star* doesn't have the power to push away from the planet once she's so close, so once we begin to brake we're committed. The Shrikes are just a bit of insurance while we're oriented for drop shuttle deployment and unable to defend ourselves."

"Yes, sir," Simmons nodded. The commander turned back to his station and began reconfiguring one of the terminals to provide updates to the missiles that were quickly leaving the *Star* behind as she gently braked on approach.

"Commander, let's figure out how to split the bridge watch up," Jackson said once his XO had finished. "We're still nearly thirty hours from orbital insertion but deep enough in enemy-controlled space I want a qualified watch up here the entire time. I want the crew fresh and bright-eyed so let's do split twelves on the bridge and Flight OPS, regular twelve hour watches for the backshops."

"I actually anticipated this, sir." Simmons reached over and pulled a tile out of the bag he always carried up onto the bridge during his watch. He thumbed through the device until he found the document he wanted and handed the tile to Jackson. "This schedule meets your requirement, but I can make changes to it if you'd like."

"You're well on top of things, Mr. Simmons," Jackson said with a nod of approval after reading through the list of names attached to the modified watch schedule. "You are clear to inform all affected crew of the changes. As per your schedule, you have the bridge, Commander." He handed the tile back to Simmons and grabbed his coffee mug from the holder near his seat.

"I have the bridge, aye," Simmons said, walking over to the coms officer with the tile so that she could begin calling up needed crewmembers.

****

Sergeant Barton stood at ease in front of the field desk, watching Major Baer as he rubbed at his scalp and groaned in frustration. Barton had been whisked into the command shelter and been asked to give a full report on what he'd seen since his patrol had been ambushed and his suspicion that they were being pinned down by a minimal Darshik presence while their main force bypassed them for the capital.

"Take a seat, Sergeant," Baer said finally. "You look like you've been through hell."

"Just tired, sir," Barton said. "I'm ready to get back at it though."

Baer smiled indulgently. "What I'm about to tell you isn't for general dissemination, clear?"

"Clear, sir."

"Intel has come up with much the same theory you have about why the Darshik haven't just tried to use their superior numbers and overrun us," Baer said after Barton had settled into his seat. "Colonel Rucker has sent out motorized patrols, including some light aircraft we scavenged from local farms, and checked out this cross-country highway your local expert mentioned.

"At first we didn't see anything. A smattering of squad- or platoon-size units here and there on the main road, but nothing of the sort or size that would indicate a larger movement. So we went further south, far past where we thought they would have time to advance, and found the trailing elements of their main body. They've *already* bypassed us, Sergeant. We're still observing them, but as of last report they're redeploying their forces to try and take one of the main entries into the city."

"Do we have any way to stop them, sir?" Barton asked, knowing the numbers weren't on their side.

"We can move out of here and begin harassing their rear guard, but we don't have enough Marines to dig them out completely. Not to mention we don't have the vehicles to get them there in time anyway," Baer shook his head. "The colonel hasn't decided what to do yet, but he's sent word to the Marines and the civilian defense force in Neuberlin and told them to be ready.

"The only reason I'm telling you this, Sergeant Barton, is that I'd prefer it if you didn't spread this around base until we have some sort of answer. Being deployed without any vehicles or support equipment was bad enough, but to have another ground force that *also* deployed without any heavy equipment completely out-maneuver us is embarrassing."

"I won't go spreading rumors, sir," Barton said slowly, "but there is something else that I think might be important to keep in mind."

"What's that?"

"If this position has been circumvented, and the Darshik forces are no longer engaged closely, we might not have that much longer to live," Barton said tightly. "They may have landed without heavy equipment like us, but they still have orbital superiority. Their starships may go ahead and eliminate us as a threat now that we know Westfall was never their ultimate goal."

"We've … discussed that as well," Baer said slowly. "But there's no way to evacuate the entire base right now."

"I see, sir," Barton said, knowing he wasn't likely to get anything else out of the major.

"Go get something to eat and grab some sleep, Sergeant," Baer said. "We're not surrendering just yet and I'll need you fresh and ready. Dismissed."

Barton stood and came to attention for a two-count before stepping back one step and turning to walk out of the soft shelter that was serving as Major Baer's office and living quarters.

"Anything new?" Castillo asked once he was back outside. The corporal and Emil were both waiting on him, having nowhere to report to for the moment.

"Nothing we didn't already know," Barton shook his head. "They're checking the Transcontinental Link, but that's about all I heard."

"I wonder if they—" Castillo trailed off as Major Baer burst from the shelter and took off towards the command post at a full sprint followed closely by his aide. Two more officers went running by as well, none of them raising an alarm or even acknowledging anybody as they passed. On instinct, Barton and Castillo jogged in the general direction everyone was running, trying to see if there was something up ahead.

"Yo! What's going on?" Castillo shouted at another corporal that was sprinting by them hot on the trail of a second lieutenant.

"The *Aludra Star* is approaching the planet!" the corporal shouted back.

"What the fuck is an *Aludra Star*?" Castillo asked.

"Wolfe, man! Captain Wolfe ran the blockade! Reinforcements have arrived!"

"I'll be damned," Barton muttered and slowed to a walk now that he knew there wasn't anything he needed to be involved in. "I would have lost that bet."

Chapter 10

"They're definitely coming down," Simmons said calmly. "Data is hours old but the thermal blooms from their engines are easy to track with the passives. Three of the picket ships are moving on us and two more ships that we hadn't detected appear to be moving to cover our jump points."

"There wasn't enough time for our transmission to the surface to be intercepted all the way out there and for us to detect their reaction," Jackson mused, looking at the mission clock on the main display that began counting the instant the *Star* transitioned in. "They detected us right away. Tactical, you are clear to go to active sensors ... no point trying to hide anymore."

"Aye, sir," Simmons said. "Active sensors coming online now."

The *Aludra Star* was ten hours from having to commit to decelerating hard to hit their optimum orbital insertion or veering off and maintaining their velocity to escape into the outer system and try their approach again. Jackson was unsurprised that more enemy contacts popped up once their presence was known; there was no way in hell they were holding this system against three separate counterattacks with four cruisers. Now he would get to see just how much they wanted to keep control of the planet's surface, or at least keep it intact. The Marines and civilians down there were hanging by a thread and he feared that if the Darshik felt they were losing their grip on the system they would just glass the surface from orbit and retreat.

It was why he'd pushed CENTCOM to try and take back the Juwel System with overwhelming force and not a handful of half-measures before giving up. He didn't have any real experience with this new enemy but he felt certain that if they forced them to withdraw they would make sure there was nothing left in the system on their way out. They needed to be quickly and decisively eliminated. For all he knew he was deploying his drop shuttles just to have all the Marines and spacers aboard get vaporized in an orbital bombardment because Fleet hadn't cleared the system first.

All of that was irrelevant now, though. When he broadcasted the coded hail and immediately received a proper reply from CENTCOM forces on the surface there was no chance of the *Star* simply flying through the system at speed and escaping out the other side. Admiral Pitt had intimated to him that there would be no hard inquiry if the *Star* came back and reported that the system was lost. He'd said it was something CENTCOM and Federation oversight were almost expecting anyway.

The conversation had made Jackson physically ill, especially coming from a flag officer that he admired so much. Oh, he understood the math and could appreciate its cold, dispassionate logic: The Federation was weak and Starfleet was decimated. Throwing all their resources into freeing a single Frontier planet made little sense when taking into account how much at risk it put the core worlds.

Jackson knew it was why he'd never be an admiral: He couldn't accept that they should just leave the citizens of Juwel to their fate because the fight might be difficult. In a way he felt that perhaps it was the fact that the Darshik *were* so beatable that made CENTCOM want to pull back and protect key infrastructure. With the Phage there had been a sense of hopelessness in the face of being so overmatched and from that hopelessness came complete freedom to fight with everything they had. There had been nothing to lose. Nothing to protect. Just a desperate flailing about until they'd gotten lucky and landed a haymaker that killed the Phage just before it could really move to exterminate humanity for good.

"New contact! Darshik cruiser clearing the terminator of Juwel; it was hiding on the sunward side as you said it would be, Captain," Simmons called out.

"Is it coming out to meet us or has it shifted orbit to put us in line of sight?" Jackson asked.

"It looks like it's under full acceleration, sir."

"So they'll swing around the planet at least one more time to get to escape velocity," Jackson nodded. "Our best intel on their cruisers indicates they don't have the power to just come straight out of a low parking orbit. Keep tracking them for now ... they're too far away to worry about and I'd rather not engage them so close to the planet."

"Do you think that's the only bogey in orbit over Juwel, sir?" Ensign Dole asked.

"Given the predictive models we have from Captain Wright's multiple encounters I would have to assume there are two more that we don't see right now," Jackson said calmly. "This one peeked around to see if it could get a reaction out of us it liked. We'll hold course and speed and make it come out to meet us."

"Aye, sir," Dole said.

The Darshik cruiser ended up making three full orbits of Juwel, accelerating and gaining altitude on each pass, before it broke away and came out to meet them head on. The range on the threat board showed it still over six hundred thousand kilometers away, so Jackson took a moment to steady himself and think about the engagement. It was his first combat action since he'd retired after the Phage War and took a job as a paper pusher for a research project and he didn't want to make a rookie mistake because he missed something obvious.

"Tactical," he said finally. "Set point defense to auto. We know they have missiles but so far they've showed us nothing our laser batteries can't knock down. Bracket the incoming cruiser and plot a targeting solution, one Shrike."

"Sir, we still have—"

"I'm saving those, Commander," Jackson cut him off. "They're too far out now anyway. They won't be able to close the gap before the cruiser is past them and I don't want a missile coming back at us chasing it."

"Aye, sir," Simmons said. "Firing solution locked in, tube one is ready to fire."

"Hold your fire," Jackson said. "Keep updating the weapon, but let's let it fully commit to this charge."

Simmons said nothing but pulled his hand back from the fire control panel. The enemy cruiser was well within the Shrike's effective range, but the ships were closing at near-relativistic speeds and accelerating. The missile would increase this closure speed even more and then be unable to make even minor course corrections if the Darshik ship executed an avoidance maneuver at the last minute. Even if the *Star* was equipped with a kinetic weapon like a mag-cannon Jackson couldn't risk firing while a populated planet was directly behind their target.

"We're getting returns from our active sensors on known targets within the system," Dole spoke up. "Data is agreeing with our passive data so far and the tactical computer is updating predicted tracks."

"Thank you, Ensign," Simmons said as the younger officer stepped in to pick up the slack for the busy tactical officer. Jackson said nothing but thought that maybe there was some hope for Dole after all. The tension on the bridge was palpable as the *Star* bore down on the planet and the closing Darshik warship. The crew was young, untested, and knew that their assault carrier was not built to go head-to-head with the enemy heavy. The only thing that seemed to give them comfort was the one thing Jackson was least confident about: him. He heard the whispers in the corridors about how they'd lucked out with the legendary starship captain taking the bridge before their first combat mission. Jackson remembered much the same attitude from the crew of his last ship, the *Ares* … many of them didn't make it back from her last mission.

"Darshik ship is continuing to accelerate, sir," Simmons said. "Thermal analysis indicates they're still running under full power."

"That makes no sense if they intend to hit us with that plasma lance," Jackson muttered. "What's our range?"

"We've broken three hundred thousand kilometers, Captain," Dole said.

Jackson thought furiously for a moment, trying to put himself in the shoes of the Darshik commander. What would he do if he had a numerical and tactical advantage? He sure as hell wouldn't rush headlong into—

"Helm! Emergency stop!" Jackson barked. "Don't be gentle, slow this ship down! Coms, sound the warning for hard maneuvering."

Almost simultaneously a klaxon began blaring in quick blasts and the engine pitch died out momentarily and then increased to a dull roar that shook the deck plates. His crew cried out in surprise but grabbed onto handholds and kept at their stations. The *Star's* internal gravity system once again couldn't keep up with the inertia created by the engine thrust and they had to hang on while the ship's relative velocity was shed off.

"Tactical, fire tube one! Target that ship!" Jackson grunted. "Just get that missile away! Helm, reduce engine power by half but keep slowing." There were some grunted replies to his commands and he saw on the tactical threat board the target ahead bracketed by a flashing red box right before tube one spit its Shrike out.

"Missile away," Simmons said as the g forces let off.

"Send an update and have it veer off to port; update its intercept angle well past what it will think is optimum," Jackson said. "That ship is going to break away hard. It never was going to try and close on us."

"How do you—"

"Send an update to the other Shrikes we released earlier," Jackson cut Simmons off. "Burn their first stage to put them within line of sight of the sunward side of Juwel. They're clear to prioritize and engage any targets they find. I'm sending you the override codes to transmit to the weapons. They'll have a safety lock to prevent them being fired at targets not classified by the ship's tactical computer."

"Captain ... isn't there a good reason for the safety interlocks to—"

"Commander, the only ships in this system are the *Star* and the enemy." Jackson waved him off with his right hand as he accessed his secure server with his left.

"Yes, sir." Simmons fell quiet and waited for Jackson to forward him the missile override codes while keeping an eye on the threat board.

"Incoming target is bearing hard to port, sir," Dole said. "It's still at full burn ... it's going to be close if our Shrike can catch it."

"Let's hope so," Jackson said. "I'd hate to be one missile short at the end of this battle. Tactical?"

"Missile targeting package updated ... confirmation from both weapons received," Simmons said. "They're away."

"OPS, how far off course did we manage to get from our original orbital insertion?" Jackson asked.

"Minimal deviation, sir," Dole said. "Sending update to the helm now to put us back on target for our optimum launch altitude and speed."

"Helm, execute your new course when you get it."

"Coming onto corrected course, aye," the helmsman reported. "Ceasing braking thrust. Engines to ahead three-quarters." The dull throb of the engines changed slightly and the hull groaned as the thrust reversed directions and the *Star* began accelerating again along her new course. It was another three hours before anything happened, but when it did it happened all at once.

"Missile pursuing Tango One has detonated; waiting for battle damage assessment from CIC," Dole reported just as an alarm went off at the tactical station.

"Our first two missiles are each tracking a target and burning their second stages," Simmons said, his red-rimmed eyes wide. "Telemetry tracking shows their targets are in a stationary orbit; they won't be evading these two."

"They can still shoot them down," Jackson said. "Do we know there were *only* two more ships hiding on the other side of the planet?"

"No, sir," Simmons shook his head. "The Shrikes only return data on the target they're locked onto."

"You have to dig into the raw telemetry feed," Lieutenant Epsen said from behind Jackson at the com station. "They talk to each other to prioritize targets when they're fired in autonomous mode so they don't chase the same one. There might be something there to indicate if there was more than two."

"How the hell do you know that, Lieutenant?" Simmons asked, his voice carrying only the thinnest trace off annoyance.

"I was a munitions officer before cross-training to be bridge crew," Epsen said. "I'm rusty, but I could take a crack at it if you give me access to the buffer in the tactical computer where the telemetry feeds are stored."

"How long will that take?" Jackson asked, eyeing the mission clock. Juwel was beginning to take shape on the display and they would quickly be past the point of no return for an abort.

"Half an hour if it's there, sir," Epsen said.

Jackson looked at Simmons and shrugged. "Give him the pointer to the telemetry buffers," he said. "We're not likely to need a com officer until we need to talk to the surface prior to launch."

"Worth a shot, sir," Simmons agreed. Jackson made a note in the ship's log to make a suggestion to Fleet Research and Development regarding the Shrikes and Hornets. The missiles had advanced sensor and com capabilities; there was no reason they couldn't be more flexible in what they sent back when fired at long ranges. The log was constantly updated on a com drone that would be fired off to Terran space if it looked like the *Star* would be lost.

Jackson fervently hoped that he would be able to carry the suggestion to the engineers himself.

Chapter 11

"We have the initial report from intel section on the enemy ship, Captain," Commander Barrett said quietly from the open hatchway of Celesta's office.

"Come in and sit down, Commander," she said, passing a weary hand over her face. "Close the hatch." Barrett closed the hatch and walked over to the chair in front of his captain's desk and sat, his back ramrod straight and his hands clenched.

"I've gone over the data on the exception report with the analysts in CIC."

"Yes, ma'am." Barrett almost flinched.

"You need to put this out of your head, Michael," Celesta said, using his given name for only the second time since they'd known each other. "I don't see that I would have done anything different with the information you had at your disposal."

"If I had been more inquisitive … or had even just put an entry in the turnover log for you to look at it … I don't know—" Barrett trailed off.

"I would have ignored it the same as you," Celesta insisted. "I need you at your best, Commander. We're flying into the complete unknown right now and I can't have this cloud hanging over my XO's head. Yes … an unexpected event happened and our mission ended up being a bust, but the *Icarus* suffered minimal damage and we lost no crew. More importantly, we know what to look for now the next time we run into that ship."

"You think this won't be an isolated incident?" Barrett frowned. "That maybe we stumbled into someone's patrol area?"

"Oh no, there's something quite unique about that ship." Celesta shook her head. "I give it even odds that we're racing it back to Terran space right now."

"That's disquieting," Barrett said. "We've forwarded all the raw data on the encounter to CENTCOM via the point-to-point drone, but CIC and our own intel folks have done a lot since then. Should we drop out of warp and send another com done?"

"No," Celesta said firmly. "And for two reasons: I want a second, unbiased analysis of the data and I also don't want to risk dropping out of warp in interstellar space. Our best astronomical mapping data gives us a clear shot to our target system, but we're still taking a mighty risk with this flight."

"The warp drive likes to avoid obstacles by its very nature and swings around anything with too much mass to be deflected," Barrett insisted. "I don't think we'll pop out and slam into a planetoid—"

"My fears are a bit more exotic," Celesta interrupted him. "The eggheads in Fleet Research and Science are good, but a lot of what they *know* about space this far out is gleaned from remote observation and best guess. I'd rather not find out the hard way that there's a localized gravitational distortion that nullifies our ability to transition back to warp.

"There's precedence for that ... we've lost more than a couple automated probes that way. The point is that the risk far outweighs the reward since we'll not get any reply back from New Sierra anyway. We press on."

"Aye aye, ma'am," Barrett said.

Celesta looked him in the eye for a long moment. "That will be all, Commander," she said just as the silence began to become uncomfortable. "Take heed of what I said. My trust in you and your ability to do your job isn't shaken from the incident, so I hope your confidence in yourself isn't either. I expect the *Icarus* to be at one hundred percent by the time we get to our destination."

"She will be, Captain," Barrett said crisply.

"Dismissed," Celesta said, turning to her terminal. "Please leave the hatch open on your way out."

After her XO walked stiffly out the hatchway she placed her hand on the monitor so the terminal could take a biometric reading and allow her access to the server the intel report was on. She didn't think she'd find any additional insights than what she got from CIC, but she was nothing if not thorough and it wasn't as if there was anything more pressing to do as the *Icarus* hummed along in warp.

Her intel crew had cleaned up some of the imagery captured by the optical sensors as the ship flew past, and Celesta could tell that it had little in common with the standard Darshik cruisers she'd been going up against. In fact, it was the first time that she'd seen any sort of major deviation in starship design from the species. While humans constantly changed their designs based on available technology or shift in mission, it seemed the Darshik had designed their heavy cruisers and stuck with them. It suggested to her that they hadn't developed much of their technology themselves and merely learned to copy it.

This new ship, however, was something different. It was actually a bit smaller than the standard cruiser and seemed … skeletal. The hull wasn't uniform and in spots she could see spars and support struts, but it looked like it was intentional and not from any battle damage. The color-corrected image also showed an embellishment on the narrow, pointed prow that was interesting: two hash marks that looked like someone had dipped two of their fingers in yellow paint and left the marks that went down and forward.

"War paint?" she wondered aloud as she began to scroll through the rest of the multispectral imagery. In them she could see other details of the ship that began to make it more clear what its purpose was. It had nearly three times the number of maneuvering jets as the *Icarus,* and her analysts were confident that most of the interior was dedicated to power generation and weaponry with a much smaller crew than a Terran vessel of similar size.

"It's more like one of Colonel Blake's gunboats than a starship," she mused, tapping the desk with a forefinger. "Or at least what what the Vruahn had built that was supposed to be Colonel Blake."

She then went through all of the radar data from the engagement and saw that the ship was impressively maneuverable and had noteworthy acceleration. From the limited data they had from the encounter Celesta was convinced the ship likely had a few nasty surprises left for them, but she'd be ready for it the next time around. The thought made her glance up at the wall display in her office that was showing the master mission clock and saw that they were still just over four days from their destination and they had no idea what they might find when they transitioned in.

****

"Come in," President Wellington said, not bothering to get up as everyone filed into his office. The President was pallid and somewhat disheveled-looking even though it was barely early afternoon. He'd been recently complaining of stomach pains and those that knew him best were becoming increasingly concerned for his health. Augustus Wellington hadn't been an especially healthy man when he took office, known for his militant distaste for physical activity and a lifestyle of excess, but it had recently taken a turn to the point that it was considered a threat to the security of the Federation. The fledgling government barely had its legs under it and losing the man whose iron will had kept it together in the early days would be a devastating blow.

"Thank you for coming on such short notice," Wellington went on, as if any of them had any choice in the matter.

"Of course, Mr. President," CIS Director Sala said, an oily smile pasted onto his face as he watched Wellington haul his bulk out of the chair and walk to the side bar in obvious discomfort.

"I want to make sure we're all on the same page so I called this informal briefing session," Wellington said as he began pouring Scotch into a glass, not offering anything to his subordinates. "Well ... let me clarify that. I want *you* to brief each other and I'll just be the person calling out topics. This territorial pissing contest between CENTCOM and CIS is over. We have no time for this sort of petty bullshit. Now, who wants to go first?"

"Our envoy was turned back at the border by ESA frigates before they were even allowed to deliver their message." Sala wasted no time diving into his brief. "They're still destroying our com drones when they enter a system and they've been quite successful in reprogramming all the existing platforms to no longer take message forwarding requests. Our Tsuyo reps say that even the failsafes have been eliminated. In other words, we're completely locked out of the ESA's com network."

The ESA, or Eastern Star Alliance, was the Asiatic Union and Warsaw Alliance enclaves from the old Terran Confederacy along with roughly half of the New European Commonwealth worlds that had broken off and formed their own government. In the aftermath of the Phage War and the restructuring after the loss of the capital world of Haven, many of the old resentments bubbled to the surface and before it could be stopped borders had been drawn up, threats had been made, and now the ESA and the Terran Federation existed in an uneasy standoff while the latter was dragged into a war with a new alien species.

"Did they open fire on the delegation?" Admiral Marcum asked. The CENTCOM Chief of Staff was wearing a civilian suit as per the request of the President.

Wellington wanted to impress upon the admiral that he was to no longer be meddling in Fleet operations or he would be replaced.

"Not this time," Sala deadpanned. "I suppose we could see that as a marginal improvement in relations."

"This isn't funny, goddamnit!" Wellington snapped. "Do I need to remind you that we're critically short of fissile material right now? We lost a major weapons depot and we have no short-term solution to replace those warheads! Will you still be so fucking funny when the Darshik are knocking down Fed worlds at will?"

"My apologies, Mr. President," Sala said, seeming to be genuinely contrite. "The levity was inappropriate for the moment."

"Just get on with it," Wellington waved him off.

"That's really all I have, sir," Sala said. "At least on that matter. We've tried every way we know of to get the ESA to at least talk to us, but they refuse to engage. We do have assets in their space keeping an eye on things, but that's all just a lot of technical detail that's in one of the briefs to be sent out this coming week."

"Admiral? Good news?"

"I'm afraid not, Mr. President." Marcum cleared his throat. "As you previously mentioned, the loss of the Bespitd Depot was a devastating hit to Fleet's readiness. We have reserves and the munitions manufacturers are working through the rest of the raw material they have, but—"

"Quick answer, Admiral," Wellington interjected. "How bad is it?"

"Ships leaving New Sierra right now are carrying a half-load complement of Shrike ship-to-ship missiles," Marcum said bluntly. "Within the next four weeks of operations we'll be pulling missiles off of reserve fleet ships to make sure the line can hold."

"That's much worse than the projections I was given last time I asked," Wellington said accusingly.

"We had to revise downward, sir," Marcum said. "First and Fourth Fleets had apparently been giving inaccurate numbers on their existing munition stores when the Shrikes first went into service."

"Why the hell would they lie about having *more* missiles than they really had?" Sala asked.

"Shrikes are very expensive and each numbered fleet is responsible for its own operating budget," Marcum said. "When the directive came out to replace older missiles with the new ship busters we gave an exception for ships still carrying the older Avengers."

"And they claimed far more Avengers than they actually had to avoid having to buy Shrikes?" Wellington rolled his eyes. "You'd think fighting a war that could have resulted in the extermination of our species would have knocked that sort of nonsense off."

"That's about the long and short of it." Marcum shifted uncomfortably. "They apparently wanted to spread the expense of the refit across the next few years. Anyway … the people involved are being reprimanded, but it doesn't change the fact we have far fewer nukes than originally estimated."

"What's the status of our latest expedition to free the Juwel System?" Wellington asked.

"As you may remember we re-tasked a group of ships from the 508th Strategic Defense Squadron to replace Captain Wright's taskforce," Marcum said, waiting for Wellington to nod that he did. "Captain Rawls was held up by a maintenance issue and his ships didn't depart the DeLonges System until eight days after they were scheduled to. Unfortunately the *Aludra Star* had moved out on her own and departed on time before Rawls could let Wolfe know they were aborting—"

"Wait, so the 508th left anyway?" Sala frowned. "And Wolfe took a single assault carrier out to Juwel alone?"

"Yes," Marcum said slowly. "Apparently there was some disagreement between Wolfe and Rawls about how to run the blockade and the *Aludra Star* moved out of formation and transitioned out of the system without word to Rawls … whom I had assumed to be the overall mission commander."

He braced for the explosion from the President he knew was coming. Jackson Wolfe, long a thorn in Marcum's side, had long been favored by Wellington. More to the point, Wolfe's legend was useful to the old fox as a political tool as long as he could trot the notorious starship captain out to appease his constituents.

Although he hadn't been technically ordered not to leave nor even officially had his ship attached to the 508th, he saw it as yet another instance of Wolfe just doing whatever the hell he wanted with Fleet equipment and personnel. This time it would likely end much as it had with his last two commands: destroyed ships and lives lost. It was the reason Marcum hated the hero culture that permeated Fleet and was perpetuated by politicians and a media hungry for stories to sell an imaginative public.

Nobody could deny the sacrifices and bravery of Jackson Wolfe during the Phage War campaigns, but he'd succeeded as much on dumb luck as from any innate ability to command a starship. While she was still on his personal shit list for the stunt she'd pulled over New Sierra, Marcum much preferred to have Celesta Wright on the bridge in a crisis. She was more steady, a team player, and in Marcum's opinion a better shipmaster. But Wright was only a hero from the war, not the hero and so Marcum found himself saddled once again with Wolfe and again left holding the bag when the captain felt he knew better than everyone else around him.

"So that means the Aludra Star and her entire complement of Marines is likely lost as well as one of our more important ship commanders," Wellington said slowly, taking a long drink and setting the glass down on the desk with a thud. "What was the nature of Rawls's technical trouble and did it affect all of his ships?"

Marcum thought very hard before answering, knowing that the President was accusing one of his captains of sandbagging in a not so subtle way. It infuriated him to no end, but it would do him no good to show it.

"I don't have the details with me, sir," he said diplomatically. "I'll have it included in your morning brief material."

"See that you do," the President said. "So … now that we know the Juwel System is likely going to be lost and we have no ability to save it, and we know that the ESA will not be coming to our aid, what do we have in the way of contingency plans for when the Darshik decide to begin pushing further into Terran space?"

For the next four and half hours the CIS Director and CENTCOM Chief of Staff brainstormed with the President to see what resources could be pooled to shore up weak points and, depressingly, which systems would have to be sacrificed to keep the core infrastructure safe. By the end of the unscheduled meeting Marcum began to fully realize just how thin the thread was they hung by. The Darshik didn't seem especially powerful from what they'd shown so far, but they'd hit humanity right at the worst time.

By the time he was walking out of the office for his ground car he had an irrational surge of hope that Wolfe might pull another miracle out of his ass and save them all. The thought was dismissed as quickly as it popped into his sleep-deprived mind. Lucky though the captain was, a single, borderline obsolete assault carrier wasn't going to turn the tide of the war in their favor.

Chapter 12

"Tango One is listing and—secondary explosions detected," Commander Simmons said. "CIC is reporting that the target is still intact but is going into an uncontrolled tumble. It looks like our Shrike may have taken out their drive section."

"Let's go ahead and take advantage of the confusion that's certainly taking place on that bridge," Jackson leaned forward. "Hit it with two Hornets; fire them from the aft tubes."

"Firing solution locked in ... firing," Simmons said. "Missiles away."

"Mr. Epsen?" Jackson said loudly.

"Two more minutes, sir!"

"We don't have two more minutes, Lieutenant," Jackson said. "Give me the odds that there are more Darshik ships sitting on the other side of the planet."

"It's just ... I ... stand by," Epsen said, his voice cracking. "One of the missiles didn't properly classify targets ... there's either three more, one more besides the two, or there was only one and it kept counting it over and over based on what the other Shrike was telling it."

"So two to one odds that we have more ships sitting on the other side," Simmons said quietly.

"OPS, give me an abort vector. Take us away at as steep an angle as you can and get us into the outer system," Jackson said in disgust. "We can't risk it this close if there's even one more. Helm, all ahead flank."

"All engines ahead flank, aye."

"Coms, tell Flight OPS to stand down and get the crews out of the shuttles and secured," Jackson said. "We're committed to having to come around again. Once you do that send an encrypted burst transmission to the surface telling Colonel Rucker we'll be at least another five days from orbit by the time we get turned around."

"Aye, sir," Epsen said.

"OPS, drop a drone and have it sit out in high geostationary orbit over the last known location of the Marine detachment," Jackson said as the ship really began to shake and rumble under full power. "Program it as a com relay between us and them, at an altitude of sixty thousand kilometers plus. Hopefully it'll go unnoticed and the Darshik won't swat it down."

"Aye, sir. Coordinating with Flight OPS now," Dole said.

The *Star* didn't carry any of the wondrous Jacobson drones that Jackson had taken for granted when he was commanding a destroyer, but she did have a small hangar with some decently advanced com and recon drones. They were packed with the latest and greatest hardware since the *Star* was a recently commissioned ship, but they weren't mission scalable like the Jacobsons. The drone he was dropping had an impressive suite of com gear, but its optics were not going to be up to the task of any detailed reconnaissance of the surface from the altitude they would have it parked at.

He watched his ship's indicated relative velocity creep up, the delta V not all that impressive considering the harsh shaking and discernible engine noise as the assault carrier tried to haul its bulk away from the green planet. With the launch bays stuffed with fully loaded shuttles she had a lot of inertia to fight when trying to veer off while so close to something as big as Juwel. His worry was that she didn't have anything left to give; if there were even two more cruisers sitting in the shadow of Juwel which moved to pursue they'd be in real trouble.

"We've lost telemetry from both Shrikes," Simmons reported. "We're still not far enough around the planet to know if they were good hits or not."

"OPS, make sure CIC is focused on getting us a look on the other side of Juwel when we go by," Jackson said as he looked at the projected flightpath up on the main display. The *Star* had her prow pointed away from the planet at nearly eighty degrees and was thrusting at full power, but their velocity had still been so high, even after the emergency braking maneuver, that they were going to sail past Juwel at speed, showing their aft quadrant to anyone waiting to take a shot.

"We have debris of sufficient mass to account for two Darshik cruisers, Captain," Simmons reported. "There are two ships remaining; neither are maneuvering to pursue. In fact, neither has even come about to face us."

"Interesting," Jackson frowned. "So they're not pursuing nor are they fleeing. Are they active?"

"Thermals indicate both have power but neither has its main engines running."

"Record it for later analysis," Jackson said. "How does our flight path look on the way out?"

"The ships coming in from the jump points are still coming but have ceased acceleration," Simmons said. "They don't seem to be in much of a hurry to get down here."

"How long until we get past the fifth planet?" Jackson asked, checking their flightpath again from his own terminal.

"Seventeen hours under current acceleration," Dole said almost apologetically.

"Helm, all ahead emergency," Jackson ordered. "I want to get us at least flying in the right direction while the Darshik picket ships are still so far out. The sooner we can shut down active sensors and the mains the sooner we can begin to plan our return trip to Juwel."

"Sir, CIC is examining the radar returns from the outer system," Lieutenant Epsen spoke up from the com station. "They're saying preliminary scans of the area around the DeLonges jump point indicate the 508th was not destroyed there."

"They should be here by now," Simmons said.

"Yes they should, Commander," Jackson agreed. "So they're either in the system and hiding, were destroyed and we aren't able to pick them out of the other debris at this distance, or they didn't leave the DeLonges System when they were supposed to."

The bridge fell quiet as the crew went about their tasks and Jackson pulled whatever information he needed directly from the CIC's threat assessment rather than bother his tactical officer for it. The ships left around Juwel by the enemy appeared to be damaged according to the high-resolution radar scans they were able to take on the flyby of the planet. That told him that the blockade wasn't just a thrashing machine chewing up Terran ships as they popped out of warp; the Fleet taskforces were still able to cause damage before being overwhelmed. Since there were still many ships patrolling the outer system Jackson had to assume the Darshik were replenishing their forces after each engagement. Unfortunately that showed a firm commitment by them to maintain their hold on the system.

The only roadblock in his line of reasoning was that if the Darshik were moving in fresh starships, why hadn't they bolstered their ground invasion forces? His brief conversation with the Marine commander on the surface, a Colonel Rucker, indicated the Darshik troops were just as underequipped as his people and they weren't seeing them in overwhelming numbers. In fact, they appeared to be clustered just outside their first and only landing area and moving slowly towards the capital city of Neuberlin. It wasn't exactly overwhelming force when you've had complete orbital superiority for months. Why no more troops? Why no heavy equipment or artillery? It sure as hell wouldn't be how he'd run an invasion and he was just a lowly ship captain.

For another ten hours under emergency acceleration the *Star* pulled away from Juwel and the incoming Darshik ships. Jackson ordered his active sensors shut down and then, once the ship dipped behind the Class II gas giant they'd been flying towards, he killed the mains and ordered the ship to go dark. Once they were coasting along with most of their primary flight systems and sensors shut down he began rotating his crew out for rest, telling Commander Simmons to come relieve him in six hours so he could grab a quick nap and be ready.

What he didn't tell his crew was that this big, looping maneuver was just to buy him some time to think. If the 508th wasn't there, and not likely to show up, their chances of successfully getting down to Juwel and deploying their cargo shrank from just slim down to none. He was beginning to get a better picture of the Darshik strategy for holding the system as their sensors were able to pick up ship numbers and deployment, but that didn't do him a hell of a lot of good since the *Star* was underpowered, outgunned, and not built to take the punishment a destroyer was.

As he wracked his brain trying to find some way to pull the ships away from Juwel long enough for him approach, decel, and launch he had to remind himself once again that the "legend" of Captain Jackson Wolfe was in reality a string of dumb luck and coincidence. In his mind he was little more than a decently competent ship captain, but against the odds he was looking at he didn't see any gambit that would move the pieces as he needed them. All they had to do was keep one ship parked over Juwel and he was effectively blocked. He wouldn't risk the complete loss of ship and crew on something that had no hope of success, and the *Star* was at her most vulnerable during launch operations.

"Coms, call down to Lieutenant Commander Sharpe and have him meet me in my office," Jackson said, standing up and stretching. "Then call the XO and tell him I'm regretfully cutting his rack time short and he needs to report to the bridge."

"Aye aye, Captain," the com officer said. Jackson had to look twice to see that it actually wasn't a com *officer* manning the station. A young enlisted spacer had the headset on and was carrying out his orders. The *Star* was so short-staffed that Commander Simmons had to get creative to provide complete coverage when Jackson ordered split-twelve watches. She didn't even look old enough to be in the service and it reminded him that real lives were at stake whatever he decided.

He waited impatiently for his XO to come up and relieve him, simultaneously anxious to leave yet dreading the dry technical details he was going to have to drag out of his Chief Engineer. Sharpe had done well with his braking maneuver that kept them from carrying their transition velocity all the way to Juwel, and Jackson wondered what other sort of outside-the-box thinking the lieutenant commander might have up his sleeve. He would give the Marines and civilians on Juwel his one best shot to get his cargo on the ground, but after that he had to be realistic about their chances of survival if he stayed. One slow ship against at least six cruisers, probably more, wasn't a fight he could win. If they couldn't come up with a workable strategy within the next day he'd have no choice but to head for a jump point and pull back into uncontested space.

****

Sergeant Willy Barton was in a clean uniform, outfitted with fresh kit, and generally felt quite good about life all things considered. He was bouncing in the passenger seat of a Tracker, a four-seat all-terrain vehicle that had survived the initial drop from the assault carrier. If it wasn't for the fact he'd been assigned to a four-man team to ride out and hunt for the larger Darshik troop movements they surmised must be out there it would feel like any other training day.

Corporal Castillo had been put in another identical vehicle and the young civvy kid, Emil, had been left back at base. Barton had admired his guts when he insisted on going out, but there was no need for him now. They had secure tiles with maps and local data, independent navigation equipment, and enough Marines to fill the vehicles with trained shooters and techs. Major Baer had been tasked with finding larger enemy formations to not only track them but mark them for a possible orbital bombardment from the assault carrier that was inbound with reinforcements.

The plan had been absurdly simple: drive east and see if they bumped into anything. The mission was more of an intel gathering exercise since Colonel Rucker had no real way to move enough Marines quickly enough to put up any sort of resistance that would be more than just symbolic. Instead he was having a handful of teams track and report while he tried to mobilize his entire force and send it south to Neuberlin in what amounted to a race with the Darshik with the disadvantage of having to use smaller, less direct roadways.

Barton felt like they should have been on the march to the capital as soon as they realized the main

Darshik force was not where they should have been; it was the only next logical target. But sergeants do not tell majors and colonels what they should be doing. The capital at least made sense in a campaign where little else did. The Darshik were aliens, sure, but there had to be some goal to landing a few thousand troops other than just marching around and shooting up the countryside while refusing to meet the Terran forces in numbers greater than a patrol. Although just a lowly ground pounder, even *he* could tell there was something significant they were missing.

"What's that up there?" a lance corporal manning the gun turret called, pointing ahead and slightly to the left of them.

"Smoke," Barton said, trying to differentiate what was smoke and what was the low-hanging early morning fog. "I think."

"You want to check it out?" the corporal driving asked, letting the vehicle roll to a stop. "We have plenty of juice to get to that highway and back again even with a detour." To emphasize his point he tapped a forefinger on the dash readout that displayed the remaining charge on the primary and backup batteries.

"Fuck it." Barton shrugged. "We're here to look for signs of the enemy, not just practice our land nav skills. Take that side road ahead and then we'll cut across the field and make our final approach on foot."

"You're the boss," the corporal said, nodding as he jammed the accelerator down hard enough to make the motors whine in protest as the vehicle clawed for traction on the gravel road.

They made it close enough to smell the smoke of something burning that wasn't wood before they had to stop and reconfigure the vehicle to travel further. The driver flipped a few switches and the Tracker rose up to provide better clearance. There was a soft hiss as the multiple air bladders in the tires depressurized so that the wheels provided a larger contact patch to the ground and the weight of the vehicle was supported by the tire's internal composite ribs. The process took less than a minute and soon they were barreling across an open field, the active suspension absorbing the bumps and ruts so completely all they felt inside was a gentle swaying.

"Oh no," Barton said softly as they got closer and the smell became more pronounced. And familiar. "Just drive up as close as you can."

When the Tracker cleared the last treeline and rolled up to a small town the corporal pulled back onto the road, not bothering to reconfigure the running gear, and drove down what looked like an idyllic main street scene … save for the pile of human bodies still smoldering in the main intersection, the smoke curling off and wafting up into the fog.

"What the—" the driver broke off, leaning over the steering wheel, his eyes wide. "I don't see any weapons lying around … these were non-combatants. They've never done this before."

"Stay sharp," Barton warned, pulling his weapon out of the rack in front of him and covering out the passenger side. "Stop here. Let's dismount and do a quick check around."

"This could be an ambush, Sarge." The lance corporal slid down into the seat under the gun turret before hopping out.

"I think they'd have hit us already if it was," Barton shook his head. "We're a four-man in a single vehicle that wasn't very quiet about approaching. Corporal Greenwood, call this in to Command and tell them we're deviating to investigate. Our schedule shouldn't slip much."

Greenwood stayed in the driver's seat as the others cautiously scanned the street lined with squat, single-story buildings, most of them storefronts. Barton tried to ignore the pile of bodies barely one hundred meters ahead of him as well as the sickly smell of burning flesh.

"We're good, Sarge," Greenwood climbed out and grabbed his weapon, clipping it onto the lanyard attached to his body armor. "The major wants us to be thorough but quick."

"Typical officer contradiction of terms," the gunner muttered as he moved forward with the rest of them.

Resisting the urge to gag, Barton could tell that the pile of human bodies were indeed all non-combatants, civilian, and likely all the residents of the small town's main street. So far in the campaign the Darshik had ignored or bypassed anybody that wasn't actively shooting at them, even to the point of leaving people behind their advancing lines. So why the brutal change of tactics?

"This was quick and dirty," Corporal Greenwood said, his face a stony mask. "They piled them up, tossed on some fuel and lit it, but there wasn't enough to actually burn the bodies completely … just smolder and smoke a lot."

"You think it was meant to be seen?" Barton asked.

"Not sure," Greenwood said. "I'm thinking more that this was an impulse decision by the alien fucks that did this and they couldn't find enough flammable liquid to burn two hundred bodies."

"Mark the location on the map and sync it with Command," Barton said. "We can't do anything for these people right now. We'll have to send someone back after us to properly bury or burn them. Let's do a quick walk through the main section of town here and then get rolling."

The Darshik weapons didn't do much visible damage when they struck something solid like the Terran kinetic rounds did, but the evidence was everywhere once someone knew what they were looking at. Tiny little scorch marks peppered the buildings and had broken out glass windows in what must have been a simply terrifying ordeal for the citizens as they were rounded up and slaughtered. Barton clenched his jaw as he remembered the Marines had been issuing "do not resist" orders to civilians since the Darshik had shown no inclination to harm them up to this point. These people likely didn't even try to fight back, assuming the aliens would just pass through town like they had been up north. After a brief look around they climbed back into the Tracker, their mood dark.

"You think we'd be able to catch up with them?" Greenwood asked as he flipped the vehicle's main power back on.

"Not the mission," Barton said tightly. "Believe me … I know how you feel, but we can't compromise our section of this patrol because we're out looking for some payback."

"Whatever you say, Sarge," Greenwood said with a snort. "I know that if I was—" the rest of his comment was cut short by the Tracker's com lighting up.

"Go for Barton."

"*Where are you, Sergeant?*" the voice of Major Baer came over the speakers.

"Still in the town of … Potsdam, sir," Barton said as Greenwood held the map up on the tile for him to see. "We're just now moving on. Nothing to report outside of what Corporal Greenwood called in earlier."

"*We've heard from Sergeant Werner's patrol and they've come across two more settlements in the same condition. All the residents dead, in a pile, and some effort made to burn them … thousands of dead so far,*" Baer went on. "*We have to assume these aren't random atrocities but a new enemy tactic. Tell every civilian you see to flee westward or to fight back however they can, but get your asses out to that highway and get the intel we need. You are not to stop at any other towns and investigate no matter what you see. Clear?"*

"Clear, sir," Barton said, the bile rising in his throat as he thought of the body count the aliens were racking up in such a short time while the Terran Federation Marine Corps drove around and looked at things, not lifting a fucking finger to take the fight back to the enemy.

"Get on it, Sergeant. Command out."

"You were saying, Corporal?" Barton asked as he flicked the com off.

"Nothing, Sarge," Greenwood said as he turned the Tracker in a tight loop, his face now more somber than angry. "I wasn't saying nothing."

"Let's just get this done," Barton sighed. "The sooner we get back, the sooner we're on the march south to kick the shit out of the … things … that did this."

"Ooh rah, Sarge," their gunner said without any enthusiasm.

Chapter 13

"We have an update from the Marines on the ground via our satellite relay, sir," Lieutenant Epsen said, the fatigue his voice indicating how tired the whole crew must be.

"Give me the highlights, Lieutenant," Jackson said. "I'll read the full report later."

"They're requesting an update on when we're making another attempt to launch our shuttles," Epsen began.

"Obviously," Simmons snorted. Jackson let it go and made a hand motion over his head for Epsen to continue.

"Colonel Rucker has decided to move his entire force south to counter the suspected redeployment of the Darshik ground forces to the capital of … Neuberlin," the com officer went on, stumbling over the strange, ancient European word. "They also are reporting that the Darshik have changed tactics. They're apparently killing everyone, civilians included, in every town they come across, piling the bodies up in the middle of towns, and lighting them on fire."

"What in the hell?" Jackson actually turned in his seat to give his officer an incredulous stare.

"That's a summary of what it says, sir," Epsen said apologetically. "The accompanying imagery is … graphic."

"So far the Darshik had been ignoring civilian non-combatants," Simmons said quietly.

"We always thought that was because they landed such an inadequate force for a planetary invasion that they couldn't risk having the populace turn on them," Jackson said, pulling up the full contents of the transmission at his terminal. "If they bypassed towns and settlements then the civilians would be more inclined to stay out of it and allow them to maintain a numerical advantage over the Marines deployed there." He caught the questioning look his XO gave him.

"I had a couple long conversations with Brigadier General Ortiz before we departed New Sierra," Jackson explained. "I wanted a crash course on the tactics of ground warfare since we'd be directly supporting them."

"Wasn't General Ortiz the same—"

"That's right, Commander," Jackson smiled tightly. "Back when he was just Major Ortiz he was the detachment commander for the Marines aboard both the *Blue Jacket* and the *Ares*. It's been everything CENTCOM can do to keep him from finding a way out here to take command of the ground campaign himself."

Jackson forced himself to go through the video and image data transmitted up from the Marines on the surface of Juwel. Graphic had been an understatement. There was little doubt that the bodies had been piled up and burned as a message, but what was it? Why resort to these sorts of atrocities when so far the human defenders hadn't even mounted much in the way of a counteroffensive?

He slid the images off his display with a disgusted swipe and brought up his own personnel roster. He sifted down until he found who he wanted and quickly read through the officer's service record before nodding to himself.

"Coms, have Lieutenant Colonel Beck report to the bridge please," he said.

"Aye, sir."

"Sir, Captain Osso is the commander of the *Star's* Marine detachment," Simmons said, clearly confused.

"And you feel I'm unaware of this?" Jackson asked, managing to keep a straight face.

"No, sir!" Simmons said quickly. "I mean … yes, sir, of course you're aware of it. It's just that Lieutenant Colonel Beck isn't officially attached to this command."

"I know he's officially listed as cargo, but I think that he'll be inclined to help us out all the same," Jackson said, not bothering to clarify his reasoning to Simmons any further. The XO realized that once Jackson had gone back to his terminal the conversation was over.

Just over fifteen minutes later Jackson heard the Marine at the hatchway issue a challenge and a rough, gravelly voice identify himself as Beck. Jackson stood just as the Marine officer stopped at the threshold of the hatchway.

"Permission to come onto the bridge, Captain," Beck said, standing at attention. He was short in stature and the smooth, youthful face did not go with the harsh voice that emanated from it. He was wearing a set of combat fatigues that were well-worn but still within regulation and he could see that they were damp in places with sweat. Apparently he'd caught the lieutenant colonel in the middle of a training session or a workout. Jackson liked that he hadn't changed once he'd been summoned, just dropped what he was doing and followed orders.

"Granted," Jackson nodded to him. "Your service record says that you were top of your class at the Yamato War College." Since he hadn't asked a question the Marine officer didn't provide an answer, just stood at the ready waiting for a request to be made.

"We have some new intel from the surface of Juwel and I'd like your opinion of it. Apparently the Darshik have adopted a new tactic … one that has me more than a little concerned."

"I'll do my best to provide any insight I can, sir," Beck said doubtfully. "But this is the closest to the enemy I've ever been and we're still in the tin can waiting to be put ashore."

"I'm hoping it's that detachment that might provide a new insight or at least a fresh perspective," Jackson said. "Colonel Rucker seems to be at a loss as to why the sudden shift in strategy. If you'll just head to that station back there I'll have Ensign Dole provide you with all the pertinent files.'

"Aye aye, sir," the Marine said and walked quickly to one of the three configurable work stations that could be set up to perform a variety of tasks when needed. Soon

Beck was logged in and reading through all the firsthand accounts from the Marines on the ground.

"Sir, I'm not trying to be contrary," Simmons almost whispered into Jackson's ear, "but that ground data has yet to even be preliminarily classified by our own intel section. Is it—"

"I appreciate your concern, Commander," Jackson said, waving Simmons off. "But he'll be climbing into a drop shuttle within the next few days and dropping into hostile territory. To deny him any and all information we have on the situation would be criminally negligent."

Simmons just nodded and walked back to the tactical station, looking over the shoulder of the lieutenant that was sitting monitoring the passive sensors.

By the time Jackson was relieved to go off watch Beck was still at the station, a look of fierce concentration on his face and what looked like copious notes made on the tile he'd requested a few hours earlier. Jackson left instructions with his relief that the lieutenant colonel was not to be disturbed or questioned while he did his work. It was a long shot that the Marine officer would see something in the limited information that his intel people had missed. He had a seasoned crew in the CIC that had proven themselves quite adept at digging needles out of haystacks, but Beck wasn't otherwise usefully employed on the *Star* and anything that might give his people an advantage was worth exploring.

****

"Captain Wolfe to the bridge!"

The call came in forty-five minutes before Jackson had planned to get up. As it was he was already awake and mentally preparing for the day and trying to decide how he would approach the problem of being the lone Terran ship in the system. It made it nearly an impossible proposition to get down to the planet when the Darshik could afford to keep patrols out in the outer system as well as ships sitting in orbit over Juwel. He didn't hear any other alerts going out after the call for him to report to the bridge, so he assumed the decision hadn't been made for him by the Darshik finding their cold-coasting ship as she skulked around near the orbit of the only system's largest gas giant.

He slid his boots on and pulled his top over his head. As he always did when his ship was in a combat situation he had been asleep in his uniform. The jog to the bridge was a short one and the Marine sentry simply came to attention as a sign of respect when he saw Jackson. His standing rules on the *Star* while underway were to not announce his presence or call the bridge to attention as he walked on or off.

"What do we have?" Jackson asked. He noted absently that Lieutenant Colonel Beck was still at his station and diligently working.

"Federation transponder codes popped up briefly and then vanished. We didn't get enough for a full identification," Commander Simmons said. "CIC says they came from the direction of the DeLonges jump point and belong to Fourth Fleet. The squawk was shut off before we got unit designation or ship registry."

"I'd say the obvious answer is the 508th has just arrived and one of their ships didn't secure their transponder prior to transitioning into the system," Jackson said, shaking his head in disgust. It was an amateur move. "That's unfortunate since we have diverted much of the attention in this system away from the jump points … that mistake will likely cause the Darshik to redeploy to the outer system and not necessarily clear out the orbital paths of Juwel."

"My thought as well, Captain," Simmons nodded.

"Shit," Jackson muttered as the tactical computer put up blinking yellow icons representing the *Intrepid*-class destroyers near the jump point. "Coms! Prepare a burst transmission that has our latest logs, position, and intel reports from both the surface and our CIC's analysis of the overall tactical picture of the Juwel System. I want it tight-beam transmitted in the general direction of the DeLonges jump point. Repeat the transmission three times, standard encryption."

"Captain, we could relay the transmission through the drone we have down at the planet and let it rebroadcast it to our fleet," Dole suggested.

"Excellent suggestion, Ensign," Wolfe said, biting back his original, disparaging reply. "However, having the drone send out a high-power, wide-beam broadcast will let the Darshik know exactly where it's at and we'll need it when we begin our approach. We also can't afford the time it would take for the signal to reach the drone and then be sent all the way back out to the outer system. That fifty-minute delay will give the Darshik ships that much more time to close in on Captain Rawls and his squadron."

Dole seemed to be perking up and at least offering suggestions and engaging of late, so it wouldn't do much good if Wolfe bit his head off in the heat of things. Despite the previous war the wheels of change turned very slowly in Starfleet and many young officers coming out of the academy still needed a lot of practical training before they were worth a damn. He was gradually coming around to the fact that Dole wouldn't need to be replaced and moved off the bridge to somewhere more commensurate with his ambition and talents, so berating him for not seeing the situation from all sides would be counterproductive. Besides, the battle was already met and it wasn't as if there was anybody down on the lower decks that could be brought up as an OPS officer at a moment's notice.

"Transmission packet ready, sir," Lieutenant Epsen reported.

"Send it," Jackson said. "Tactical, we're broadcasting our position right now, so if the Darshik are good enough to pick this out of the noise from this gas giant … better be ready for anything."

"We're ready, Captain," Simmons nodded. "However, the planet is a double-edged sword in this case. It's helping to hide our signature, but even at this distance the interference it's throwing off is playing hell with our passive sensors."

"Understood," Jackson said. "But I don't want to come out from behind it just yet, nor do I want to light us up by firing the mains. We'll gamble on the fact the tight-beam burst transmission to the outer system wasn't detected."

"Yes, sir."

The *Star* had been chasing the gas giant in a heliocentric trailing orbit since they'd come onto the new course and shut the engines down. The planet was typical of its type in that it generated a lot of radiation that helped to hide a ship the size of the assault carrier from long-range radar scans. The downside, as Commander Simmons had pointed out, was that it also effectively blinded them, the passives being overwhelmed by the interference the closer they got.

The tactic had been a bit of desperation on Jackson's part, an underpowered ship outnumbered by at least six to one in contested space ... he had no choice but to run and hide while he figured out his next move that wouldn't result in the pointless loss of the *Star* with all hands aboard. Now that the escort destroyers had arrived he was thinking furiously about how he could use that to his advantage even with Rawls's squadron blundering into the system like the proverbial bull in the china shop.

The main issue he saw was that Ed Rawls was very enamored with the fact he was put in overall command of the mission. He'd already shown he was unwilling to take suggestion or to even concede that he might not have the experience that others under him had. Rawls had spent the Phage War as the OPS officer aboard a Merchant Fleet ship that was supporting mining operations in a system far, far away from the Frontier. Jackson didn't hold that against him, but he did bristle at the fact the prematurely promoted senior captain refused to see that he simply wasn't qualified to strategize the retaking of the Juwel System.

"Sir, incoming transmission," Epsen said twenty minutes after they'd sent their burst packet. "Wow … this is a high-power broadcast, Captain. Everything in the system will hear this one. It's not even encrypted."

"Who's it from?" Jackson asked, already suspecting the answer.

"The flagship, sir. The broadcast originated from the *Relentless*."

"Put it on the overheads," Jackson sighed. He did the math and knew that the transmission must have been sent as soon as the 508th charged into the system.

"*Attention enemy ships unlawfully operating within this Terran-controlled star system,*" Captain Rawls's voice came over the speakers. "*Our taskforce has arrived to ensure your exit from this space … that can either be by concession or by force. We will allow your ships to withdraw, but any further hostile acts will result in immediate retaliation from my battlegroup.*"

"That's the end of the transmission, sir," Epsen said in a quiet, stunned voice. Jackson opened his mouth twice but made no sound as he tried to process the utter stupidity he'd just been witness to. The problem was there were so many layers to the stupidity that when he peeled one off to marvel at it there was another one right under it.

"I'm ... actually speechless," Simmons said from the tactical station, his face mirroring the shock of everyone else on the bridge.

"Perhaps the senior captain has some overall strategy we're not aware of," Jackson said, finally finding his voice. "This changes nothing for us in the immediate future ... we continue to plan and prep in order to safely deploy our drop shuttles and then we get the hell out of this system. Understood?" The ragged chorus of confirmations was decidedly unenthusiastic.

Jackson thought he understood why Rawls had pulled such an idiotic opening gambit upon his arrival. He was afraid. Despite his swagger and bluster back on the New Sierra Platform, he didn't want to actually fly his ship into combat. He hoped his message would convince the enemy to leave without a shot fired. It was a foolish, misguided hope considering the Darshik had been chewing up Terran battlegroups at the DeLonges jump point for months.

The broadcast did offer Jackson an insight into how Rawls intended to fight the Darshik in the Juwel System: He didn't. He now realized he couldn't count on the 508th to provide any sort of meaningful cover, escort, or diversion in order to allow the *Star* to get back to the planet and complete her mission. He marveled at the overt display of incompetence and cowardice. What the hell else could go wrong on this mission?

"Captain, I think you'll want to look at this," Lieutenant Colonel Beck said from his elbow. The Marine looked like he hadn't slept in over a day and Jackson had a chill run up his back as he instinctively knew he was about to get the answer to his unspoken question.

Chapter 14

"What do you have for me, Colonel?" Jackson asked, indicating for Beck to retake his seat so he could more easily manipulate the imagery he had presented on the terminal monitor, obviously prepared to give an impromptu briefing on his findings.

"Yes, sir," Beck said, his voice crisp and alert despite the signs he'd been up and working for over a full day ship's time. "I believe that the bodies being stacked and burned by the Darshik are a form of psychological warfare."

"I surmised that myself when I saw the stacks of dead non-combatants, Colonel," Jackson deadpanned, unimpressed.

"Yes, sir," Beck said again, unruffled by Jackson's response. "But I don't think this was something they came up with. When I went back through all the mission data I saw that Rucker had his Marines burning Darshik bodies with a plasma torch after each engagement. This was done for precautionary reasons since we don't know if the Darshik's biological material carries pathogens or parasites that are a risk to human physiology, but the Darshik have apparently interpreted this as psyops being perpetrated by *our* side and are mimicking the action."

"You have my attention now, Colonel," Jackson nodded. "Go on."

"The timing of this change in tactics, not to mention the specific targeting of the civilian population, makes little sense given that nothing has changed on our side to drive it," Beck went on. "In fact, the Marines are in a weaker position now than when they first deployed … there has to be something else driving the aliens to this extreme.

"After analyzing the engagement patterns, the number of troops used in each, the lack of support from orbiting starships, and the suspected targets … I don't think this small pocket of alien troops flanking Westfall is executing the enemy's primary mission. The limited enemy contact, along with hit and run tactics designed to keep the Marines spinning in place, makes me believe this all is nothing more than a diversionary tactic meant to keep the only sizable ground force on the planet focused on the wrong thing."

"And what would be the right thing, Colonel?" Jackson asked.

"I couldn't begin to speculate given the lack of information available to us on the *Aludra Star*, Captain," Beck said. "We have a … distressing … lack of intel from the usual sources for such a long-running operation. I understand Colonel Rucker's full force didn't survive the insertion, so he's lacking the usual complement of drones and aircraft, but trying to plan around just what his Marines are seeing on the ground is … challenging."

"Diplomatically put, Colonel," Jackson said drily. "So your assertion is that we're completely missing the big picture in the ground campaign and that the Darshik move on Neuberlin is a diversionary tactic?"

"I'm positive of it, sir," Beck nodded. "Neuberlin is a strategically unimportant city. I know it's the capital, but all that's there is the governmental seats of power and the banking industry. There's nothing there that would amount to anything if you were trying to subdue a planet with such a small force. You'd have to strike at the heavily industrialized places and power generation sites, anything that could be used to resupply and fortify the defending forces arrayed against you. From what I can tell half the factories that have been shut down on Juwel only did so at the direction of the human government, not any enemy attacks."

"So if you were to speculate, what would you say they're up to?" Jackson asked. "They've committed a lot of ships to holding this system against three serious tries by the Federation to retake it."

"There is one thing I noticed from the reports of the early invasion, the landing before the first Marines were deployed," Beck motioned to the terminal. On it Jackson could see he'd accessed some of the intel briefs that had made it back to New Sierra regarding the initial incursion by the Darshik.

"Before the collapse of the civilian information networks and news media there were reports that Darshik starships were firing on any aircraft moving along the western coast of the main continent." He pointed out the area on a map. Juwel only had one large landmass that covered nearly twenty-eight percent of the surface; the rest was one contiguous ocean and dotted with thousands of tiny islands.

"So there was something along that coast line they were … protecting?" Jackson asked.

"I think maybe more so out in the water," Beck said. "The ocean, according to the records on this ship's servers, is relatively shallow save for a few deep trenches on the opposite side of the mainland. Right off the western coast the average depth is only around twenty-five meters all the way out for a few thousand kilometers before the continental shelf ends and it drops off."

"I see," Jackson said noncommittally while looking over the information on the screen.

"Unfortunately, Captain, I cannot give you any firm conclusions," Beck apologized, "only an educated guess based on the information available. However, regarding the original matter you asked me to look into: I would say with ninety-five percent probability that the new Darshik tactic of killing and burning civilians is a direct response to a misunderstanding of the same actions taken by our Marines."

"So I need to see what the hell is going on over here," Jackson ran his finger along the monitor down the line representing the western coast, nearly four thousand, five hundred kilometers away from where everyone was focused on Neuberlin. "And pass it on to Colonel Rucker if your theory pans out … not that he has any way to move his forces over there."

"No he doesn't," Beck said. "But we can deploy our drop shuttles right into it. I realize that our mission is to reinforce Rucker's people but depending on what we might find there it may be necessary to split our forces and leave the defense of the capital to the Marines already there."

"That won't go over well," Jackson said sourly. "But I can't fault your logic. Very well, Lieutenant Colonel … let me see what I can do about getting you the intel you need. Go get some rack time, you look like you really need it."

"Thank you, sir," Beck said, climbing back out of the seat.

"Ensign Dole! Please add Lieutenant Colonel Beck to the bridge access list," Jackson spoke up. "And make it so his credentials will log into this terminal if he needs it."

"Aye, sir."

"I regret having to divide your attention, but I'll likely need you up here again as we plan for our approach and deployment over Juwel," Jackson said to the Marine officer.

"Of course, sir," Beck nodded. "Wherever I'm needed most."

After Beck left the bridge settled into a quiet hum of activity while the *Star* continued to drift along, slowly closing in on the gas giant. Jackson walked over to the OPS station so he could talk to Dole without shouting from the opposite corner of the bridge. He had a vague idea of how to get at least a limited amount of intel, but it wasn't a guarantee.

"Sir?" Dole straightened as Jackson walked over.

"Bring up the specs on the drone we left over Juwel." Jackson laid a hand on the ensign's shoulder. "Specifically the imaging equipment it's carrying." Dole brought up a new window on the leftmost monitor and quickly brought up a scrolling spec sheet of the small spacecraft sitting in high geostationary orbit above the planet.

"It doesn't have much," Dole said, looking over the suite of imagers the drone had available. There were two visible spectrum cameras, one wide-field and the other a more long-range instrument but still nothing that could do the job at the craft's current altitude. There were two other multispectral imagers including one mid-wave thermal camera that also had insufficient magnification power for the job.

"It wasn't meant for this sort of high-altitude information gathering," Jackson sighed. "We're going to have to move it. Go ahead and coordinate with Flight OPS and set a mission profile that will allow me to get high-res imagery of the western coast and the ocean along that side of the continent. The sooner the better."

"Aye, sir," Dole said and slid his headset on, pulling up his com panel as he did.

"Let me know when—"

"Captain, another incoming transmission from the *Relentless*," Epsen interrupted loudly. "This one is directly to you … text only."

"Send it to my station," Jackson said, walking quickly back to the command chair.

Captain Wolfe,

In your status update I see that you haven't yet deployed your drop shuttles despite being in-system for days. Please explain. Your failure to accomplish the Aludra Star's primary mission puts the entire taskforce at risk. I will not authorize the 508ᵗʰ to remain here indefinitely while you remain in the outer system apparently unwilling to risk an encounter with what you yourself described as a collection of derelicts.

I was given overall command of this mission and I intend to see it done with as little collateral damage as possible. Starfleet cannot afford to lose any more destroyers attempting to liberate a single star system. Please send me your planned course back to Juwel and your projected timetable. My ships will remain in the outer system to provide cover for your withdraw.

Senior Captain Rawls

CO, TFS Relentless

Jackson just blinked at the message as he read it a second time. He'd provided Rawls with specifics in a synopsis and all the raw data from his encounter; he should know exactly why they didn't deploy. What the hell was he talking about having his ships remain in the outer system? Not only were they more vulnerable out there to attack from the Darshik cruisers, but that wasn't why they were sent in the first place. They were to provide escort and clear the way for the assault carrier as a destroyer is meant to do, but Rawls had made it clear he had no intention of risking his ships with unnecessary contact with the enemy. He actually planned to just fly circles near the jump point and wait to see if the *Star* could deliver her cargo or was destroyed in the effort.

"Un-fucking-believable," Jackson muttered a bit too loudly and drew concerned looks from some of the crew.

"Sir?" Simmons asked quietly.

"Our escort has arrived," Jackson said, struggling to figure out how to inform his crew their destroyer escort was being commanded by a feckless coward. "Senior Captain Rawls is ... unsure ... of how to proceed in order to ensure the *Star* can safely deploy the drop shuttles."

"I understand, sir," Simmons said with a nod. "What do you plan to do?"

"We have time for one more exchange given the com lag before we have to begin our course correction back for the planet," Jackson said, already typing on his monitor. "We've been drifting cold for too long and the Darshik had a decent idea of our course vector when we aborted our approach the first time. Too much longer and we risk sitting helpless and their ships have demonstrated an uncanny ability to sneak up on Terran ships trying to sit dark."

"Yes, sir," Simmons said. Jackson ignored the questioning look from his XO and continued to type.

Senior Captain Rawls,

The explanation for our launch abort is clearly spelled out in both my synopsis brief and the mission data we forwarded. Given that you have tactical authority over the mission and your ships, I can only suggest that you begin steaming for Juwel at best possible speed. You are highly vulnerable in the outer system and will be unable to clear any enemy ships from our flight path from your current patrol location. Additionally, the com lag will put us at a significant disadvantage given the Darshik ability to warp-hop within the system.

We will be firing main engines within the hour and will begin our second and final run on the planet before we will have no choice but to abort and push for an escape jump point.

Senior Captain Wolfe

CO, TFS Aludra Star

Jackson read through the message twice, rejected the idea of softening the language and encrypted it himself and tagged it with the classification of "EYES ONLY: COMMANDING OFFICER."

"Coms, I'm sending an encrypted packet to you," he said over his shoulder. "Send it immediately, tight-beam burst to the same target area as the last. Address it to all ships in the 508th taskforce." He said this last part as almost an afterthought. It was petty to be sure, but there was no reason that the other captains shouldn't be aware of Rawls's decision since it would affect them as well. At least that was the thin justification he used when in reality he just wanted to expose the squadron commander's cowardice in the face of the enemy. It was a serious accusation, but after some of the things he'd witnessed unqualified COs do in the last war to save their own skin it was something he had zero tolerance for.

"Transmission sent, sir," the ensign that had replaced Lieutenant Epsen said.

"OPS, tell Engineering it's time," Jackson said. "Prepare to fire the mains and begin bringing our primary flight systems online. Tactical, make sure you're coordinating closely with CIC and watching the passives for even the slightest hint that something is sneaking up on us."

"CIC has doubled their watch and is using the auxiliary stations to ensure there is always a redundant set of eyes on each passive system, sir," Simmons said with confidence. "If it's able to be seen, we'll see it."

"Was that your idea?"

"Yes, sir."

"Good man," Jackson said with approval. "Let them know down there that I appreciate the extra effort and the people of Juwel damn sure do as well."

"Yes, sir … I'll pass that on." Simmons sounded somewhat surprised. Praise of any kind from Captain Wolfe was rare so an overt expression of pleasure with something they did was unheard of.

Jackson leaned back and began to worry about all the things he wasn't aware of. What were they missing on the planet that Beck seemed sure existed? What was the full strength of the Darshik fleet presence in the system? Would Captain Rawls suck it up and do what he needed to do in order to accomplish the mission and get them all home safely?

It was the nagging of a thousand important little details that aged starship captains prematurely. While he still looked fit and trim with just a touch of gray at the temples, Jackson very much felt the weight of responsibility pressing down on him. Stranger yet he found the weight comforting. He'd missed it while sitting behind a desk pretending he was an administrator of a research project in one of the most secure systems of the Federation. He could lie to his wife, Jillian, all he liked, but the truth was he never felt more alive than at times like this.

He felt power thrum through the ship as the reactors began feeding power to the *Star*'s flight systems, and his resolve strengthened. He would find a way to accomplish his mission *and* get his crew back home to see their families again … he would get back home to see his wife and children again.

Chapter 15

"You look like shit … when did you get back in?"

"A little over an hour ago and then I saw your message to come straight here the moment I did," Pike said. The CIS agent was drawn-looking and had the sunken-eyed look of someone who hadn't had much sleep lately.

"I know you'll be filing a full report later with Director Sala, but did you get anything?" President Augustus Wellington asked. Pike was technically on permanent detached duty to Wellington and had been since the current President was a senator in the now-defunct Terran Confederacy. When the current head of the CENTCOM Intelligence Section approached Wellington and asked that Pike be brought back into the fold for an extended mission he had approved reluctantly. Pike had an uncanny ability to show up where he was least expected and a knack for gaining intel on things that powerful people tried very hard to keep hidden.

"Despite all the rumors I just can't find anything in the ESA that suggests they've made some great technological leap in ship design," Pike said. "I've been to every shipyard I could find, including the four they tried to keep hidden in the old Confederacy days, and the new hulls are slightly derivative from what they already had in service when their numbered fleets were part of CENTCOM.

"Energy readings, thermal signatures, warp transition flashes … it's all the same. Since they're not shooting at each other I can't say for certain their weapons are unchanged, but it would be a safe bet. Sorry, boss, the rumors of advanced starships streaming out of ESA shipyards appears to be unfounded."

Wellington stiffened as Pike casually called him *boss*, something he utterly hated, but didn't bother correcting him this time. "Damn," he said, turning around to face the sidebar. "Sala made such a compelling case for it too. Had defector testimony from three people who were apparently not connected to each other and their stories held up to scrutiny."

"May I remind the esteemed President of the *United* Terran Federation that I always was highly suspect of the good director's claims?" Pike yawned and accepted a glass of what he assumed was Scotch from the President.

"You never made a clear case why," Wellington said.

"*Three* defectors out of the ESA, all arriving separately and all claiming to have worked on highly secret ship building projects?" Pike scoffed. "No way. And then to claim they have no idea where the secret shipyards are? Then how the hell did they leave? Navigating through space requires you know where you were and where you're going. And how the hell did they get out of the ESA? There are no more starliner flights and Fed ships are forbidden. They're either plants by the ESA or they're working for Sala."

"I don't think it was Sala," Wellington shook his head so hard his jowls kept on after his head stopped. "If they're ESA agents what was the goal?"

"Who knows?" Pike shrugged. "Could have been to catch someone like me snooping around the locations we were given. It'd be a convenient excuse to start a war and they know the Fed is weakened and distracted with the Darshik problem at the moment."

"It would be nice if the intel flowed both ways," Wellington snarled. "They know every detail about what's happening on New Sierra and we don't even know who the fuck is in charge over there. Amazing."

"They control their media and communications a lot more strictly than we do," Pike said, stifling another yawn. "Is that all?"

"That's all … get out of here and get some sleep," Wellington said. "Don't get too comfortable. I might be calling on you soon."

"Better prod the Tsuyo techies to get the Broadhead back up to snuff." Pike rose. "Five months of constant operation has her a little beat up."

"Not to mention you being stuck in those confines the whole time," Wellington waved him off. "They'll probably have to strip the upholstery out and fumigate it."

Pike laughed over his shoulder as he walked out of the Presidential office. It was the one in Haven Hill, the residence of the Federation's leader, rather than the executive suite at the Praetorsta, the building where the parliament convened. Wellington rarely used that one, convinced it was being monitored at all times. Pike had never found any evidence that it was, but he wasn't a tech expert by any means. His skill was getting in someplace, gaining the information he needed, and leaving without a trace.

The ride back up to the New Sierra Platform was unusually smooth as the scheduled shuttle, lightly loaded this late in the evening, climbed effortlessly into the night sky. Pike reflected back on the mission he'd been sent out for and still couldn't figure out if he'd been played, and if so, by whom? The premise of advanced starships coming out of Eastern Star Alliance yards was thin at best, but Wellington seemed to have swallowed it whole and sent him on a very long, very boring, and ultimately pointless fact-finding mission deep into ESA space.

He'd forgotten how much he hated taking the "cattle car" to get down and back from the surface. Usually his Broadhead would automatically dock in its secure, private berth and he'd be on the station without so much as waving his ID to a Marine sentry or submitting a biometric scan. Now he was in line behind seven other people as two Marines and one dweeb from Fleet Security patted down and questioned every person coming aboard as if they were a threat, never mind the fact they'd gone through an identical procedure just to get on the shuttle on the surface.

Once through the dehumanizing ordeal, his false credentials passing scrutiny, he made his way to the cramped office he had down in the intel section that he suspected used to actually be a janitorial closet and logged into his terminal. After sifting through his messages to see what his workload would be like the next few days he looked up the docking schedule for the platform to check on the off chance the *Icarus* was currently docked to the station. It wasn't. In fact, it hadn't been back to the DeLonges System since it had left with Ambassador Cole for the unnamed world on the Frontier.

"Strange," he murmured, checking the schedule and seeing that the destroyer was long overdue and nobody had seemed to flag an official inquiry about it. He began to dig deeper, at first out of idle curiosity and a desire to see if it would be convenient to see Celesta Wright, but the further he went the more concerned he became.

The first warning that something was off was that he was forced to keep digging deeper into his bag of credentials to provide the necessary security clearances to proceed. Eventually he had to enter in a set of access codes he'd only used twice before that came from the authority of the President himself. As far as he could tell he was reading mission data for the *Icarus* that even Fleet Admiral Pitt would have trouble accessing, so he knew he had to tread carefully. He was under no delusions that he was immune to the consequences of abusing his access. As long as he was useful to Wellington he was protected, but if he stepped in it and became an embarrassment to the administration he would find his ass flapping in the breeze.

He sucked in a breath when he saw that the *Icarus* had been dispatched with Ambassador Cole aboard to meet with the Ushin again at their behest. The destroyer went out alone. No escort, no resupply convoy to meet it halfway ... that was a long flight for a ship of that class. Even the logistics of the mission aside, it made little sense to send a mainline warship as a consular ship if trying to vie for peaceful relations was the goal. Pike was about to close out the files when he saw the date the mission started; it was long enough that he was certain the ship must have run into trouble.

The next file he dug into set his mind at ease, but only slightly. A point-to-point com drone had been received by the DeLonges com platform from Celesta's ship giving a post-mission brief. He saw that the captain reported her overall mission a failure but sent back loads of sensor data regarding some unknown class of Darshik ship that had seemingly appeared out of nowhere and taken out the Ushin delegation before she could make contact. The *Icarus* had sustained minor damage and the strange ship had fled the engagement before Celesta could come about and return fire.

"This *is* strange," Pike said aloud in his closet/office. He had memorized all the attempts by Fleet R&S and Tsuyo Research Division to develop predictive models and psychological profiles of the new enemy. While most were beyond useless, there were some analysts that had provided some useful information when it came to Darshik military strategy, and the engagement Celesta was reporting didn't match. A single ship, skillfully commanded, nimble and stealthy … it flew in the face of the bludgeon the Darshik preferred when facing a Terran force.

The sensor imagery from the *Icarus* during the single pass the enemy ship made didn't do much to clear up the confusion for Pike. It looked nothing like the blocky cruisers they'd faced from the Darshik so far. In fact, it seemed to be a strange hodgepodge of dissimilar shipbuilding philosophies. The decorative hash marks along the prow seemed to be just another indicator that this was no ordinary Darshik fleet cruiser.

"A rogue?" Pike asked, flipping through the imagery. "Or some sort of specialized strike unit?"

The screen suddenly flickered and went out, a warning bar stating that he was accessing restricted material flashed, and the system forcibly booted his terminal off the secure network. He shrugged and reached over, unplugging the processing unit from the network spoofer he had sitting on the floor and slipping it into his pocket. After making a note of which set of false access credentials had been compromised he stood and left the office.

He wasn't overly worried about being caught snooping around. The warning message had been a response from the secure network's automated protection system when it decided it didn't like the tenacity with which he was digging into sensitive material. He could have bypassed the lockout, but he had what he needed. With any luck the intrusion would be logged and never looked at by anyone in Fleet Security. His network spoofer and CIS-issued credentials would ensure they'd have a virtually impossible time tracing the access back to his little office or him in particular. He'd toss the terminal processor into the recyclers to eliminate the hardcoded serial number it transmitted with any network request and he'd take that particular set of credentials out of rotation.

Whatever Celesta had decided to do after the encounter with this Darshik hotshot, it hadn't been to return to New Sierra. The failure to report back hadn't triggered an investigation or a search and rescue operation yet, so either CENTCOM knew exactly where the *Icarus* was or they'd decided the ship was likely lost and didn't want the sensitive mission to see the Ushin public knowledge by announcing it through normal channels. The hell of it was that even with all his resources Pike couldn't think of whom to ask discreetly. Chief of Staff Marcum despised him, Fleet Admiral Pitt wasn't a huge admirer either, and President Wellington wouldn't be too pleased he'd gone on a fishing expedition through classified data because his maybe-girlfriend was possibly missing.

He arrived at his spartan quarters and as soon as the door clanged shut the exhaustion he'd been carrying around since being summoned to the planet surface overwhelmed him. He kicked his shoes off and was asleep in less than a minute, sprawled out on the couch, one leg hanging off. The agent would occasionally twitch or mumble as he was tormented in his dreams by visions of a *Starwolf*-class destroyer being reduced to slag by a Darshik warship with twin hash marks on each side of its pointed prow.

****

Interstellar space was a terrifying place, Celesta concluded. There was the nothingness of the void between the planets, but the gaps between the stars was truly humbling. The *Icarus* had been forced out of warp by a variance in the forward distortion ring that the computers couldn't correct while the drive was running. Her Chief Engineer, Commander Graham, had quickly isolated the problem and assured her it would be quickly corrected. It didn't make her feel any less queasy about sitting powerless in deep space.

The Darshik ship had done more damage than previously thought with its glancing blow, and once they'd been in warp flight for the better part of three days the issue began to make itself known. The power cable that was spooled out to feed the port, forward emitter had taken damage, not from the plasma lance itself, but from bits of the hardened alloy of the ship's structure that were blown inward by the hit. The cable assembly had been inspected, but the damage had been undetectable until the drive powered up. The cable was damaged just enough that it caused interference with the drive's control system.

The *Icarus* carried four spare warp drive emitter power cables so it wasn't a catastrophic failure, just a time-consuming one. First the emitter had to be fully retracted, the hatch closed and the chamber pressurized, something it normally wasn't. Then crews would climb in and dig out the old cable and detach it from the emitter/arm assembly. Once the new cable was installed Engineering would redeploy the emitter and then begin the forty-three-hour process of testing and calibrating the entire drive. Since the new cable would have a different impedance, no matter how miniscule, it required the full calibration so the new numbers could be entered into the drive controller tables.

To add insult to injury, when Celesta had ordered another of their point-to-point com drones launched to make sure someone at CENTCOM was aware of their position in deep space they found even more damage. The launch bay had been hit and the metal that had been broken loose inside had damaged the launcher for the nine drones she had left. They still had all their standard com drones, but they would be of no use in their current position.

"What update do we have from Engineering?" she asked for the tenth time since coming on watch four hours prior.

"They just finished the extension and retraction operational test, ma'am," Accari said. "The emitter/arm assembly cycled ten times without any binding or problems. Engineering is preparing to power up the drive and begin the calibration. Commander Barrett says they may have it done in twenty-eight hours if all goes well."

"Commander Barrett?" Celesta asked, just then noticing that her XO was absent.

"Yes, ma'am," Accari said. "He's been coordinating the efforts down in Engineering so that Commander Graham can be with his crews in the forward port warp emitter bay."

"I see," she said. She didn't say so, but Barrett being down in Engineering was likely slowing them down more than helping. He was a tactical officer and before that had been an OPS officer ... he'd always served on the bridge of a starship and his background wasn't in engineering. Still, she doubted Commander Graham would tolerate him being underfoot if he was actually slowing his crew's progress. He felt personally responsible for that strange Darshik ship's warp transition flash being overlooked, and it was that same ship that killed their mission and damaged the ship. If it made him feel better to sit with the people fixing the ship so be it; it was a sentiment she well understood and he wasn't needed on the bridge otherwise.

"How are we with mapping out local space and getting a fix on our position?"

"Our position has been verified; we drifted just over three hundred thousand kilometers off course," Accari said. "Commander Graham assures me that it was because of the drive variance that eventually shut us down. High-power radar scans have verified that local space is clear dead ahead out to a distance of sixty-two million kilometers, and accelerometer data isn't indicating any unusual gravimetric anomalies. CIC and Science have both cleared us for transition along our current course."

"Very well," Celesta nodded, still fidgeting. "Make sure everyone is rotating out for extended rest periods. Even if we were tracked out of that system I think we're exceedingly safe sitting out here in the middle of nowhere."

"Aye, ma'am, I'll handle it," Accari said.

"You have the bridge, Mr. Accari." She rose quickly, startling the ensign sitting at the tactical station. "Let me know if I'm needed."

"I have the bridge, aye."

Her restlessness was not only unprofessional and distracting for her crew, it was contagious. There was no reason to think they were in any danger in the random place their drive had failed, so there was no reason to get them worked up and agitated. It wasn't the situation they found themselves in that galled her, it was the unshakable feeling that things were going very, very badly in the Juwel System.

Celesta had complete faith in Captain Wolfe, perhaps more so than he had in himself, but the *Aludra Star* was an obsolete ship the moment the bottle broke on her hull during the commissioning ceremony. Not only that, but she was an assault carrier, not a destroyer, and certainly not a battleship. If the 508th hadn't been able to clear the blockade it wasn't likely that Wolfe had been able to get the slower, lightly armed ship all the way down to Juwel to deploy his drop shuttles. But she knew he'd try anyway.

It was this gut feeling that had her constantly uneasy and snappish while she waited for her skilled crew to repair the *Icarus* and turn her back over to her captain so they could be on their way. Three *Intrepid*-class destroyers were nothing to sneeze at, but she had little faith in the men who commanded them, even knowing them by reputation only. She just wished CENTCOM would take the Juwel invasion seriously. There were two *Dreadnought*-class boomers sitting in the DeLonges System that could be moved in to deliver a crushing blow to the ongoing blockade.

As she walked the corridors of her ship, intent on passing along words of encouragement and checking on the general readiness of the crew, she knew it wasn't logistics that kept CENTCOM from deploying their big guns to save the people of Juwel. It was fear. After the attack on the DeLonges System the halls of power on the New Sierra Platform positively reeked of it. The hollow excuses they used for holding the bigger ships back—to use less ships to protect more assets while deploying the smaller destroyers forward—were pathetically transparent. And so here they were again it seemed: the whole of the Federation made weaker by the timidity and fearfulness of the people put in place to protect it.

"The more things change the more they stay the same," she snorted in disgust, startling two enlisted spacers as she walked in front of a side corridor, her face a thundercloud of anger that she couldn't keep from showing.

"Maybe *I'm* the one doing more harm than good wandering around the lower decks," she mumbled to herself, taking the next cross corridor to make her way back to the lifts that ran up to the superstructure. She would contain her outbursts and foul mood to her office until the *Icarus* was ready to get underway.

Chapter 16

Jackson Wolfe paced the bridge, his nerves stretched thin as his people went about their jobs, not needing him to provide guidance as the *Star* was made ready to get underway. Lieutenant Colonel Beck was back up on the bridge working over the data that was coming in from the drone Jackson had ordered repositioned. Surprisingly it had taken the Darshik twelve full orbits of the little craft, broadcasting real-time telemetry, before they finally destroyed it.

Not surprisingly, Colonel Beck was also an expert at aerial imagery analysis and was skillfully making use of the *Star's* formidable computing power to analyze all the high-res, radar, and multispectral data to try and coax some sort of motive out of the mess for the Darshik's bizarrely run ground war. Jackson instinctively felt that Beck was correct in his assessment of the issue despite having zero experience commanding troops on the surface or fighting a ground engagement himself. He was also becoming quite impressed with the cool, calm Marine lieutenant colonel who went about his work with a smooth efficiency that delivered results while seeking no accolades. It was a breath of fresh air in a time when Starfleet was still struggling to purge a *lot* of bad officers from its ranks in the wake of the failures during the Phage War.

"Main engines are available, Captain," Ensign Dole reported. "All plasma chambers are hot and the nozzle constrictors are stable. Engineering reports the powerplant is now providing full combat power."

"Excellent," Jackson said. "Tactical?"

"All expendable munitions are responding and passed self-tests, laser batteries are charged and primed, and our orbit-to-surface guns are ready, Captain," Commander Simmons said. "Sensors are ready to go active at your command; still monitoring passives."

"Very well." Jackson forced himself to sit down. "Go ahead and retract the towed sensor array and secure it. OPS, plot us a course that puts us in a decaying orbit intersecting Juwel. Don't be overly aggressive with your flightpath, I want to conserve velocity without needing to light up the sky with the mains any more than absolutely necessary. Coms, any word from the 508th taskforce?"

"Nothing has come back to us, sir," Epsen said. "We've been receiving chatter on a Fleet channel that looks like the three ships talking to each other but nothing directed our way."

"Were you able to decipher anything being said on that Fleet frequency?"

"No, sir," Epsen said. "We couldn't pick up enough to determine the encryption they were using. I can tell you it wasn't any of the codes that were in rotation for this mission, however."

Epsen had given him the information he'd wanted without being asked, and the answer made him clench his jaw in frustration. Rawls and his commanders were talking amongst themselves, broadcasting for the entire galaxy to hear, using encryption codes he wasn't privy to. That didn't bode well for how the mission would likely be executed from there on out. The Darshik were no doubt closing in on their positions. They knew the Terran ships were in the system and enough time had passed without a mad rush or the system being flooded with high-power active sensors that Jackson was certain they were planning some nasty surprise for the handful of ships that had squeezed in past their picket line.

They were almost certain to be in for the fight of their lives soon and Rawls was still playing fucking games and trying to pick a side strategy that would allow him to not actually bring his ships into harm's way. The former Merchant Fleet officer was in for a rude awakening. Although the Darshik weren't especially advanced, they were dogged and they were aggressive. Jackson knew that the four Terran ships in the system had already delayed too long to just simply escape; the Darshik would be moving now to cut off their routes of egress, the known jump points, and using their other assets to begin corralling them into a kill box where they could bring their plasma lances to bear. He was still determined to get his shuttles to the surface where they needed to be, not to mention unload the *Star* of forty percent of her current mass, but he knew they'd have to fight their way out.

"Have we received a Link request from the 508th ships?" Jackson asked.

"No, sir," Dole said. "Our Link transponder isn't broadcasting while we're observing EMSEC protocols, but we should still be receiving the telemetry feeds from the three destroyers."

"Shall I send them a request to activate their Link connections, sir?" Epsen asked.

"Negative, Coms," Jackson sighed. "We're beginning our own course correction and I'd like to remain hidden as long as possible. Let the 508th be as much of a distraction as possible for the time being; whether they're doing it intentionally or not, they've been making a hell of a racket near the system boundary. OPS, how long until we're ready to fire engines and start back downhill to Juwel?"

"Forty-three minutes until we intersect our projected flightpath down," Dole said, still tapping furiously at his terminal. "I've sent the new course to your terminal and the helm, sir."

"Very good." Jackson stayed his hand from checking over the ensign's work immediately. He would have plenty of time to make sure there weren't any snags in the young officer's new course without giving the impression he didn't trust him to do his job and was looking over his shoulder at every turn.

"Captain, a word, sir?" Colonel Beck said quietly from Jackson's left.

"Of course, Colonel." Jackson motioned to the seat Beck was standing behind. "What can I do for you?"

Beck produced an oversized tile and took the seat, bringing up a series of images to show Jackson, many of them the same photo with different processing enhancements to highlight detail.

"The Darshik have something off the western coast that they're protecting with orbital bombardment and the distraction of the undermanned infantry push towards

Neuberlin," Beck said, showing him a structure of some sort that was clearly visible just under the water's surface.

"What is that?" Jackson asked, leaning in for a closer look at the three accompanying false-color images Beck had put up with the original picture captured by their now-destroyed drone.

"Without a frame of reference this is just a guess … but I think this is an atmospheric processor," Beck said hesitantly. "And if you'll look at the scale of how big this one is—"

"It's the size of a damn fleet carrier," Jackson whispered as he saw the scale lines Beck had imposed over the image.

"Yes, sir," the Marine nodded. "In my unqualified opinion, this is likely being used to modify enormous volumes of atmosphere as it passes through the machine."

"Terraforming," Jackson grunted. "We have atmospheric composition data from a Darshik world thanks to Captain Wright's mission, and Terran worlds aren't a match."

"Yes, sir," Beck said calmly. "I looked that up. The drone we launched didn't have the capability to analyze the gas composition around the machine remotely, but with the help of your Engineering section I was able to make an educated guess that three such machines would be able to shift the atmosphere enough that the Darshik could live there within five to ten years. A lot of that depends on the machine's efficiency and capacity, of course, but Lieutenant Commander Sharpe was fairly confident in his numbers given velocity and volume of air capable of coming out of that main stack."

"So over the next five years Terran flora and fauna will quickly choke off and die ... including the humans that live there," Jackson said.

"Essentially, sir," Beck said. "Maybe not quite that quickly, but humans sure as hell wouldn't be able to stay there without the aid of a rebreather."

And just like that, Jackson now fully understood the Darshik strategy for Juwel. Along with that understanding was the realization that it would be very difficult to stop with the assets they had in the system currently, doubly so given the difficulty he was already having with Senior Captain Rawls.

The strategy was as brilliant in its simplicity as it was brutal in its execution. There was no need for an invasion force large enough to displace the humans on Juwel, they just needed to keep them focused on the distraction of the Darshik ground forces while they slowly shifted the atmosphere to the point where the humans that couldn't evacuate with the blockade in place would asphyxiate and die over the course of half a dozen years. By the time they realized what was happening it would be far too late for them even if they managed to destroy the single atmospheric processor that was almost up and running.

"Given the state of Starfleet right now and CENTCOM's reluctance to commit a larger force to repel the Darshik in this system, a strategy of conquest that takes years doesn't seem so farfetched," Jackson said slowly. "If we can't accomplish our mission now, then by the time Fleet gets around to fielding another underpowered battlegroup to come back out here it will be too late."

"That's my take on it as well, sir," Beck said. "But … I'm just a lowly ground pounder."

"False modesty is *not* a virtue, Colonel."

"Yes, sir."

"It would seem your mission has just changed," Jackson said. "Given this new information and the degree of accuracy you feel you have with the help of Lieutenant Commander Sharpe … deploying your forces to reinforce Colonel Rucker doesn't make a lot of sense now."

"I'm relieved to hear you say that, Captain." Beck nodded. "I'm formally requesting that my mission objectives be changed and the *Aludra Star's* drop shuttles get us on the ground near that processor."

"No offense, Colonel, but I don't think your group of Marines are going to be much of a threat to something that big," Jacksons shook his head. "We'll have to hit it from orbit and I wouldn't want you too near the thing when we do."

"I'm confused then, Captain," Beck said. "Where would you have us put down if not Neuberlin and not the coastal area where the processor is?"

"I want to put you in between these two coastal cities." Jackson gestured to the two large cities, each built up around natural harbors on the western coastline. "They aren't building that massive of a construct with no ground support. I think we're missing a large number of camouflaged troops, engineers, and construction crews to support the effort."

"You want us to take them out?"

"I do," Jackson said. "More specifically, I would like you to consider my suggestion to take them out. I have no authority over the ground campaign and the *Star* is here to support your efforts. I think there's a sizable Darshik force down there supporting and defending the construction of this processor, and I also think there's a decently high chance that we won't be able to destroy it from orbit depending on what insertion vector the defending ships force us on to safely deploy your shuttles.

"As I said, your force as it stands simply doesn't carry enough firepower to take out something as large as we're seeing in these images. If I can't get Captain Rawls's ships down here or the *Star* is forced to correct course, I can't guarantee I'll be able to put weapons on target."

"It seems I have some planning to do, and quickly," Beck nodded. "With your permission, sir?"

"Dismissed, Colonel," Jackson nodded. "Coms! Send *another* burst transmission to the *Relentless* and tell them I would appreciate it if they would activate their Link connections so I can at least use their active sensor picture to help plan our approach."

"Aye, sir."

"And then prepare to send another to the Marines on the planet surface." Jackson sighed. "We have some bad news for them."

Chapter 17

"Incoming burst transmission from the *Aludra Star*, sir!"

"About fucking time," Colonel Rucker snapped, grabbing the tile from his com operator and reading through the message quickly once, then again more slowly.

"Good news, sir?" a lieutenant from Intel asked hopefully.

"There's good news and bad news," Rucker shook his head. "It seems the attack on Neuberlin is just a diversion, so our success or failure to hold the line will not determine if Juwel falls."

"And the good news, sir?"

"That *was* the good news, Lieutenant." Rucker slapped the tile into the chest of the sergeant who had brought it to him, causing the NCO to grunt. "The not-so-good news is that Colonel Beck's relief force will not be deploying to reinforce us. Captain Wolfe is going to drop them somewhere along the west coast to try and counter what the Darshik are really up to … something about changing the atmosphere."

"So we're on our own," the lieutenant mumbled.

"What we are, *Lieutenant,* are Terran Federation Marines … and we will continue to perform our mission until the last of us falls," Rucker said with some venom in his voice. If there was anything he hated more than losing, it was defeatism. "Now go get me Major Baer."

"Yes, sir!" the lieutenant snapped, happy to be given an avenue of escape.

Colonel Rucker watched him go for a moment before turning back to the map display showing the suspected enemy positions as his outlying patrols began feeding him intel. All his planning had revolved around Colonel Beck swooping in within the next week with his fresh Marines, heavy artillery, ground vehicles, and maybe a nice round of orbital bombardment from the *Aludra Star* as she streaked past on her way back out of the system.

Now, instead of trying to hold their position while clinging to the hope of reinforcements, he and his Marines just became a speedbump and they'd barely slow the Darshik on their way to Neuberlin. But the more he thought about it, why try to defend Neuberlin at all? If the intel from Wolfe was solid, all the Darshik infantry had been sent to do was tie up the Marines here and provide a convincing cover, not actually invade the capital.

He brought up another window that provided a running count of how many Marines he had left, how they were equipped, and what ground transportation was available to him. It galled him that he had absolutely no aerial assets to move quick-reaction forces or evacuate wounded if overrun, but he put that aside and focused on what he could control. He might have been dealt a shitty hand on a mission that would likely be his last from the looks of things, but he'd make sure his Marines wouldn't go down without a fight the Darshik wouldn't soon forget.

****

"What's the word, Major?" Sergeant Barton asked as Major Baer walked back over to 2nd Platoon's cordoned-off area. He'd been at the colonel's hastily called mission planning brief for the better part of an hour.

"We're moving out," the major said. "But not to Neuberlin and not in a single force."

"What the fuck?" Castillo raised his head up from where he'd been napping. "There aren't enough of us here to hold off a determined group of elderly pensioners trying to get to a Sunday buffet, what the hell are we going to do by dividing the force further?"

"That's 'What the fuck, *Sir*,' Castillo," Baer said. "And get off your fat ass when you're speaking to me." Alejandro Castillo scrambled to his feet and snapped to attention.

"*Sir*, what the fuck, *sir*?" he said crisply. Major Baer just rolled his eyes.

"We've received intel that Neuberlin isn't the primary objective," he went on. "Instead of allowing them to grind us into the dirt in a futile last stand to hold the city, we're *not* advancing en masse to the capital. Instead, we'll break off into at least ten elements and begin harassing their rear guard and right flank. We are not to engage in a standing fight with them; the colonel wants us to stick and move all up and down their lines."

"How is this any less futile than trying to beat them to Neuberlin and digging in?" Barton asked.

"If the enemy is only trying to tie us up here then this will not only give us a greater chance of survival until such time as CENTCOM decides to send actual reinforcements but it will keep them out of a major urban area," Baer said. "The point now is to try and slow them or get them to cluster up and not give them the chance to make any more bonfires out of the civilian populace. Understood?"

"Not at all, Major," Barton shrugged. "But I think we get enough to get moving. Where do you want us?"

"Just be ready," Baer said. "We'll get specific orders shortly but get your gear together for a seventy-two-hour patrol. I doubt we'll be coming back to this base so grab any other personal effects you don't want to leave behind." He turned and left, Barton assumed to grab his own gear from where he was bunking in the command center: a building that looked like it might have been used to store farm machinery at one point.

"You heard the major." Barton stood and stretched. "I want to be ready for anything within the hour."

He didn't say anything to the younger enlisted Marines in his care, but there was a lot left unsaid by Major Baer in the short "briefing." The fact they were abandoning both the base and the defense of Neuberlin said one thing, and only one thing, to the veteran NCO: something had happened and the Marines aboard the *Aludra Star* were not coming. While it was well outside his area of expertise his first assumption was that, despite being commanded by a legendary captain, the assault carrier had been destroyed trying to run the Darshik blockade.

Despite having served in the Marines, both Confederate and Federation, he knew next to nothing about ships battling in space. Hell, he'd only been on a starship twice in his life: once leaving Columbiana to enlist and then again to deploy out to Juwel. The expense of operating the big ships and the losses taken in the Phage War meant that most of his training had been done on planetside simulators, really just long buildings set up to look like starships, and then some zero-g and vac-suit training on orbital platforms over the planet DeLonges. But even with his limited grasp of the subject he could read between the lines when listening to the loose-lipped officers of the intel group: The Darshik picket ships were many and the *Aludra Star* had arrived alone.

This brought up a few unpleasant realities, at least from the limited view Barton had of the overall situation. First was that the division was already running low on consumables, most importantly ammunition for their weapons. While Juwel was a well-armed planet they didn't use compatible weaponry, almost all of it being a sort of antiquated cartridge type that couldn't be adapted for the firing mechanisms of the Marines' carbines and machine guns that used electrically fired, caseless ammo. They could use the civilian weaponry, of course, but that would almost certainly drag the population into the fight in greater numbers, not just the few advisors like Emil. How long would the Darshik continue to play these games if the population rose up against their paltry ground forces? The answer was likely not at all, and major cities would be bombarded from orbit until all resistance was crushed.

The other logistical concerns aside, Barton knew that this new strategy of quasi-guerilla fighting was just pissing in the wind. An intelligent alien race didn't waste the resources to fly massive starships out to Juwel and blockade the system to march around in the countryside in perpetuity. There was a goal they were working towards and he doubted it involved humans being allowed to live peacefully on the surface for much longer. But absent any other valid options he would saddle up with the rest of his Marines and continue to do his job as best he could and deal with the Darshik endgame when and if it came while he was still alive.

"That's a pretty serious face you've got there, Sarge," Castillo said, letting his pack slide off his shoulder to the ground. "You know something we don't?"

"What's that?" Barton shook his head. "No … you know the drill. We won't be given any critical information until Command thinks we need it."

"So … at least twelve hours after it would have been useful."

"Exactly."

The mobilization went surprisingly smooth considering they had to completely reorganize the division into twelve strike teams that seemed to be based on random selection rather than pulling logically from the organizational chart. Barton didn't necessarily have a problem with that since it kept him matched up with Corporal Castillo as well as two other friends of his from 3rd Platoon that he knew were solid fighters from the limited action they'd seen on the planet so far.

Colonel Rucker wasted no time in dividing his officers up among the strike teams, Major Baer specifically asking for Sergeant Barton's team, and getting them into vehicles with nothing more than a rough area of responsibility with limited overlaps in the coverage. The colonel was very specific that they were to avoid the locals at all costs to avoid drawing attention to those in the outlying towns that hadn't evacuated. He also didn't want any excess com chatter. The Darshik couldn't break their encryption yet, at least to their knowledge, but a lot of radio transmissions broadcasting across the countryside and an empty base would suggest to all but the densest of military strategists that the humans were up to something. Rucker didn't want to force their hand and cause them to lash out at the civilians again in order to draw the Marines out or disrupt their plans. He'd also given them some clue as to why they weren't being reinforced by the troops on the *Aludra Star*.

"The point of this maneuver, Marines, is to confuse the enemy and keep them fixated on us … not the civilians and not Colonel Beck's group when they drop along the western coast," Colonel Rucker said, standing on the tailgate of a large agricultural off-road vehicle and wearing a hodgepodge of his uniform and commandeered civvy garments. Barton looked around and saw that the senior staff was similarly kitted out and wondered why they would be dressing like civilian guerilla fighters if the point was to keep the Darshik from attacking the locals.

"You may be wondering about our new … uniforms," Rucker said, giving voice to Barton's unspoken question. "You're encouraged to do the same with anything you might find useful or which breaks up the appearance of what the Darshik will recognize as a standard CENTCOM battle uniform. It might seem counterintuitive, but we're going for maximum confusion here. We want them spinning in circles and worrying about who is attacking them and from where it might come. The overarching goal is to try and collapse their lines back down upon themselves so the entire force bunches up into a defensive knot. This will keep them out of the population centers and also conveniently package them for an orbital strike from the *Aludra Star* when Captain Wolfe makes his approach within the next few days—." The rest of Rucker's words were drowned out by a loud cheer that went up at the mention of orbital fire support soon. Barton maintained his silence, staring hard at the colonel and watching his facial tics to try and determine how honest he was being with them. Was Wolfe really coming back?

"Settle down, Marines!" Rucker cut over the cheering. "For OPSEC purposes I can't divulge the nature of the threat to the west, but just know that the Darshik have larger designs on this planet than just a few raids on outlying towns and marching into the capital. Fight smart, fight hard, and show no mercy when you have the chance to inflict damage and maybe we'll all make it back home when this is over. Get with your team commanders for your specific assignments and get moving. I want this camp broken down and abandoned within the next three hours. That is all."

Rucker turned and hopped off the truck without another word, grabbing his own carbine from where it leaned against one of the massive rear wheels and pulling himself up into the passenger seat. Without so much as a wave to his Marines the truck's drive engaged with the dull throb of worn motors and it rolled slowly away from the gathering and towards where another group of Marines had been standing apart from the assembly. Barton recognized two of them as spec ops operators on loan from CENTCOM Special Operations Command, the umbrella unit that ran the NOVA program as well as the handful of specialized Marine units.

He frowned as the group boarded the truck in a calm, orderly fashion and continued on through the front gate of the camp. Colonel Rucker appeared to be gathering up their most experienced and highly trained people for his own team. Barton liked the old man and hoped that it was because he planned to lead from the front and not what a more cynical NCO would think of a senior officer in the same situation: that the colonel was bringing along the best people to cover his own ass while the others slogged it out with the enemy.

"There's that ugly face again," Castillo punched him in the shoulder. "What is it this time?"

"Just thinking," Barton said.

"Why?" Castillo asked, seeming to be completely serious. "Nothing good ever comes of it. Come on, Sarge … we need to get our shit on the truck and get the hell out of here. We don't want to be the last team here and have to clean up this mess."

"True enough," Barton agreed and hustled after the corporal. It had been nearly four days since they'd had any contact with the enemy, and he was wondering what they were up to out there. The *Aludra Star* had been able to get some low-resolution pictures of the area with a drone it had do a few flybys, but from what he'd been told by the intel guys there wasn't really anything they could make out. The drone had been focused on something happening along the western coastline and the images were being transmitted down as a favor. Apparently the spacecraft hadn't survived more than three passes, so the Darshik warships were still sitting up there, just waiting for Wolfe to try and make another run. Barton didn't put much faith in heroes or legends, but he fervently hoped that just a bit of what was said about the infamous starship captain held true and he was able to get through and provide a little support.

Chapter 18

"Incoming message from the *Relentless*, Captain," Epsen said, interrupting the conversation Jackson was having with his XO.

"Just read it to me," Jackson said wearily. He'd been up for thirty-two hours straight and he was beginning to feel it. The *Star* had been delayed in turning back in for the inner system and he still had no damn idea where the Darshik ships were and that made him very edgy.

"Captain Rawls says they're not running active sensors and are observing stealth protocols as per standard operating procedure, sir," Epsen said, looking uncomfortable. Jackson's cheeks flushed as he could just imagine the condescending tone Ed Rawls used when giving his com officer the message to send.

"That idiot is broadcasting radio like a com platform and isn't even running his radar to search for local threats," Jackson muttered, struggling to maintain his detached professionalism in front of his crew.

"Coms, please send this reply," he spoke up after clearing his throat before looking at the ceiling for a moment. "Disregard, Coms … we've already been too lax with our emission security. Maintain com silence."

"Aye, sir," Epsen said.

"OPS, status on our primary flight systems?" Jackson asked. When they'd fired the engines up to begin their run back down to the planet the secondary attitude thrust system had failed to respond. The backup system was fed by its own, isolated power system so that even if all three main busses failed they would still be able to point the ship in the direction they wished and use the emergency chemical rocket boosters to get the ship out of danger. Theoretically.

The irony of them being forced to hold because the bulletproof failsafe system wasn't responding wasn't lost on Jackson. He just hoped it wasn't an omen of things to come.

"Engineering has finished with the repair and is almost ready to begin testing," Dole said. "Lieutenant Commander Sharpe said it was a minor problem, but he wants to test all the jets anyway."

"Tell him he can test while we're underway," Jackson said. "We're not waiting. Helm! Come onto new course, all ahead full."

"Coming onto new course," the helmsman said as he executed the preprogrammed script that would swing the *Star* onto her new heading. The computer had been continuously updating their course correction as they continued to drift during the repairs. "All engines ahead full, aye!"

An instant later and the comforting rumble of the main engines running up could be felt through the deck plates, and the tracks on the main display began updating with their new course and countdown timers to specific waypoints and mission thresholds.

"Tactical?"

"We're still tracking three Darshik cruisers via the passives, sir," Simmons said. "Two near the planet underway in a high orbit and another lurking out between us and the DeLonges jump point. He's oriented so that we see the main engines fire every so often, and the computer has been maintaining a predictive plot from there despite what looks like his best attempts to be silent."

"That ship is sitting and tracking the 508th ships," Jackson said, hands on his hips and eyes narrowed as he studied the tactical plots arrayed on the main display. "They're not overly worried about us; they'll rely on the ships over Juwel to counter any moves we might make, but he's sitting quiet and watching those three destroyers."

"Maybe they lost track of us, sir," Dole offered hopefully.

"Possible, but unlikely," Jackson said with an indulgent smile. "They have ships spread out all over this system and despite how careful we've been I'm afraid they've had plenty of opportunity to triangulate our rough position from our com traffic. It was one of the reasons I wanted us tucked up behind that gas giant: Any starship approaching us would have interacted with the magnetic field enough that the passives should have easily detected them."

The crew fell silent and Jackson continued to watch the threat board, listening to the ship groan slightly as she fought against her own inertia and the gravitational pull of the massive planet ahead of them to come onto the course he had ordered. He looked at the clock and saw they had at least thirty hours before they hit their first threshold and had some decisions to make.

"XO, you have the watch," Jackson said, the exhaustion of the last few days weighing down on him. "Stay on duty for another four hours and then call up your relief; after that I want you in the rack for at least eight hours. Understood?"

"I have the bridge, aye," Simmons nodded. "Don't worry, sir … you won't see me up here again before I need to be. It's been a long watch."

"That it has, Commander," Jackson agreed. "Carry on."

His feet felt leaden as he trudged off the bridge on the way to his quarters, even his artificial leg seeming to move slower than normal. It was at times like these he keenly felt that he was getting older and he didn't appreciate the feeling. His wife, Jillian, teased him that he'd better start looking into the Tsuyo rejuvenation treatments if he expected to keep up with their twins. He'd always taken mild offense at the ribbing, the age difference between the two of them something he was self-conscious about just below the surface, but he had to concede that she might have a point.

He remembered not too long ago pulling fifty-six-hour watches with nothing but coffee and adrenaline to keep him awake, sleep for six, and then come back on watch ready to kick some Phage ass. It just wasn't fair. He felt like he was finally figuring things out and developing true wisdom as a shipmaster, and now his body was letting him down.

Once he reached his quarters he nodded to the Marine sentry that had followed him from the bridge, standard procedure when the ship was at general quarters, and decided that the extra time for a shower was well worth it. Three days in the same uniform meant he certainly wasn't setting an example for his crew when it came to dress and appearance. War or not, there was no excuse for looking rumpled when on the bridge of a starship.

Ten minutes after he'd entered his quarters he was lying on his rack and snoring softly, the sound of the engines lulling him to sleep. His sleep was fitful despite how tired he was, visions of tens of millions of people slowly suffocating on a planet that was slowly being poisoned running through his head.

****

"*Captain Wolfe to the bridge, Captain Wolfe to the bridge.*"

The call over the intercom was repeated again, the computer's flat, dispassionate voice not telling him if it was an emergency or not. He figured since he was being summoned via the intercom and not messaged over his comlink it had to be something serious. He was already sitting on his rack pulling his boots on, intent on hitting the wardroom for a quick breakfast before going on watch, but the call to the bridge put all thoughts of food out of his head.

He rushed through the hatch and ran to the bridge, feeling the ship through his boots and knowing they were still underway, but the engines were silent. Either they had propulsion problems or they'd hit their initial velocity and were now cold-coasting. The *Star's* layout had the captain and XO quartered on the command deck within a few seconds of the bridge, a feature Jackson wished all warships had. The *Blue Jacket*, his first command, had his quarters two decks down in the superstructure and required he take two separate lifts. But back then warships were designed without their designers considering that the ship might actually be in a war.

"Report!" he barked as he slowed to a walk just before passing the Marine sentry onto the bridge who, since he was armed and wearing a cover, saluted him as he passed. His own escort took up position just inside the hatchway.

"The 508th has engaged the enemy, Captain. Our own status is unchanged." Commander Chambliss, the *Star's* Flight OPS department head, rose from the chair and made room for Jackson. The assault carrier was so lightly crewed that he'd been pulling in officers from all over the ship to cover watches on the bridge, as long as they were technically qualified. Chambliss had actually commanded a light frigate as a lieutenant before deciding to accept promotion in rank for a chance to serve on the larger mainline ships. When Jackson found this out he immediately put him into rotation for bridge watch.

"Go on," Jackson said, sitting and logging into the terminal and giving it a second to populate his preferences.

"The Link connection went active just after you'd gone off-watch," Chambliss went on. "It took some time for the handshakes and decryption routines to bounce back and forth before we began receiving a steady, valid telemetry stream. As soon as we were able to ascertain the posture of the 508th ships we called you to the bridge. They've gone active sensors and all weapons are live. No fire has been exchanged, but there are four Darshik cruisers converging on their position."

"That's not too bad of odds," Jackson mused. "The Terran destroyers can use their stand-off weapons to reclaim a numerical advantage and then use their laser batteries so as not to expend all of their missiles in the opening salvo of this battle."

"It will all depend on what tactics Captain Rawls decides to employ, sir," Chambliss said. Jackson just gave him a flat stare at his statement of the obvious, unsure if there was some hidden meaning in the comment.

"Yes, Commander," he said slowly, "I suppose it will. Is there anything else?"

"No other than that it was—Oh! There was one other thing that the passives picked up," Chambliss said and pulled a sensor log snapshot up for Jackson to look at. "The opticals picked up what was first categorized as a transition flash, but it was much too weak to be a Darshik cruiser or one of ours." Jackson studied the initial analysis CIC did of the occurrence and was impressed by how thorough they'd been.

"There could be one thing that made this," he said, tapping his chin with his forefinger. "You ever heard of a Broadhead, Commander?"

"Just the usual conspiracy theory garbage, sir," Chambliss frowned. "I know they exist, of course, but I don't put a lot of credence into the Tsuyo propaganda of what they were supposedly capable of."

"I've had some first-hand experience with them," Jackson said. "I've even seen the second-generation Broadhead with my own eyes. What I don't know, unfortunately, is whether this transition flash is consistent with the newer class. If it is—." He trailed off, frowning.

"Sir?"

"It's just that the original Broadhead didn't have a transition signature this pronounced," Jackson said. "In fact, on more than one occasion I had one sneak into a system I was actively scanning and never detected its arrival. I have a hard time believing the newer ship would be a step backwards in regards to its ability to penetrate a system unseen."

"Maybe there was a malfunction with the drive?" Chambliss guessed.

"Impossible to say given my complete lack of knowledge of the craft," Jackson shrugged. "Catalog it and have CIC on the lookout for a new player in the system … maybe the destroyers will pick something up with their active sensors and we'll see it over the Link. If it's who I think it might be I would expect we'll get a coded message within the next few hours."

"Yes, sir," Chambliss said. "If there's nothing else, sir, I'd like to go back down to Flight OPS and relieve Lieutenant Zao."

"Of course, Commander," Jackson said. "I have the bridge. Dismissed."

"Here they go," Ensign Dole said a moment after Chambliss had gathered his things and left the bridge. Jackson looked up to the main display where the Link telemetry was populated on an overlay of the system and saw that the *Relentless* and *Racer* had both fired two Shrikes apiece at the incoming Darshik ships.

"Too far out still," Jackson grated under his breath. The Shrikes were good, but the Darshik point defense was such that given enough time they could usually counter the missiles with laser fire before they got close enough to do any damage. He watched the battle on the Link and found it frustrating knowing that everything he was seeing had already happened over three hours ago. They'd originally been much closer but the taskforce and the *Star* were now on divergent courses and the com lag was increasing.

The fact that Rawls was moving his destroyers *away* from the planet they were supposed to be escorting the assault carrier to was infuriating, but not as much as watching the three ships get caught up in the same trap near the jump point that had already chewed up two other battlegroups. They'd only managed to get into the system thanks to the noise the *Star* made on her initial approach and likely the surprise Jackson had caused by transitioning in so far into the system, something Terran vessels never did.

Instead of taking that advantage, clearing the jump point, and getting his ships in play, Rawls's hesitated and hung back near the dubious safety of a jump point his ships were in no position to even use. In the process he'd allowed the Darshik to re-establish their picket lines. Even now, against four ships, the three destroyers could push hard down the well and come about, allowing them to engage the cruisers at speed instead of hanging back flat-footed where they were at the mercy of the closing ships. The next twelve hours of the engagement would likely decide the success or failure of the entire operation.

"Sir, message coming in from the *Relentless*," the chief manning the com station in Lieutenant Epsen's absent said. "They're reporting they've engaged the enemy."

"Thank you, Coms," Jackson said. "Send no reply. We'll monitor their progress through the Link."

"Aye, sir."

Jackson checked their position, course, and speed and saw they were dead on where they were supposed to be and quickly approaching their first mission threshold. In the next six hours he would have to decide just how committed he was to rushing down to Juwel. The arbitrary waypoint would be when the engines were fired and they were accelerated again to the approach velocity they would carry until they had to brake hard for drop-shuttle launch.

He debated with himself about bringing up his active sensors for two hours to clear the immediate area, weighing the tradeoff of stealth for situational awareness. The chance that the *Star* had escaped notice as she skulked about in the outer system for the last few days was good as they'd not detected any directed radar pulses hitting the hull, but they'd lit the sky up with their engine burn as they escaped the gravitational influence of the gas giant they'd been trailing. He also toyed with the idea of broadcasting a coded-burst message during the window the sensors were transmitting as he was almost certain Agent Pike had made an appearance in the system and that his Broadhead had caused the strange transition flash.

After a few more moments of looking at the pros and cons of his current options he decided to just leave things as they were. The *Star* was gliding silent and dark after executing a drastic course change, if there was a Darshik cruiser shadowing them it would have also had to execute the same maneuver and they would have easily picked it up. Even if they'd been spotted, a likely scenario, he didn't think there was any way another ship would be able to get within weapons range unseen given their relative velocity and a course that had them flying steeply back down the well towards Juwel. Although at times it was the most difficult thing in the world to have, patience was the key to winning battles in space when things happened over the span of days. A rash decision could have a ripple effect that ensured a mission's failure long before he would ever even realize his mistake.

****

Senior Captain Edward Rawls knew that he had royally screwed up.

When that insufferable Wolfe had decided to take the *Aludra Star* off on his own instead of staying in the convoy with the rest of the taskforce he'd felt confident that they'd arrive to find no assault carrier and thus, no reason to remain in such a hostile system. He genuinely felt for the people of Juwel, but he also felt the half-measures taken by CENTCOM to recapture the system meant that ships and spacers were just being wasted in a political PR game. As such, why should he needlessly risk the remaining three ships of the 508th to support such a weak strategic goal?

When Wolfe had come to him with some half-insane, half-impossible plan to transition their ships into the Juwel System well beyond the system boundary, and any acceptable margin of safety when operating a warp drive near a primary star, he'd firmly put his foot down. He'd been given overall command of the mission but, infuriatingly, the *Aludra Star* hadn't been officially attached to his taskforce. That meant the notorious loose cannon had been able to detach his ship and do whatever the hell he wanted including violating a litany of Fleet regulations regarding chain of command and operational protocols.

He'd been beyond surprised when they'd transitioned in and found no Darshik armada facing off against them ... right up until he realized that was because the *Aludra Star* had not only made it into the system safely but was engaged with enemy forces down near the planet. A cold lump of fear settled in his stomach when he realized he would not be able to just swing his ships back around in a wide loop and haul ass out of the system, and he hated himself for that fear that he seemed unable to control.

"Sir, both of our missiles have been intercepted," his tactical officer reported. "One of the *Racer's* got through, one Tango listing and secondary explosions observed." The tactical officer's icy calm brought back Rawls's self-loathing with a vengeance and he hated the man for it. How the hell could he be so calm when he had to realize his captain was in way over his head?

"Bracket both ships closing from our port and lock on two more Shrikes," Rawls said crisply. "Have the firing solutions continuously updated, but hold your fire. We need to get in closer to give our missiles a chance."

"Aye, sir," the tactical officer said. "Missiles locked, firing solutions updating continuously and ready to launch."

"Good. Coms! Notify the *Resolute* and *Racer* that we'll be accelerating down into the well, firing as we close the range," Rawls said. "We're sitting targets here and we need to push ahead to support the operations over Juwel. Any word from the *Aludra Star*?"

"No, sir," the com officer said. "We received the last burst transmission requesting we activate our Link and haven't heard from them since."

"CIC reports no explosions or detected weapons fire within the system," his OPS officer offered. "Lieutenant Commander Yu thinks Captain Wolfe is running silent on their next approach to the planet. They detected the engine flare from the assault carrier as it pushed out of a holding orbit behind the larger of the two gas giants."

"This changes nothing," Rawls said. "We press ahead. Nav! I need a course down to the planet for the taskforce ... no need to worry about stealth or conserving propellant."

"Aye, sir. Plotting—"

"Transition flash on the boundary!" the tactical officer called out.

"Darshik reinforcements?" Rawls asked, his heart sinking and the icy lump rolling over a few times. If it was indeed Darshik forces that meant his hesitancy and—fuck it, he may as well admit it—cowardice had let his entire taskforce get boxed in with enemy warships pursuing and waiting dead ahead. He almost wished Wolfe had been given overall mission command and had absolved him of making these impossible choices.

"Transponder coming in … it's a Federation ship, sir!" his com officer's elation was contagious. "Resolving now … it's the *Icarus*!" A few bridge officers smiled widely and Rawls heard a few quiet cheers. Rawls had to admit, he would have cheered himself had he not been so surprised. Either way, now that Captain Celesta Wright had joined the battle with her powerful *Starwolf*-class destroyer he felt a surge of confidence and hope where moments ago had been only fear.

"Coms! Please welcome Captain Wright to the Juwel System," Rawls said. "Nav, where's my course?"

"Plotted and sent to the helm already, Captain," the specialist first class said. "Course has also been sent over the Link tactical channel."

"Confirmation received from both the *Resolute* and the *Racer*, sir," the com officer said.

"Very well," Rawls said. "Helm, all ahead full. Tactical, stand by on Shrikes."

"All engines ahead full, aye."

The *Relentless* surged ahead and the change on the bridge was palpable. They'd yet to even talk to the captain of the *Icarus* and Rawls could tell the crew's uncertainty at what they were doing had been replaced with a confidence knowing that one of the Federation's most-decorated and combat-hardened starship captains was there with them.

Chapter 19

"What in the hell are the escorting ships doing bunched up along the perimeter?" Commander Barrett wondered aloud as the Link connection established with the 508th ships. "And where is the *Aludra Star*?"

"She's not on the Link, sir," Lieutenant Accari said from the OPS station. "I'll check the mission logs from the—RDS has just come online. Engineering has cleared the *Icarus* for maneuvering."

"OPS, dig in and see if you can quickly see where the *Aludra Star* is," Captain Celesta Wright said. "But don't waste a lot of time on it … I just want to know if she's still in the system and still on-mission or if Captain Rawls has any idea what happened to her."

"Checking now, ma'am," Accari said.

"Tactical! Full active sensors," Celesta stood. She was supremely annoyed that the 508th ships were still so far out in the system and had not moved down to clear the jump point. She'd expected to transition in and have millions and millions of kilometers to maneuver and get her bearings, but now three Darshik cruisers were still in the immediate neighborhood and she had no idea what the status of the mission was.

"Incoming message from the *Relentless*, ma'am," Lieutenant Ellison said.

"On the overheads, if you please," Celesta said, not turning back to her com officer.

"Captain Wright, this is Captain Rawls aboard the Relentless. I ... We are very glad to see the Icarus join the fight. Right now the Aludra Star is further down in the system preparing for her second attempt to make orbit over Juwel and deploy her shuttles. Captain Wolfe arrived before we did and was chased away from the planet once and there are an unknown number of enemy ships in the system. They have some that are transmitting active radar and others that appear to be hiding.

"Captain Wolfe has been in contact with the Marines on the surface of the planet and so far they are holding out so the mission is still critical. I've transmitted the mission logs we've received from the Aludra Star along with our own over the Link. We are currently accelerating to meet the formation of Darshik cruisers below us and will then proceed on to Juwel. Please advise as to what capacity the Icarus will be supporting. Relentless out."

Celesta didn't say anything for a moment, looking at the main display as the mission clock came up through the Link along with all the pertinent countdown timers each ship had shared. The Aludra Star was conspicuously absent and she knew Wolfe must be hiding out in the weeds, not wanting to broadcast his position needlessly. Her eyes narrowed as she realized the 508th destroyers must have been loitering along the perimeter for days while the assault carrier was trying to push in and make orbit. No wonder Wolfe was running silent; his escort had left his ass flapping in the breeze while they huddled around the jump point and waited for him to either crash upon the rocks or pull another miracle out of his bag of tricks. Either would suffice if Rawls's main objective was to give the appearance of doing his job without putting his ship in any real danger.

Was this push down into the system a result of guilt finally getting to him, or was it the Darshik ships breathing down his neck and he was getting panicky? Celesta pulled her terminal around and discreetly pulled up the service record of Ed Rawls, at least the one that was available to all field grade officers, and read the highlights. She wasn't really digging for dirt, she just wanted to see what his experience and training had been before being put on the bridge of a destroyer. What she found did nothing to assuage her suspicions as to why the escort ships were hanging back.

"Coms, open a direct channel to the *Relentless*," Celesta said.

"Go ahead, ma'am."

"Captain Rawls, this is Captain Wright aboard the *Icarus*. We're reviewing the mission logs now, but in the meantime I think we need to press ahead as quickly as possible so that we can clear the orbits over Juwel prior to the *Aludra Star* arriving.

"I'm in position to take out the two cruisers bearing at you from your fore, port quadrant. When you see the *Icarus* begin to close in I would suggest you veer your formation towards the remaining two ships and concentrate fire on them. The Darshik cruiser-class vessels are quite susceptible to damage from our laser cannon. If we get in close and make quick work of these four we can be on our way while keeping our standoff weapons in reserve. *Icarus* out." She turned and made a chopping motion across her throat to let Ellison know to kill the channel, but the double-chirp over the speakers told her he'd beaten her to the punch.

"Nav! I want a tactical intercept of the two tangoes directly ahead of the *Relentless*, maximum performance," she said. "Tactical, maintain active sensors and ready all weapons. We're going to hit them hard and fast and try to salvage this mess so Captain Wolfe has a chance to make it through. As soon as you have valid returns from the targeting radar bracket them and begin plotting a firing solution. We'll use one Shrike each … we don't have the time to play around and draw them in for the laser batteries."

"Aye aye, ma'am," Lieutenant Commander Adler said crisply from the tactical station. "Do we want to have the *Relentless* try again for one of the tangoes?"

"We'll be down there and past before the *Relentless* can get close enough to bother with a kill shot," Celesta said. "Just pipe our targeting info onto the Link and the *Relentless*'s tactical officer should get the hint. I don't want to cause further insult by calling over again."

"Yes, ma'am."

"Course plotted and ready, Captain," the chief at Nav said.

"Helm, let's go," Celesta leaned back in her seat. "Sound alarms and engage the RDS, all ahead full, maximum velocity of .15c. Be ready to haul us back down so we can deploy our missiles."

"All engines ahead full." The helmswoman grinned as she gave the general warning alarm three short blasts and advanced the throttle for the reactionless drive system. The surge of acceleration from the gravimetric subluminal drive pushed them back as the acceleration overwhelmed the artificial gravity field generator's ability to nullify it. They'd long ago learned that the drive was capable of such violent and abrupt maneuvers that the new standing order was to give the general alarm three short blasts before executing a maneuver if possible, the crew now understanding that meant hold onto something solid.

The *Icarus* shot forward, reaching almost four hundred g's of acceleration within seconds as the reactors poured power into the improved RDS pod attached to the aft section of the hull. Rumor was that Tsuyo had developed a much more robust gravimetric compensator and the new class of Terran starship would put up numbers that made the *Icarus* all but obsolete. Celesta briefly lamented about how quickly space combat was changing, the timetables compressing so that engagements were over in mere hours rather than spanning for days and weeks.

"We have positive tracking locks on both tangoes, weapons updating," Adler said.

"We're at target velocity, RDS to null," the helmswoman said. Celesta noted that she was the only one to adopt the new vernacular for the drive system. Her other starship drivers still called out thrust power levels despite the fact the RDS produced no thrust.

"Tactical, do you want helm control or can you call out our decel while we're in so close to the targets?" Celesta asked, shaking her head at the power of the new drive. *Close* was a relative term since they were still over thirty-seven million kilometers away.

"I'll call out decel, Captain," Adler said. "We'll have plenty of cushion and the Shrikes are forgiving to slight variances in our relative velocity."

"Very well, you have command authority until weapon release." Celesta leaned back. The next hour went by quickly as the *Icarus* bore down on the two hapless Darshik vessels. They realized far too late that there was something very, very different about this new arrival and turned to try and regroup with the other two, but the *Icarus* was already there.

"Helm, braking thrust!" Adler called out. "Two hundred and fifty g's."

"Two hundred and fifty g's all reverse, aye!" The power level to achieve this wasn't as drastic as the acceleration had been, and Celesta could barely detect the inertial shift. She watched the main display as the *Icarus* shed relative velocity so quickly she seemed to almost stop in space.

"Tactical, you're clear for weapon release at your discretion," she said, pressing her palm to her terminal so the computer could take a biometric reading for command authorization to fire weapons.

"Firing! Missiles one and two are away … both Shrikes are squawking, burning hot and clean," Adler said. "Impact in … thirty-four minutes."

"Coms, let the *Relentless* know that as soon as these targets are clear we'll be turning downhill," Celesta said over her shoulder. "Tell Captain Rawls I'll look for him once his taskforce dispatches the remaining two."

"Aye, ma'am," Ellison said.

"How do you think this will play out with Captain Rawls having overall operational command of the mission, or at least his escort force, and us coming in unannounced and uninvited?" Barrett asked quietly.

"It's honestly something I haven't the time to worry about," Celesta said candidly to her XO. She'd been trusting Barrett's discretion more and more the longer they served together, so she relaxed her instincts to filter her comments when talking to him. "Rawls can either get with the program or get out of the way. He may have already screwed this mission up beyond our ability to get it back on track. What I can't figure out is why Wolfe didn't just usurp command ... Rawls seems like he'd be amenable to someone with combat experience calling the shots."

"From what I'm reading in the mission logs it sounds like Wolfe made his case for an approach Rawls vetoed, and then the captain said, 'fuck it,' and went off on his own," Barrett said. Celesta smiled slightly as there was no doubt to whom people who had served with Wolfe were referring to when they said *The Captain*.

"It looks like he pulled some insane stunt to transition that assault carrier into the system *deep* down the well ... much more risky than anything he'd tried in the past with the *Ares*."

"Including when he flew that same ship through the atmosphere of a planet?" Celesta said, arching an eyebrow.

"Easily," Barrett said, not catching the humor in her voice. "This was an all or nothing gamble and he must have had a *lot* of faith in his navigator and chief engineer."

"Impact missile one! CIC is doing battle damage— Impact missile two!" Adler interrupted herself as the sensor feeds came in. "Stand by … Tango Two is completely destroyed, Tango One is flagging and venting atmosphere. Shall I target the remaining ship again?"

"Negative, Tactical," Celesta said as she read the same scrolling battle damage assessment from CIC that Adler was. "It's out of the fight for—"

"Tango One has exploded," Accari said calmly. An instant later the threat board updated and the target disappeared from the display and was replaced with a larger navigational hazard warning icon as the debris cloud spread.

"As I was saying, it's out," Celesta said. "Helm! Heel over, seventy-two degrees to port, ten degrees inclination and roll in gently to ahead full!"

"Hard to port, aye!" the helmswoman said. "All engines ahead full." Celesta watched as she gently rolled the throttle on the RDS up. No point in needlessly abusing the ship or her crew by slamming the drive to full power when she just wanted to get heading downhill and find the *Aludra Star*.

"Nav, plot an indirect course down to Juwel," Celesta ordered. "I want to shallow out near the orbit of the sixth planet and then try to come up behind the last known position of the *Aludra Star*—OPS, get him that info—and then we'll accelerate past Captain Wolfe's assault carrier and clear his orbital lanes so he can deploy his drop shuttles. Any questions?"

"No, Captain," the specialist said. "Plotting course corrections now."

"Helm, you're clear to execute your new course when you get it." Celesta leaned back. "Tactical, we're not hiding from anybody at this point so keep the sensors active. Coms, please inform the *Aludra Star* that we'll be coming around onto the same course we assume they're on and will overtake them to the planet to provide an escort and that the 508th taskforce *should* be following us down."

"Aye aye, ma'am."

"I guess it's a good thing we did decide to fly straight here instead of routing back through New Sierra," Barrett said. "This was right on the edge of being a total loss."

"It seems that way," Celesta said quietly. "Not that CENTCOM has put much of an effort into reclaiming this system. All the boomers and newer class ships are sitting in berth while obsolete or reserve units have been dribbled out in small numbers for the Darshik blockade to use for target practice, not to mention the chance to refine their tactics against Federation ships."

Barrett didn't answer but his face clearly indicated that he was thinking very hard on what she'd said. It wasn't as if it was a big secret that CENTCOM had whiffed on the Juwel System. The core systems were fearful and were keeping most of the military power back to cover their asses, but in the meantime they were chumming the waters by letting the Darshik take and keep Terran star systems. If they didn't punch back hard here and now she had no doubt that it would only be a short matter of time before they began seeing strikes deep into Terran space.

****

"New node coming up on the Link, sir," Dole said.

"Who is it?" Jackson asked, only mildly curious. He assumed Pike would be popping up now that he either had done what he'd come to do or had seen something he thought they'd missed, which would be a fair assumption.

"It's the *Icarus*, sir," Dole said, blinking in surprise.

"What?!" Jackson said, walking over to the OPS station to look for himself. "What the hell is she doing here?"

"I don't know, Captain, but she's already firing on the enemy that's bunched up near Captain Rawls's taskforce." Dole pointed to the intermittent telemetry feed streaming in. "Do you think CENTCOM sent Captain Wright to back up the 508th?"

"I don't think Celesta Wright is acting on specific orders from CENTCOM, no," Jackson shook his head. "She's here of her own volition I'm sure of it. But, this is an opportunity to get this mission back on track … the *Icarus* is equipped with the latest reactionless drive system that can put them down at the planet well before we could make it there even under full acceleration."

"Should we send them a message, sir?" Epsen asked.

"No," Jackson said after a second of thought. "Captain Wright will be able to determine pretty easily what my plan is from the mission logs we sent the *Relentless*. We'll wait until the *Icarus* closes and makes contact first."

The next four hours went by uneventfully as Jackson kept one eye on the battle taking place near the system boundary with the 508th destroyers and another making sure his crew didn't become distracted or complacent. The *Star* wasn't the stealthiest of ships, and although she was coasting dark and maintaining com silence the Darshik knew they were there. The aliens weren't going to just forget about them because of a little skirmish up away from the planet. No ... they'd been far too quiet and too passive about seeking out his ship. Jackson knew there had to be some nasty surprise in store for him.

"Captain, we're approaching Waypoint Bravo," Ensign Dole said, covering a yawn with his hand. "All mission parameters are still in the green, sir."

"Very well," Jackson said. "Helm, you're clear for your first velocity change when we cross Waypoint Bravo. Keep the engine output down to thirty-three percent."

"At Waypoint Bravo engines ahead one-third, aye," the helmsman said.

Jackson had put in six incremental bumps in velocity so they didn't have to burn the engines at high power for an extended period of time. It would put them down over Juwel when they needed to be, and he had wanted to allow the 508th taskforce time to catch up should Rawls have been so inclined to come down and actually provide an escort. As it was now he expected to be overtaken by the *Icarus* at any time, and he was infinitely more comfortable with his old protégé racing down ahead of him and clearing out any enemy ships.

"OPS and Coms … get your relief up here and then go grab some rack time," Jackson said. "Same for you, Tactical."

"I'm okay, Captain," Commander Simmons said.

"I wasn't asking, XO," Jackson said sternly. "I want first watch fresh and ready when we come onto our final course correction. We'll have to go full active sensors at that time and everything will be coming at us fast."

"Yes, sir," Simmons said and nodded at Epsen to call up his relief for him.

"Next I want—"

"Sir! We just lost the *Racer*!" Dole exclaimed, pointing up to the main display where the Link telemetry was. At first Jackson thought the other ship had just dropped off the Link, but as he looked at the last good update he could see the *Intrepid*-class ship took two hard hits in rapid succession before disappearing.

"Damn," Jackson whispered. "They outnumbered and outclassed the remaining two cruisers ... how the hell did the *Racer* get hit that hard?"

"Message coming in from the *Relentless* on the fleetwide channel," Epsen said.

"Just tell me what it says," Jackson said, still watching the raw data that was scrolling across the screen.

"Captain Rawls said the *Racer* had been pursuing the last Darshik cruiser that had broken off and was trying to escape," Epsen said. "He's not sure exactly what happened because the *Racer* was between them and the enemy ship, but he's assuming the cruiser got in a lucky shot ... the target was also destroyed in the encounter and the rest of the 508th is coming down towards Juwel."

"Damn!" Jackson repeated, this time with a little more heat. He felt helpless and it wasn't a feeling he was ever comfortable with regardless that there was little he could have done had he been there. Nor could he really fault Captain Rawls for the incident from what he was seeing on his display. Rawls had moved his ships into an offensive formation that allowed them to cover each other with overlapping spheres of fire, exactly as he would have done, and they'd still lost a ship. He barely knew Captain Sanders, the *Racer's* CO, but he still felt the loss of so many spacers keenly.

"Okay, get back to what you were doing," he said, seeing his crew had paused and seemed to be waiting for him to give them an order. "We can do nothing for the 508th and Captain Rawls is doing the right thing by following the *Icarus* down to meet over the planet; it'll allow us to concentrate what firepower we have and assume a more offensive posture. Call your reliefs up and go get some rest."

"I'll be up to relieve you in four hours, sir," Simmons said as he walked by; his relief was already reconfiguring the tactical station, having already been on the command deck.

"Make it six," Jackson said. "I'll have Commander Chambliss come up and cover the watch in a few hours to make sure we're both ready for the planetary approach."

"Yes, sir," Simmons nodded.

After the bustle of the relief watch officers filtering onto the bridge and getting turnover from their counterparts Jackson was left in relative silence; he saw the lights had dimmed down and taken on a slightly red hue to signify night hours. The eggheads at Fleet R&S insisted that maintaining a sense of "day" and "night" was critical for humans who might not breathe natural air or see sunlight for over a year at a time. Jackson was skeptical, but since they were the experts he left things as they were.

He went to the back of the bridge and poured himself another steaming mug of coffee before settling into one of the two auxiliary stations that were tucked into the corner. After logging in, he pulled up all the data that had come over the Link regarding the engagement that had claimed the *Racer* with all hands aboard. Something just didn't smell right to him about the whole thing and he couldn't quite put his finger on it. He had to admit he had very little experience against this enemy, but he never ignored his instincts when they were screaming to him that something was not as it seemed. But what was he missing? Could it really be so clear cut as the *Racer* approaching too recklessly and getting hammered with a Darshik plasma lance? Maybe Celesta Wright, with her much more extensive experience facing the aliens, would have some other insight to the engagement he was missing.

Chapter 20

"Something is … off," Celesta said as her tactical officer went over the *Racer's* engagement with her again. "But I can't see what it is from the limited sensor coverage provided by the other two ships. The *Resolute* isn't even using active sensors."

"I really can't give you any more than that, ma'am," Adler apologized. "In addition to the limited coverage we're only seeing sensor snapshots over the Link and not the full telemetry stream due to the com lag."

"Do you think it would be worth having CIC go back through the raw data?" Celesta asked. The Link transponder continuously tried to keep the time stamps on the incoming data streams synced so that the crew could see events in a timeline in context, but what usually happened was that it could only put up snippets of data when one of the sources was as far away as the *Racer* had been. In order to get a complete picture of something that happened on the other side of the system, Celesta would have to assign someone the task of going back into the archived data and digging up the proper timestamp and data source.

"I'm not sure I see any benefit from that, Captain," Adler said carefully, apparently not used to being asked her opinion. "The lack of detail is more from the sparse radar coverage on the target by the *Relentless* than us missing something in the Link stream. Captain Rawls was positioned so that the Darshik cruiser was directly behind the *Racer,* and when the destroyer exploded the debris completely obscured the area beyond to both radar and IR optics."

"Understood." Celesta kept the disappointment from her voice. She had been testing Adler with the question and, unfortunately, she hadn't been impressed with her tactical officer's answer. When facing a lack of answers one always wanted to err on the side of being thorough. Lieutenant Commander Adler's tendency to take the path of least resistance apparently held true even if she wasn't going to have to do the work herself.

"If you don't mind, Captain, I think I'll see if CIC can spare the manpower to do that analysis," Barrett spoke up. "To satisfy my own curiosity while we're transiting the system to meet up with the *Aludra Star*."

"Very well, Commander," Celesta nodded. "Proceed." Commander Barrett had shown once again that he was very much in tune with her and could read between the lines of what she said and what she actually wanted. It was a rare gift to have an XO she could so completely lean on and it pained her to realize that he wasn't going to be able to stay by her side on the *Icarus* for much longer. He'd grown beyond the role of executive officer and was ready for a command of his own.

"Mr. Accari ... how far away from the *Aludra Star*'s presumed position are we?"

"We're just shy of five hundred and fifty million kilometers away from where the tactical computer thinks the *Aludra Star* is currently, ma'am," Accari said.

"Coms, please open a channel on the fleetwide," she said.

"Go ahead, Captain."

"*Aludra Star*, this is Captain Wright aboard the *Icarus*. We're closing to within five hundred million of your assumed position on our way to Juwel. We're currently reading three cruiser-class enemy ships in orbit with an unknown number still within the system. Please break com silence when you are prepared to coordinate your launch run with us. *Icarus* out."

"How long do you think until we get a response, Captain?" Barrett asked.

"I'm not certain," Celesta admitted. "Wolfe has been cautious since that assault carrier made transition. He may not want to tip his hand even now, maybe especially so since the Darshik have already taken out one of our ships."

"I can imagine," Barrett said, nodding.

****

After listening to Captain Wright's message, Jackson looked at the main display to see where the *Icarus* was relative to the *Aludra Star*. The *Icarus* had put on an impressive display of acceleration and speed and was a lot closer to his ship than Celesta thought she was. The projected position on the Link showed him over half a billion kilometers away, but in reality the *Icarus* had already closed to within a hundred and fifty million and was still accelerating.

"Damn that ship is fast," he muttered before turning back to his com officer. "Coms, open a channel to the *Icarus*."

"Go ahead, sir."

"Captain Wright, this is Wolfe aboard the *Aludra Star*. Welcome to the party. We're activating our Link transponder now ... there's no real advantage in trying to hide right now since you're about to overtake us on the way to Juwel. Has our favorite CIS spook made contact with you yet?"

"Link Transponder coming up now, sir," Simmons said quietly after pointing to Dole. Jackson nodded his approval to his XO.

"*It's good to hear your voice, sir,*" Celesta's voice came back over the channel after a brief delay. "*We have a lock on you now via the Link. I wasn't aware the agent in question was in this system. Has he made contact yet?*"

"I'm assuming he's listening in right now," Jackson said. "He hasn't made contact yet, but we picked up a transition flash some days ago that didn't correspond to anything the size of a Darshik cruiser and it certainly wasn't one of ours. My assumption is that it's his new specialized ship."

"*Sir ... I'm sending you a sensor data file of a transition flash and I'd like your CIC to compare the two.*" Celesta's voice had taken on a tight, almost pained quality even as Ensign Dole nodded to indicate he was receiving the file in question.

"Stand by, *Icarus*," Jackson said and made a chopping motion to Epsen.

"File being sent to CIC now, sir," Dole said. "Lieutenant Maan has made it her highest priority." The results of the comparison didn't take long as it was only visual spectrum data being compared. CIC's computers made quick work of chewing through it and comparing the two occurrences trillions of times once the answer made its way to the bridge.

"CIC puts the two transition flashes as ninety-six-point-two percent that they were made by the same ship," Dole said. "There's some margin of error due to the *Icarus* having better sensors, the distance involved, and the region of space—"

"Thank you, Ensign," Jackson cut him off. "So it's the same ship ... and judging from Captain Wright's tone it *isn't* from a Tsuyo Broadhead II. Coms, if you would reopen the channel."

"Channel open, sir."

"Captain Wright, this is Wolfe ... my CIC has confirmed that these transitions flashes are from the same ship," Jackson said. "Would I be correct in assuming you know who this ship belongs to?"

"*It's not ours,*" Celesta's answer came back a few minutes later. "*The Icarus was on a mission to try and reopen talks with the Ushin, and when we arrived to meet their delegation this ship showed up. It took out the Ushin consular ship and punched a few holes in my hull before disengaging and disappearing. I'm sorry, Captain ... I may have led that ship right to you.*"

"I doubt that, Captain." Jackson waved away her comment with his hand even though it was an audio-only channel. "I can't imagine this invasion is a secret among the Darshik military hierarchy. Let's focus on what we can control. What can you tell me about this new arrival?"

"*It's fast, sir,*" she said. "*Also nimble and very stealthy; we didn't even pick up a thermal signature from its engines. It seems to be stripped down to the bare essentials to do just one job and that's as a hunter-killer. I'm sending over the data from our encounter so you can see it for yourself. I'll also have it forwarded to Captain Rawls's taskforce.*"

"Another unknown variable isn't exactly good news," Jackson said. "Are you going to be able to clear our orbital path yourself?"

"*Yes, sir.*"

"Then let's get to it," Jackson said. "We'll adjust course and speed to get down there as fast as we can and still brake to launch the drop shuttles. A word of warning: this ship is nowhere near as fast as a destroyer, much less one with an RDS."

"*I'll keep that in mind, sir,*" Celesta said with what sounded like a choked-off laugh. "*We'll escort you all the way down past the inner asteroid belt before breaking off and engaging the targets in orbit. It's not likely the 508th ships will arrive in time for the festivities.*"

"Very good, Captain," Jackson said. "We'll come up on the power and switch to active sensors for now. Once we get closer and have a more current picture of what's happening over Juwel you can decide how best you want to proceed. *Star* out."

"The file came from the *Icarus* over our direct connection and not the Link, sir," Ensign Dole said. "I'll need your command authorization to decrypt it."

Jackson stepped to his terminal and provided the necessary access code and biometric reading to allow his OPS officer to access the decryption routines he needed to unpack the data Celesta had sent over.

"Let's see what we're dealing with, Ensign," he said after giving Dole a few minutes to extract the files and get them on the *Star*'s servers.

"Stand by, sir," Dole said and began furiously working on the controls at his station. A few seconds later and the image of a ship the likes of which Jackson had never seen popped up on the main display.

"Were these scaling marks made by the *Icarus's* crew or us?"

"Captain Wright's intel people did that, sir," Dole said. "They also did the false color enhancement. In the original image all the detail of the aft end of the ship was obscured."

Jackson took a moment to really take in the image of the hunter-killer ship that was even now in the system with them, likely stalking one of the ships in their small armada. The thought sent a chill up Jackson's spine. He saw the hash marks along the front of the prow and recognized them for what they likely were: warpaint. This ship was captained by someone who saw himself as a warrior or, more likely, a hunter. If it had managed to get the drop on the *Icarus* and punch holes in her while escaping *and* making it all the way to Juwel he knew it wasn't a ship to be taken lightly.

"Tactical, I want full active sensors," Jackson said. "Coms! Get a message to the *Relentless* regarding this new player ... get the data from OPS that the *Icarus* sent over and include that. I want to make sure it doesn't get overlooked by just dumping it onto the Link."

"Aye, sir."

"Helm, maintain course but open up the taps." Jackson sat back in his seat. "All ahead full. OPS, recheck our course once our velocity tops out."

"All engines ahead full, aye!" The *Star* surged gently as her two active primary main engines throttled up. Jackson watched on the main display as the flashing green icon representing the *Icarus* also accelerated to catch them, the destroyer's awesome speed causing him a moment of irrational envy due to his ship's more modest capabilities. They were approaching close enough to the target now that he felt like something was about to happen. The Darshik would be foolish to let them get too close to Juwel now that they'd fought so hard to keep it. The question was, would it be the standard cruisers they were used to, or the new player that had already bloodied Celesta Wright's nose?

Chapter 21

"I feel I have to advise at this time that the Juwel System looks like a complete loss."

"And you base this on what?" President Augustus Wellington said. The elected leader of the United Terran Federation had puffy, bloodshot eyes and his lips were almost a dark purple color. Pike was as concerned about the man's health as he'd ever been since entering his service. He watched the exchange with a practiced indifference, trying to blend into the furniture as CIS Director Franco Sala made his case.

"We're well overdue for any updates," Sala said. "Not even so much as a com drone has made its way back to revise the original timetable for the operation. The *Intrepid* and *Vega*-class ships were never designed for this sort of extended duration mission without logistical support, which they've not called for." The director slouched in his seat and heaved a dramatic sigh that Pike knew the man thought conveyed genuine concern but sounded more like he was trying to blow out a trashcan fire.

"In the absence of solid intel stating otherwise I think we have to conclude that our latest battlegroup met with the same fate as the previous two. Was this not the threshold we'd agreed upon in order to say that the Juwel System was not recoverable?"

"Perhaps, if we insist on only trying three times to liberate a Terran system from an alien invasion force, then we should try a little harder during these attempts," Fleet

Admiral Pitt said. Pitt was at the meeting as a replacement for Chief of Staff Marcum in his absence. He was on a trip that was supposed to be classified at the highest level, but Pike knew that Marcum was doing a progress inspection on the Federation's newest generation of warships, three new classes getting ready to enter service.

He struggled to suppress a smile at Pitt's bluntness. The man was a master tactician and yet he couldn't grasp even the most basic tenets of safely navigating the political minefield he found himself in.

"Meaning what, Admiral?" Wellington asked, his eyes narrowing dangerously. Pitt either ignored or missed the warning signs.

"Only that we've sent three small expedition-sized taskforces comprised of mostly obsolete ships and reserve commanders, sir," Pitt said firmly. "We have two Dreadnaught-class boomers sitting in orbit over New Sierra that could probably clear the system out on their own. If I might be so—"

"I think we've heard enough, Admiral." Wellington waved him off then used the same hand to wipe at his face. "All I'll say is that were it up to me, and only me, the *Amsterdam* and the *New York* would be flying to Juwel with you on one of them at this moment. But there are other considerations at play and those ships don't belong to you or me."

"I—yes, sir," Pitt said, catching himself before he could lodge further protest. Pike thought he just might have a future in the snake pit of capital politics if he could see when he was already beat.

"What we need to discuss is whether we—and by *we* I mean *I*—go before Parliament and announce that the effort to free the Juwel System was not only a failure but a total loss of the military assets we threw at it. A failure up to and including the apparent death or capture of one legendary starship captain we pulled out of mothballs as a morale booster," Wellington ran out of steam quickly and looked around the room despondently. "Is that what we're going to do?"

"I feel that any further delay would be counterproductive, Mr. President," Sala said. "Captain Rawls's taskforce is well overdue ... if they'd been able to secure the planet or even push the Darshik out temporarily we would have heard about it."

"Okay then," Wellington said, standing and pointing at Sala and Pitt. "You two can go. I need to talk to Mr. Lynch a moment in private."

Pike was actually surprised, having assumed that the deception was unnecessary as Pitt and Sala were well aware of who he really was, although legally Aston Lynch was just as real as Pike or any of the other half-dozen personas he wore like clothes.

"Why do I feel like I'm not going to like what comes next?" Pike asked as the door boomed shut to the Executive Office, as it was unoriginally named.

"What do you think happened in the Juwel System?" Wellington asked, ignoring the attempt at levity.

"I'll admit that Director Sala makes a compelling case as to why we could safely assume the mission is a total loss," Pike said carefully, sensing that a misstep on his part could see him flying off to someplace he'd really rather not visit.

"But?" Wellington prompted.

"But ... I've learned to not bet against Jackson Wolfe," Pike said, knowing he'd likely sealed his fate. "Given all he's been through I have a hard time believing that it would be this enemy that brings him down."

"We all get older, slower, sometimes a little too sure of ourselves," Wellington said, hands clasped behind his back. The action drew his shirt and jacket tight around his torso, a decidedly unflattering look. "But in this case I agree with you. I'll admit I've utilized the captain's reputation and legend for my own purposes from time to time, but he seems to have a knack for turning what should be a route into a victory."

"Yes, sir," Pike said neutrally, refusing to tilt one way or another until he found out what his boss wanted of him.

"No later than two days local time after you get back to the Platform I want you in your ship and heading out to the Juwel System," Wellington said.

Shit!

"Of course, sir." Pike was quite proud of how he kept his emotions out of his voice. He'd just returned from a mission into the Eastern Star Alliance that could only be described as pure hell. Doing a quick turn and flying into the teeth of a hostile alien blockade wasn't the best idea he'd heard lately.

"I need you on this, Pike," Wellington said with as much genuine emotion as any lifelong politician could muster. "I can't argue with Sala's logic but something feels … off … about all of this. I'd send a Prowler out but I'm not sure how much success they'd have sneaking in and back out. Just pop out there, take a peek around and see if our forces have indeed been wiped out, and then get back here and report to me. In fact, report *only* to me."

Pike was fuming as he walked out of the executive residence to the waiting jump shuttle that would take him to the base where he could catch a ride to the Platform. Just *pop out there?!* Could a man that was the duly elected leader of a star-faring race that had spread across dozens of planets really be so ignorant as to what surveying an entire star system entailed? When trying to observe without being observed it was impossible to simply jump in, sit there and watch, and then leave … at least not if you wanted to capture anything to make the trip worthwhile.

Even as his anger subsided he was already making plans as to how he could best go about this new assignment. Part of what mollified him a bit was that he suspected the *Icarus* was also on its way to the Juwel System. Maybe he'd be able to talk to Celesta Wright alone and find out what the hell happened during her attempted diplomatic mission.

****

"It just got here via com drone!"

The outburst made Dr. Badu jump and he turned to glare at the project assistant that had just burst in.

"*What* just arrived via com drone, Miss Foss?" he asked acidly.

"The analysis of the organic material we pulled from the debris of the battle in this system," Foss went on, completely oblivious to Badu's tone.

"We sent samples to at least fifteen labs across—"

"Yes, yes," Foss waved him off, the dismissive gesture causing the research scientist's eyes to bulge. "I'm talking about that weird one. The blind samples we sent to that Fleet group … you know, the—" Foss trailed off as she struggled to think of the name.

"Perhaps they put their name on the packet they sent back?" Badu asked wearily. He was already interrupted so he stood up and took the courier package from Foss, turning it over to look at the printed routing label that had been attached when the transmission had been received and classified by the New Sierra Platform's com office.

"It's right here … Sector 17, whatever that is," Badu frowned. This carries the stench of Fleet Intelligence on it. "I'm not sure I understand; why are you so excited for *this* particular analysis given the fact none of the others have been able to provide much insight?"

"Because we were given instructions to contact that good-looking aide to the President when this one came in," Foss beamed. "Aston Lynch." Badu just stared at her blankly as he turned the packet over in his hand a few times, resisting the urge to roll his eyes at the exuberant project assistant who still clung to the trappings of youth. He despaired of ever making a serious researcher out of her despite her aptitude.

"I've already contacted him," she said, smiling again. "Would you believe the luck that he's actually on the station? He's on his way down to this section now."

"That is strangely fortuitous," Badu said absently, still wracking his brain to remember what Sector 17 was.

****

"Ah, Mr. Lynch, wasn't it?" Dr. Badu said as a well-dressed man who looked to be in his early thirties walked in with an air of dismissive arrogance swirling around him. "It's good to see you again."

"We've never met, Doctor," Lynch said flatly. "The Sector 17 analysis came back, I presume?"

"Yes, it has." Badu took a closer look at Lynch. Unlike most people in his career field, he was very observant of people and had a natural skill reading them. He realized that this *Lynch* was wearing his entire persona like a costume. The clothes, the sneer, the clipped manner of speaking … it was all an act. Badu saw the hard look in his eyes, his over-muscled physique the tailored suit didn't fully hide, and the fluid manner in which he moved. In an instant the research scientist put it all together and realized he was looking at someone from either Fleet Intel or CIS, maybe even an actual Agent, if those really even existed.

"If I might ask, what exactly is Sector 17? No harm now that the results are back, is there?"

Lynch gave him an unreadable look for a moment before shrugging almost imperceptibly. "It's an advanced AI emergence program," Lynch said. "The project principal has shown itself to be quite adept at finding patterns in things that most humans cannot."

"Fascinating," Badu said, tearing open the courier packet and pulling out the single data card held within. He slipped the card into the reader on the table that housed his lab's main holographic projection display and waited while his credentials were verified. All classified data was tightly controlled and stored only on the servers in the bowels of the Platform; the card that was delivered was simply the first of four verification steps that would allow him to access the specific data he needed.

"There's a message from Project Manager Danilo Jovanović. Would you like to see that first?"

"Sure," Lynch shrugged, his mask slipping a bit and his impatience showing.

"This is Danilo Jovanović, Project Manager for Sector 17." The face of a man who looked far younger than any project manager Badu had ever seen was projected up in front of them. "When I saw that Aston Lynch had requested the Cube run through this analysis I bumped it up as a special favor. I apologize for the delay, but we had to have some specialized equipment delivered in order to properly compare the samples that were sent. The samples were sent blind and there was no context or labels given for each, so when you view results keep in mind that we had nothing to do with any potential mix-up."

"I wonder what that means," Lynch said.

"I think I see the issue," Badu said, frowning as he read. "The summary analysis says it plain as day: The samples were from unique individuals, but belonged to the same species."

"What?! Impossible! We gave them Ushin *and* Darshik organic samples, yes?" Lynch asked.

"Yes," Badu said firmly. "We were extremely careful in how they were handled, packaged, and distributed. The control markers we put on each of the samples is clearly listed here." He was about to go on to describe their isolation procedures and how it was impossible for there to be cross-contamination but Lynch had already moved on, pacing around on the floor and muttering to himself. His head snapped up suddenly and when he looked at Badu all traces of the polished, urbane Aston Lynch were gone. Whoever the man really was, he was dangerous.

"Dr. Badu, I realize you have a tight schedule and deadlines to meet, but this is more important than you could possible know," the man said. "I need two compete summaries made of the data that the Cube has sent in this report, one in complete layman's terms and another with enough pertinent detail to be credible for someone trained in a scientific field ... and I need them both by this time tomorrow."

"I'll put two of my people on it right away," Badu said. He'd been ready to argue on principle alone—who the hell was this guy to come in and order him around?—but he remembered that he'd come in earlier fully credentialed as an aide to President Wellington. Whatever his suspicions about the man might be, it was obvious he operated within circles at the highest levels. Giving him too much push back might not be too smart on his part if he wanted to keep his job on the Platform.

"I appreciate that," Lynch said with a nod, still seeming distracted. He pulled a card with a memory chip embedded in it out of a jacket pocket and handed it to him. "Here are the best ways to reach me. Please send your reports directly to me; they'll automatically encrypt when you try to connect to any of these addresses. I'll likely be on the Platform still, but if I'm not I'll still be within the DeLonges System. Thank you again, Doctor … as I said, it's critical."

"We're happy to do our part, Mr. Lynch," Badu said and shook the proffered hand.

****

"Agent Pike, what can I do for you? Or is it Aston Lynch today, judging by the clothes?"

"Thank you for seeing me on such short notice, Admiral," Pike said respectfully, closing the door behind him. "Admiral Marcum is not so accessible in a pinch."

"Marcum puts up roadblocks to keep the low-level riffraff out," Admiral Pitt said. "*You* have trouble because he doesn't like you."

"The feeling is mutual," Pike sighed. "But that's not why I'm here."

"Obviously. So I repeat … what can I do for you?"

Pike looked at him speculatively for a split second before continuing. "You're aware of what Captain Wolfe was doing after he left Fleet and was—"

"I am," Pitt smiled slightly. "I was there when that … thing … woke up, for lack of a better word. So yes, Agent, my clearance is high enough to be privy to Project Prometheus in the first place *and* I'm well aware of what Wolfe was doing on the *Pontiac* with that Vruahn hardware."

"That greatly simplifies things," Pike nodded. "When both Tsuyo Science Division and Fleet R&S were hitting a wall analyzing the organic material we pulled from the wreckage of the Darshik and Ushin ships in this system I took it upon myself to have a sterile set of samples sent to Sector 17—Project Prometheus—and see if the Cube had any insights our scientists were lacking."

"By sterile you mean—"

"No context given as to where they came from," Pike clarified. "The people and the Cube in Sector 17 had no idea what the samples were other than organic material of similar size and structure."

"What did that thing find?" Pitt leaned forward anxiously, actually pushing aside the work he'd had in front of him when Pike had walked in. The agent took another breath before pushing ahead.

"The Ushin and the Darshik are the same species," he said. "The organic composition of the remains was inconclusive in the labs here on New Sierra, but the Cube was able to discern their genetic structure. Apparently, although carbon-based, the aliens don't have DNA structured like our own so it wasn't immediately recognized."

"But the Cube *did* recognize it?" Pitt asked.

"Recognized it almost instantly and then was able to break it down to discover there was zero genetic variability between what we thought were two different species," Pike said. "The Cube stated with a ninety-nine-point-nine-nine-nine percent certainty that they are the same, which is as close as it ever comes to saying there is no other possibility. It was even asked about the probability that the Darshik and Ushin are offshoots of each other, divergent species with a common origin, and the answer was no."

"Clever bastard, isn't it," Pitt shook his head. "And to break down an alien genome that fast."

"They've found that sometimes when presented with new challenges the cube will *unlock* pockets of dormant knowledge it didn't know it possessed until trying to solve the problem," Pike said. "I think this might be one of those times. For all we know the damn thing knows the Ushin/Darshik race intimately and could point out every planet they hold in the span of minutes."

"Interesting speculation, but why are you bringing this to me?" Pitt asked. "I'm not an idiot but I'm certainly not a xenobiologist nor someone in a position to make policy based on this new information."

"Two reasons." Pike held up two fingers. "First, I'm out of my depth here. What I've told you is just a snapshot of the scientific data we now have on this species. But there are profound political ramifications now that we know they're the same people. Why do they identify as separate? Why are the Ushin trying to get us to fight the Darshik, and then betray us within the span of weeks? It just gets muddier from there the more you think about it."

"And the second reason?"

"I'm shipping out within the next twelve hours," Pike said. "The President wants me to fly out to Juwel and find out what the hell happened to our latest taskforce. I'm preparing a full brief to send down to the surface, but I wanted to tell someone I trust in person about this before I leave. There's a decent chance I won't come back from this trip, and I don't want something like this being lost in the shuffle of bureaucratic incompetence."

"Blunt enough," Pitt nodded his approval. "Okay, Pike … I'll hand-deliver your brief to both Wellington and Sala as well as make sure Marcum gets a copy. Beyond that"—Pitt splayed his hands open in a gesture of helplessness—"I can't make any promises. Wellington keeps his own council and Sala is working some sort of angle I can't see."

"I noticed he gets very nervous when you talk about moving assets out of the DeLonges System," Pike nodded. "But I chalk that up to a misguided sense of self-preservation rather than any sort of nefarious design."

"Interesting way to talk about your boss," Pitt said with one arched eyebrow.

"I work for the President currently," Pike sighed. "If I live through the coming months *and* Wellington steps down as he's indicated then I'll likely hand over my Broadhead and sack of false credentials and be on my way."

"Right into the open arms of Tsuyo Corporation as a security consultant, I'm sure," Pitt said sourly, standing up and extending his hand across the desk. "Good luck, Pike. You may be a slimy spook, but you've always been straight up with me and I appreciate that."

"Likewise, Admiral." Pike grasped the outstretched hand. "Don't let the politics of this place suck out your soul."

Pike left the office and quickly made his way down to the lifts that would take him to the lower docking complex. He'd already put his bags in the Broadhead and had it warmed up and ready to leave the instant the hatch closed behind him. As the lift car descended away from the upper decks of the station he thought about what it was he might actually find when he got to the Juwel System. Could Wolfe have really been so arrogant as to blindly charge into a trap and get his ship destroyed? He had to amend his last thought with a reminder that Wolfe had actually lost every ship under his command so far; not exactly a stellar record.

When the lift doors opened he stepped out and made his way down to the first of two automated security checkpoints that would require he enter a six-digit code to pass. The Platform was ostensibly secure, but there were layers of protection built into even some non-classified areas just to keep honest people honest. He was almost to the archway that led to the docking complex when he caught sight of a familiar face for the second time even though they were going through great effort to remain hidden.

"I hope you NOVA pukes are better at shooting than sneaking," he called over his shoulder. "What the hell do you want, Essa?"

"When did you see me?" NOVA Team Commander Amiri Essa stepped out of a doorway and walked up to him, still dressed in casual civilian attire that left little doubt his affiliation. Full service dress would have been less obvious than the ubiquitous cargo pants and collared pull-over operators seemed to prefer when on duty and not in battle dress.

"Since you tried to dive into a hallway when I came out of Pitt's office," Pike said, turning around. "How did you know I was heading down here?"

"Dumb luck," Essa admitted. "Heard a rumor the President was sending someone to scope out the Juwel System. I saw you walk into Pitt's office and put it together from there."

"What the hell? That was a private meeting with the President! How could—you know what? Never mind," Pike said disgustedly. "So you snuck down here because you couldn't stand the thought of not saying goodbye?"

"Funny. No, I was coming to ask if you wanted company," Essa said.

Pike looked at him for a moment, trying to see if it was a setup for a joke he wasn't getting. "Why do you want to go to Juwel?" he asked. "Or more specifically, who told you to go to Juwel? Nobody *wants* to go out there, including me."

"Okay … General Ortiz wants me to check things out," Essa admitted.

"Ortiz is a Marine general," Pike said. "You're a Fleet puke. Who authorized this?"

"Ortiz pulled some strings and got me put on detached duty to his office, but he has no way to get anyone out to Juwel," Essa said. "This was two weeks ago and I've been wracking my brain trying to figure out how to insert onto a hostile world with no Fleet backup. Imagine my delight when I saw you and realized where you were going."

"Hence the sneaking around and the backpack that looks like a seventy-two-hour bag from the way it's bulging out at the sides," Pike sighed. "Look, Amiri, I'm going to do a quick in and out. I'm not landing on that planet and my ship doesn't have any drop pods assuming you're suicidal enough to climb into one."

"Fair enough," Essa said. "But I'll be damn sure closer than I am right now and your ship could get there a lot faster than some civilian transport I scam into taking me. Who knows? Maybe I'll get lucky and you get shot down over the planet, we *have* to land there, and then I can complete my mission."

"The fact that you're the best and brightest of the NOVA program terrifies me to no end," Pike said.

"Thank you."

"Wasn't a compliment," Pike said. "Fine, I'll let you ride along. You've got time to go pack a bit more thoroughly. I'll have to put a call in to provisioning and have more food, water, and air brought aboard before we leave. I only allotted for one passenger for a short-duration trip."

Essa stared at him for a moment, no doubt trying to detect if Pike was being straight with him or not, before turning and heading back the way he came at a run.

"Don't say I didn't warn you," Pike said to the NOVA's departing back before keying in his security code.

Chapter 22

"Shit! Contact!"

"Calm yourself!" Jackson barked. "Where is it?"

"It just appeared off our port flank, coming in fast!" Ensign Dole reported. "Range is ninety-two thousand kilometers and accelerating … it looks like a standard Darshik cruiser."

"Coms! Alert the *Icarus* we have been engaged," Jackson said calmly. "Tactical, bracket that ship and stand by on all laser cannon batteries; make sure the computer is continually tracking and updating. We're too close for missiles so don't even bother plotting a firing solution."

"Aye, sir," the shaky voice of a lieutenant J.G. that was filling in for Commander Simmons came back. Jackson recognized her from CIC but had never spoken to her before she was tossed onto the bridge watch rotation.

Jackson took a moment to look at the updated tactical display and realized what had happened: once he'd lit up the sky with his active sensors the Darshik were able to accurately pinpoint his location and jump in on him. He also saw that the *Icarus* would not likely arrive in time to stop the enemy ship from opening fire on the *Star* and his lasers had an effective range just barely greater than the enemy's plasma lance. They were more for point defense than anything else and were wide-focus, underpowered cannons.

"Helm! The instant I give the order roll the *Star* eighty-two degrees to starboard," Jackson said. "No confirmations, just shove her over. I want our keel facing the incoming."

"Aye aye, sir!"

"Captain, the *Icarus* is coming toward us at full power, but Captain Wright says she won't be within range to fire a Shrike before the enemy ship will be too close to risk it," Lieutenant Epsen said.

"Tell Captain Wright that she should be able to take her shot once it passes beneath us," Jackson said. "Tactical! It's very important you keep tracking that ship no matter how rough the ride gets. The moment it crosses into range open fire immediately, don't wait for orders. Just stay calm and focus on the small part you can control in this, Lieutenant. We have a matter of minutes so I don't have time to get Simmons up here to relieve you."

"Yes, sir," she said more confidently this time. He saw that she was setting up firing scripts on her terminal so he stopped worrying about her freezing up.

"Helm, I'm going to be giving you corrections fast and furious," Jackson said as the enemy inexorably closed on them. There was no avoiding this engagement. "Just do what I say, when I say, and we'll come out of this fine and the *Icarus* will clear this nuisance from our flightpath. Remember to listen for the order to roll the ship."

"I'm ready, Captain," the helmsman said.

"OPS, sound the alarm," Jackson said, sitting back into his own seat and pulling on the restraints. "I want everyone strapped down for this." Dole didn't reply but Jackson could hear the harsh klaxon blaring in the corridor beyond, three sharp blasts to let everyone know to strap in and hold on.

The enemy was at such close range that all the updates he was seeing on the main display were in real time. It was still coming in under full power … good. Jackson felt a calmness settle over him as he knew exactly how he would counter the mad rush. Either it would work or it wouldn't, but his path was set and along with that certainty was an absence of panic. He still felt fear, of course. Anyone staring down an enemy warship that wasn't afraid was either a liar or clinically insane.

"Helm! Thirty degrees inclination, all engines ahead emergency!" Jackson barked as the enemy crossed to within fifteen thousand kilometers. The ship pitched up relative to the ecliptic and the engines slammed past full power. Unfortunately the assault carrier didn't make course or speed changes all that quickly and they wouldn't even come close to clearing the enemy before it was well within range, but Jackson had expected that.

"They're within range of their—"

"Helm! Roll!" Jackson shouted, cutting off his OPS officer. The *Star* ponderously rolled to starboard, exposing her ventral surface to the incoming ship. For a few seconds nothing happened … and then all hell broke loose.

The deck heaved as the ship was hit full on with the enemy's primary weapon. The sound was horrendous as the *Star* bucked and shook. Alarms were blaring at every station and a few screens winked out completely. There were harsh thumps felt throughout the deck and a moment later the lights on the bridge went out and Jackson felt himself go weightless in his harness.

"Main Bus B is out!" someone shouted. Dole? "Starboard main engine is venting and shutting down!" Mercifully, the buffeting subsided and Jackson didn't hear any decompression alarms amid the cacophony so he forced himself to remain calm and tried to focus on the main display, which was miraculously still functional and feeding data. The icons representing the *Star* and the enemy ship merged briefly as they passed each other.

"Tango One is ranged! Firing!" a clear, confident voice rang out amid the chaos and Jackson looked up as his relief tactical officer, her face almost serene in the soft light of her terminal, worked the starboard cannon batteries up and down the Darshik cruiser as it flew by.

The closure speed had been quite high so the engagement was over in the blink of an eye, but it had been costly. Jackson could tell the *Star* had been badly damaged in the exchange despite his best efforts to minimize it, and the enemy may very well have flown through their degraded laser fire with nothing more than a scorched hull finish. How many spacers did he lose in that skirmish? He closed his eyes for a moment, not wanting to know.

"Damage control!" he barked out when he opened his eyes again. "OPS! Start taking stock of how badly we're hit."

"Target destroyed!" the tactical officer called out. She'd never taken her eyes off her instruments. "*Icarus* took it out with a single missile shot. Telemetry shows it was a Hornet."

"Impressive," Jackson said absently. "Keep tracking local space, Lieutenant. Coms! Convey our gratitude to the *Icarus*, if you please. OPS!"

"Damage control reports coming in now, sir," Dole said. "Engineering reports Main Bus B will be back up in minutes, artificial gravity in less than twenty once the bus is up, and no estimate on starboard main engine."

"Casualties?"

"Three dead in Forward Launch Control," Dole said in a tight voice. "There are also a handful of minor injuries ranging from burns to bruising."

"What the hell was anyone doing in either of the launch control rooms? We're not even close to the planet?!" Jackson was struggling to control his temper. The *Vega*-class had three launch control rooms that were located just in front of each of the main launch bays. It allowed them to keep watch over the shuttles leaving the ship, but they were right up against the ventral hull plating.

"That was their duty station when at general quarters, sir," Dole said, glancing around at others on the bridge.

"Please have those compartments vacated," Jackson said quietly. "Tell Commander Chambliss that nobody is to be down there until we're actually beginning launch ops. Understood?"

"Aye aye, sir."

"And tell Lieutenant Commander Sharpe he has twenty minutes to start getting me a total status on the condition of this ship," Jackson said. He wished he could get up and walk around, but he didn't feel like creating a hazard by bouncing off the walls in zero g. He felt sick to his stomach. He'd lost people before in combat and it was never something one got used to, but to have them die because he was too incompetent to make certain that nobody was needlessly in harm's way was almost too much to bear. Those spacers had trusted him to do the right thing and he'd lined up the ship so that they took the brunt of the shot. Had he been thinking clearly when he devised his strategy he would have also ensured that any compartments close to the ventral hull armor were evacuated. So stupid.

"Captain," Epsen said quietly. "The *Icarus* is coming up alongside us. They said they'll fly close formation until we're underway again and then they'll continue on to Juwel."

"Thank you, Lieutenant," Jackson said. A few minutes later and there were some thumps and bangs of load contactors engaging throughout the command deck. The lights blinked on and off twice before coming back on for good, and the terminals that had been knocked out all flicked on, the affected subsystems rebooting now that power was restored. It wasn't long after that Jackson began to feel the gentle pull of gravity as the generator started and the field came up in strength. As soon as he could he popped off his restraints and stood up, coming off the floor a few inches before bouncing back down in the weak gravity.

"Coms, get the XO up here on the double," he said before turning to the tactical station. "Lieutenant ... Quintana, your performance during the engagement was exemplary. I'll be sure it's noted in your record."

"Thank you, Captain." Quintana said, a flush creeping up her neck. Simmons burst onto the bridge just then, also flushed but not from having had his CO compliment his skills under fire.

"Captain ... I ... Sorry I wasn't—"

"You weren't supposed to be up here, XO," Jackson held his hands up, palms down. "Just review the sensor logs and see if there's anything new we learned from this scuffle. That bastard jumped right in on top of us so there wasn't any time to swap out personnel."

"Yes, sir." Simmons still looked chastened despite Jackson's assurances.

Once the final reports trickled in they could see there was surprising little damage other than right at the point of impact. Unfortunately the heat from the plasma lance had liquefied the armor in that area and the result was that Launch Bays Five and Six had their hatches welded shut along the leading edges. They didn't really have the time to try and cut through the cooling alloy so Jackson sent out engineering crews with explosive charges to blow the edges clear. It seemed counterintuitive to intentionally light bombs off on the hull of his ship, but he was banking on the hope that the plasma hadn't penetrated too deep. Hopefully the relatively small charges could blast the gaps clear enough for the doors to open.

The starboard main engine restarted without trouble although Engineering was at a loss as to why it shut down in the first place. With Main Bus A and the emergency backups still operational there should have been plenty of power to maintain plasma containment and the nozzle constrictor fields. But, for reasons unknown, the engine had performed an orderly shut-down after venting its plasma chamber harmlessly into space. Jackson told Lieutenant Commander Sharpe to put troubleshooting the engine on low priority and to concentrate on getting the ship ready to fight as quickly as possible.

"Why did you roll the ship when you did, sir?" Commander Simmons asked as the two of them ate from boxed meals that had been delivered to the bridge.

"The *Vega*-class has unusually thick armor on the ventral hull," Jackson explained. "It's an especially dense alloy as well. It's made to resist the friction of skimming through an atmosphere during launch operations as well as protect the ship from ground fire coming up. I'm dubious about that second part since the launch doors would be wide open, but it was the most logical place on the ship to allow that cruiser to hit us since we couldn't get away. Sort of like a boxer leaning into a punch he knows he can't duck."

"I see." Simmons chewed his sandwich, looking off for a moment. "How did that compare to other times you've exchanged fire with enemy ships?"

"Other than when that first Phage Super Alpha blew the prow completely off the *Blue Jacket* that was the hardest hit I remember taking," Jackson said honestly. "I'm genuinely shocked she held up so well after taking a beating like that." He didn't bother to tell his XO that the hardest hit he'd actually taken was the one he didn't remember; when he'd rammed that same Phage with what was left of the *Blue Jacket* and intentionally sent her reactors super-critical. He'd taken so much punishment he had no memory of the incident afterwards. He self-consciously flexed his artificial lower left leg, his remaining souvenir of the encounter.

"Sir, Engineering is clearing us to get underway," Dole reported twenty minutes later. All total, the ship had only been adrift for six hours.

"The launch bay doors?" Jackson asked.

"Clear, sir," Dole nodded. "They're not as quick as they were, but they open and close smoothly."

"Good enough," Jackson nodded. "Coms! Tell the *Icarus* we're coming back on course for Juwel and they are clear to range ahead. After that send a message to the 508th ships and alert them to our revised schedule. It shouldn't affect them, but let's keep them in the loop."

"Aye, sir."

"Seems strange after an encounter like that to not be limping home," Simmons said quietly. "But here we go, right back at it." Jackson glanced over but couldn't read his XO's expression.

"It's what we do, Commander."

"Yes, sir, it is," Simmons agreed and slid into the seat at the tactical station after relieving Lieutenant Quintana.

****

Captain Ed Rawls had just allowed himself to relax a bit as the *Relentless* and *Resolute* flew hard down into the system towards Juwel. Watching the *Icarus* easily take out two Darshik cruisers along with his own ships' success with the other two had allowed a thread of confidence to worm its way into that icy ball of fear he'd been carrying around. He'd been afraid since they left the DeLonges System if he was completely honest with himself.

Combat with starships hadn't been anything like he'd imagined it would be. He'd read all the firsthand accounts from the Phage War, of course, and had tried to put himself in the heads of Wright, Lee, and even Wolfe though he had mixed thoughts on the Earther. Sometimes he thought he seemed to show genuine brilliance despite his heritage, other times he seemed like the bumbling, lucky, unlikable halfwit some had said he was. He'd also spent the requisite time in the simulators on DeLonges before taking command of the *Relentless* when he'd been told that he was being transferred to Starfleet from Merchant Fleet, but none of these things had prepared him at all for the first time he squared off with an enemy ship.

The problem with simulators was that instructors weren't willing to tie up the machine for weeks, so the timetables were always compressed to mere hours and it was the same with reading accounts of other commanders. He finished Wright's accounts of the war in a day, but single battles would take up to three weeks. What he found in reality was the distances involved, and thus the time, could almost break you. When a target was located and the ship was put on course for an intercept the adrenaline automatically started pumping and there was an almost unbearable anxiousness to get to it … but the target could be thirty-six hours away at full acceleration. You can't stay on an adrenaline high that long, you really can't even stay awake that long and be of any use once you get within weapons range.

When he'd read Wolfe's official account of the war from the Archives he'd thought the man a fool. A lucky fool, but a fool nonetheless. Instead of insights into his strategy or his thought processes during critical decisions, the man rambled on and on about making sure he was rotating his crew out for rest and down time as often as he could and making sure he was also taking care of himself. He talked about forcing himself to remain calm and cool even once the first shots had been exchanged instead of the thrill of battle or his philosophy on war in general.

But now, after his first taste of battle and having not accorded himself with honor or courage, Rawls began to understand what the Earther was talking about. Battle in space was an endurance contest. Could you wear your enemy down before your own stamina gave out? He also finally understood what made the implacable Phage so very terrifying compared to these impulsive Darshik.

"Captain I'm getting … something … in the returns from our aft-starboard quadrant." His tactical officer broke into his thoughts and caused his heartrate to spike again.

"Define *something,* Mister," Rawls snapped, instantly regretting his tone and taking a deep breath to reset himself. He saw how his XO looked at him out of the corner of his eye and had an irrational burst of anger towards him too.

"I'm sorry, sir," the lieutenant commander said. "It could have been a false radar return, but it was something that the computer wasn't able to classify. Normally it would filter out ghosts like that."

"Okay, what was it doing? Was it pacing us, closing, or flying away? Did we at least get that much?" Rawls asked.

"It appears it was closing tangentially, but it's almost impossible to tell since there's no frame of reference for the object."

"What about thermals?" Rawls asked. "If there's something near and closing we should see its engine plume easily."

"Nothing at all on the thermals during that time," the tactical officer said. "OPS?"

"Confirmed," the ensign at the OPS station said. "Thermals, visible spectrum ... neither picked up anything where the radar image was."

"Bundle everything during the event and put it on the Link," Rawls said, breathing easier. "I have a feeling we were seeing a false echo from the *Resolute*. Let's stay sharp, though, we're flying deep into enemy-held space. Good call bringing it up, Tactical ... take nothing for granted."

"Yes, sir," the lieutenant commander said.

Rawls had just begun to relax again from the apparent false alarm when everything went to hell again.

There was a flash on the main display that he instantly realized was a light source hitting the dorsal hull plates.

"Fuck!" his tactical officer practically screamed, all thoughts of professional decorum out the airlock. "The *Resolute* is gone!" Rawls saw the icon for his other ship on the Link status turn amber, then flash red and disappear.

"What happened?" he asked irrationally. "Was she hit with something?"

"We don't know yet, sir," the tactical officer reported. "I'm still clearing our local space."

Rawls opened his mouth and closed it twice but said nothing. He felt completely helpless but the lieutenant commander was right; clear the area and then worry about what might have happened to the *Resolute*.

"Commander Bevin had just been selected for captain, too," his XO whispered next to him, referring to the CO of the *Resolute*. He didn't chide his inappropriate comment as he was still processing the fact that he'd now lost two-thirds of his taskforce and had yet to even remotely accomplish his mission.

"Local space is clear, Captain," the tactical officer reported.

"Confirmed," OPS said unprompted. "At least as clear as it was before the *Resolute* exploded."

"Do we know what happened yet?" Rawls asked.

"Yes, sir," OPS said. "This was just sent up from CIC." The main display shifted to a shot of the *Resolute* flying off their starboard flank, trailing by a few thousand kilometers. The image jumped and Rawls realized he was watching a video clip. The video was slowed down significantly so they were able to clearly see a Darshik plasma lance burst through the port, dorsal surface on the Terran destroyer, piercing it like an arrow. The explosions rippling under the surface of the hull were grotesque in the slowed-down clip, but Rawls refused to turn away. For a split second light could be seen pouring out of hundreds of rents in the *Resolute*'s hull before she was engulfed in a flash.

"That's all there was?" Rawls said, his mouth dry. "They didn't send up anything on the ship that hit them?"

"They think they saw something on thermals as the blast subsided, but nothing definitive." The OPS officer shook his head slowly. "They also didn't detect anything leaving the area."

"We were just hit by that ship Captain Wright warned us about, the one that snuck up on her and punched holes in the *Icarus*," Rawls said. "There's no other explanation."

"How could it hide its approach and escape so completely? We're at full power right now." Rawls turned to his XO as the realization of what happened hit him like a bucket of ice water.

"Isn't it obvious?" he asked.

"No, sir … I've never even heard of any ship being so quiet."

"Yes you have," Rawls said. "There's one in the system right now: *Icarus*."

"You mean—"

"Yes, that bastard has a reactionless drive. Coms! Send a message to the *Aludra Star* and the *Icarus* warning them Captain Wright's phantom is in play and has just taken out the *Resolute*. Tell them we suspect it's utilizing some type of gravimetric subliminal drive and it isn't showing up on radar before it hits. OPS, bundle the data from the engagement and sent that as well."

"What orders now, sir?" the tactical officer asked. Rawls saw that they were approaching their maximum subluminal velocity, knew they couldn't see the enemy ship coming, and realized they were all alone out in the outer system.

"Shut down the actives; passives only," he ordered. "OPS, secure the Link transponder. I want *no* EM emissions coming from this ship after our transmissions to the rest of the fleet go out. Helm, engines to zero thrust, steady as she goes.

"We're just going to become as silent as possible, everyone … but we're pressing ahead with our mission. We have a job to do and we don't honor those we've lost on the *Resolute* and *Racer* by cutting and running when two other ships are still here fighting and that ghost ship is still on the loose. We'll fight smart, but we're still going to fight. Any questions?"

There were none. Just a handful of grim, determined faces staring back at him. Rawls took his seat and, strangely, felt calm and clear-headed. He'd just lost a good friend in Commander Bevin and was now alone and being hunted in hostile space, but all he could think about was trying to get the *Relentless* where she could do the most good and not wanting to sacrifice anyone else because he wanted to save his own skin. He was still afraid, but the panic had subsided and he felt ready for whatever was coming next.

Chapter 23

"I think it's safe to say something has changed!" Castillo shouted over the fading sound of the explosion that had shaken the ground beneath them.

"No shit!" Barton shouted back as he reloaded his weapon. Over the last six days they'd done as Colonel Rucker had ordered, hitting Darshik patrols in sneak attacks and even taking out a site that appeared to be an enemy bivouac, killing them all as they slept standing up.

But over the last forty-two hours there had been shift in the aliens' tactics: They were now coming for the Marines and coming hard. The good news was that they were no longer messing about killing unarmed civilians. The bad news was that with the aliens' superior numbers the Marines didn't stand much of a chance over the course of the next few days. Even when they tried to hit and run like they had been the Darshik would doggedly pursue them, tracking them until they could reengage. Barton had to assume that something had shifted in the battle for control of the system out in space, but damned if he could figure out what that might be one way or another.

Another explosion ripped through a building down the street, the one they had been hiding in moments ago, the concussive blast taking Barton's breath away. Shit. They were getting closer and they seemed to be much more proficient at tracking where their fire was coming from than they had before. He realized that the ineptness displayed by the enemy in the early days of the campaign were likely a ruse as the squad they'd engaged was systematically picking them off.

"We're going to need to move," he called to Castillo. "Withdraw everyone, pull straight back. I'm going to try to get to the major and see what he wants to do."

"Got it!" Castillo waved for him to go as he used hand signals to withdraw the rest of the team before the Darshik used their light artillery to take out the squat commercial building they were hiding behind.

Barton ran down a back alley directly away from where they knew the small Darshik unit was for two blocks before cutting left and hustling up the street towards Major Baer's last known position. The damn Darshik had surprised him with that last barrage and he'd been so close to the artillery shell when it exploded that it killed his com with a small piece of shrapnel piercing the battery. Either really bad luck or really good luck depending on how one looked at it, since the comlink transceiver had been attached to his harness right over where his heart was.

Two more blasts rocked the neighborhood, a small place that looked like it used to be mostly machine shops and other light industry, and Barton was just distracted enough that he ran full bore into the black-clad Darshik soldier that had stepped out from a small alley. The alien was looking the other way when Barton slammed into it, throwing it forward and knocking it off balance. Despite its greater bulk the Darshik was surprisingly light.

Unfortunately Barton also had not expected the impact and his carbine slid out of his grip and hit the pavement, his gloved fingers sliding off the stock as he desperately grabbed for it.

"*Grresshhh!*" The deep, undulating hiss that came from the alien turned Barton's blood to ice. It was recovering and had already turned around, beginning to raise its weapon when Barton reacted out of pure, adrenaline-fueled panic.

"Fuck you!!" he roared and pulled his sidearm, charging at the alien again and slamming into it before it could raise its energy weapon. They both went down in a tangle and the alien tried to push Barton off, the human realizing that he'd pinned the weapon across the thing's chest between them. He put the muzzle of his pistol between where the helmet met the neck of the combat suit and pulled the trigger again, again, and again. He kept pulling until the pistol stopped firing, just making a whirring sound, and the Darshik quit thrashing below him.

He pushed himself up off the dead alien and, on shaky legs, backed away towards the wall of the building nearest him. His muscles were cramped up and he felt lightheaded after the hard adrenaline shock his system had just taken. Before he could go and collect his primary weapon he had to turn and empty his stomach onto the sidewalk.

"Get your shit together," he said to himself, spitting out the rest of the bile and wiping his mouth on his sleeve. He reloaded his pistol and holstered it before picking up his carbine and checking it over to make sure his stupid ass hadn't damaged it when he blindly ran into an enemy scout.

He picked up the Darshik energy weapon out of curiosity and looked it over, pulling it as far away from the body as the power umbilical would allow. After fifteen seconds of not being able to figure out how the damn thing worked he tossed it back on the ground, spit on the alien corpse, and continued down the street on still-trembling legs.

Barton didn't get much further when a new set of explosive sounds reached him, these much further away and different than the concussive shells the Darshik had been lobbing at them. He looked towards the source and his empty stomach twisted up into knots. Large columns of vapor stretching up into the sky seemed to be appearing as if by magic over the city of Neuberlin, each accompanied by a thunderous *CRACK!* that shook the ground.

"You sons of bitches," Barton whispered as he watched the capital of Juwel being attacked from a starship in orbit, laser fire raining down on one of the most populated cities on the planet. The beams were superheating the air when they were fired, causing shockwaves to emanate away from the vapor columns they created each time one was fired.

Feeling equally enraged and helpless, he turned and continued on to try and find Major Baer. If they were about to make a last stand—and it seemed like that was the case—he was determined to take out as many of these alien fucks as he could before they got him.

****

"Any word on why the *Resolute* dropped off the Link?" Jackson asked. He was on his fifth or sixth mug of the potent coffee they had in the ward room and he was starting to get a bit fidgety.

"Nothing, sir, and there is no indication that the *Relentless* is engaged," Dole said. "I'm assuming there might have been a malfunction, but I've never seen both primary and redundant Link transponders fail simultaneously."

"I have," Jackson said. "Just keep monitoring it. We won't jump to conclusions until we know anything. How long until our final course change?"

"Just over four hours, Captain."

"Tell Commander Chambliss and Lieutenant Colonel Beck they're clear to begin prepping the shuttles for launch," Jackson said. "Let Chambliss know he's authorized to power up all his shuttles via the umbilicals but to make sure Engineering knows before he puts a heavy draw on the power MUX."

"Aye, sir."

"Captain! Big com packet coming in from the *Relentless*," Epsen called. "They're saying the *Resolute* was destroyed by an unknown bogey and that they're going silent but are still coming down to Juwel as fast as they can."

"There they go," Dole said, pointing to the Link status block on the main display. The icon for the *Relentless* went amber just as the *Resolute* dropped off the board altogether.

"Damnit!" Jackson ground out. "Coms, send that entire packet down to CIC and tell them I expect a full brief ASAP ... I want to know what the hell happened out there and then ask the *Icarus's* com officer if they received the same thing."

"Aye, Captain."

The next forty-five minutes were tense as he waited for his CIC to pull a cohesive story out of the data dump the *Relentless* had sent. They were getting close to the point of no return and this mission was still very much up in the air. The *Icarus* was well past them now and actually had to decelerate so she didn't reach the planet too far ahead of the *Star*. Jackson was mildly embarrassed by that but didn't show it in front of his crew; he'd already had too many slips of the tongue disparaging the *Star* when she didn't perform like a destroyer would have. A lot of the crew had been with the ship for years and he was the outsider. They'd made it clear non-verbally early on that the comments didn't pass unnoticed and weren't appreciated.

"Sir, this is Lieutenant Jelinek," Simmons walked up with a young officer in tow. "He'll be conducting the briefing regarding the loss of the *Resolute*."

"Lieutenant, am I correct in assuming that you're about to deliver bad news given that you came up here yourself?" Jackson asked.

"It's moderately horrible, yes, sir," Jelinek said.

"OPS and Coms! Get Captain Wright on a video channel and pipe it here to the bridge," Jackson said, ignoring the muttering he heard. It was unorthodox for captains to confer with each other in plain view of their crews. That quasi-tradition began because most COs could barely agree that space was cold and the arguments over even trivial matters tended to escalate into full-blown fights. When large egos collided the results were predictable, but Jackson and Celesta had enough mutual respect and history that he felt comfortable having her sit in on the brief and add her input when needed.

"Captain Wolfe," Celesta greeted him as the video resolved on the main display. She was also sitting in her command chair on the bridge of the *Icarus* and Jackson felt a momentary pang of loss as it looked so much like his old ship: *Ares*. "Thank you for inviting me to your intel brief."

"No problem, Captain," Jackson said. "It's good to see you again. Lieutenant Jelinek … you may proceed."

Over the next twenty minutes Jelinek quickly laid out a concise recreation of what happened based on Rawls's firsthand testimony and the sensor logs of the *Relentless*. The news was bleak. The Darshik "specter" was apparently a lot more capable of a ship than even Celesta had known it to be. In addition to being able to get into a system with a miniscule transition flash it appeared to be extremely stealthy and operated a gravimetric subluminal drive similar to the one the *Icarus* used. Even the plasma lance seemed to be especially powerful compared to the cruiser-class ships they were used to tangling with, having completely speared through the *Resolute* and rupturing two reactors within seconds.

"This ... is not welcome news," Celesta pinched the bridge of her nose. "The damn thing could be sitting between us right now and we likely wouldn't even know."

"It's as bad a scenario as I can imagine," Jackson agreed. "Why is there only one ship with this sort of capability though? Why are the other Darshik warships comparatively weak and this one can gut a Terran destroyer with one shot?"

Celesta just shook her head. "All I know is I'm more thankful to still be here than I originally thought," she said. "That ship had a free pass on the *Icarus* but only hit her with a glancing shot. What do you want to do about this, Captain?"

"Nothing *to* do," Jackson said. "We'll have to hope we have some warning before it strikes, but if it left the *Relentless* intact we can bet it's on its way here now that we're approaching so close to the planet."

"Agreed," Celesta said. "We'll try to—" She was interrupted at the exact instant Lieutenant Epsen began waving frantically for Commander Simmons.

"What it is?" Jackson asked him as Celesta leaned out of frame for a moment.

"Sir, word from the surface," Epsen said. "The Marines are declaring an emergency and are calling on any assets in the system to help. The Darshik are firing on the capital from orbit and the troops on the ground are now coming after them in earnest. Colonel Rucker said he's lost most of his force and can't keep them out of the city now."

"Captain Wolfe—"

"Celesta, go!" Jackson cut his former XO off. "Take out every ship over that planet! We'll get there when we can."

"Yes, sir," she nodded and the video feed was cut.

"*Icarus* is moving off now, accelerating at … damn!" Dole said softly.

"Yes, she's a fast ship," Jackson said. "How far out are we now?"

"Final course correction coming up in seventy-two minutes," Dole said. "We'll begin braking shortly after and then slide into our orbital lane."

Jackson just nodded, replaying what the Marines had said in his head. The ground troops were now attacking the city and its defenders in earnest. The atmospheric processor was still an important target, but at what cost? People were dying *now*; the processor alone would take many years to make a dent.

"Coms, have Colonel Beck report to the bridge, please," Jackson said, making his decision. Now he just hoped the Marine officer saw it the same way.

****

"Tango marked as derelict is locked on!" Adler said. "One Shrike, ready to launch."

"Fire!" Celesta said.

"Missile one is away," Adler said. "Flying hot and clean."

"Lock onto the cruiser that's sitting over Neuberlin and bring the auto-mag online," Celesta ordered.

"Aye aye, ma'am!" Adler said with a feral smile.

The auto-mag was the latest iteration of the venerable mag cannons that had served aboard Terran warships for over two centuries. This version wasn't mounted on an articulating turret and the ferrous shells it spit were smaller, but it could belch out twenty-five rounds in rapid-fire succession before it needed to cool and be reloaded. It was not a subtle weapon and anything the multi-ton rounds hit at near-relativistic speeds was decimated. Even the Phage Super Alphas couldn't withstand salvos from such weapons.

"It looks like it's just those two cruisers over Juwel right now, ma'am," Accari reported, taking the initiative as usual and helping the tactical officer with her workload while the ship was in battle. "That leaves one accounted for in the local area, three total from the initial sitrep we received from the *Aludra Star*, and our Specter friend."

"Keep scanning," Celesta said. "That bastard is out there still. Hopefully we can draw him out with this attack and keep him off the *Star* or the *Relentless*."

"Yeah ... *hopefully*."

Celesta narrowed her eyes but couldn't pinpoint where the sarcastic muttering had come from. Barrett, however, turned and gave a hard look to someone along the back row of terminals followed by some uncomfortable coughing.

"Auto-mag is loaded, charged, and locked on, Captain," Adler said. "Ranging data is constantly updating."

"Is the target still firing on the planet?"

"Affirmative, ma'am," Accari said.

"Tactical, you are clear to assume helm control when ready," Celesta said. "I want ten rounds fired immediately so that helm control is relinquished when we make our first pass over the planet."

"Stand by," Adler said. "Assuming helm control … tactical computer has the helm."

"Confirmed," the helmswoman said.

"RDS to zero thrust … adjusting attitude … still adjust—Firing!" The deck shook with each round that was fired. The cannon was hard-mounted to the ship's structure so everyone aboard could feel each shot.

"Shrike One has detonated. Stand by for BDA," Accari said.

"All rounds away," Adler talked over him. "Safing auto-mag and relinquishing helm control."

"Confirmed, I have the helm."

"OPS?"

"Derelict is ... destroyed," Accari said in relief.

"Helm, come eight degrees to port, ten degrees declination," Celesta ordered as she watched the main display. "All ahead full."

"Coming to port, all engines ahead full, aye."

The RDS surged again and soon the *Icarus* was racing towards the planet far too fast to even think about making orbit, but that wasn't Celesta's plan. With the Specter still out and hunting, she didn't want to present too easy of a target. She assumed the *Icarus* was much faster after their previous tangle, so she would fire, pass the planet at speed to assess the damage they caused, and then use the awesome power of her subluminal drive to perform a maneuver that was impossible for any other Terran starship. She was going to come to a relative stop, come about, and be back over the planet before the *Aludra Star* even managed to plane out after her braking maneuver. She grinned slightly as she thought about Wolfe watching her destroyer on his tactical display while riding along in such a comparatively tepid ship.

"Impact in ten," Adler called. The planet was now a brighter speck moving quickly among the other specks in the corner of the main display that showed an external view. It was twelve seconds later when they saw a brief, bright flash from that speck.

"At least four rounds hit it," she said. "Likely the first four and then there was nothing left for the remaining six. OPS?"

"Confirmed, Tactical," Accari said. "CIC shows four good hits and radar data is showing an expanding debris cluster where there used to be an enemy ship."

"Excellent work, everybody," Celesta said. "Helm, maintain course and acceleration and we'll visually confirm kills on our flyby. Coms! Tell the Marines on the ground and the *Aludra Star* that we've cleared the sky for them."

"Aye aye, ma'am," Lieutenant Ellison said.

"Now the hard part," Barrett said from her left.

"Indeed," Celesta agreed. "Now we have to deal with our ghost."

Chapter 24

"The *Icarus* just destroyed both ships over the planet. Captain Wolfe should have a clear shot to launch his shuttles."

"Good," Rawls said. "Then we'll move into an overwatch role since we won't get there in time to provide cover nor does it look like we need to. Captain Wright seems to have pulled the teeth out of the Darshik blockade."

"Still no sign of the ship that took out the *Resolute*," the relief tactical officer said.

Rawls looked nervously at the main display and then the mission clock. They were close to the planet now and both the other Terran ships in the system were making no attempt to sneak around, both blaring active sensors and the *Aludra Star*'s main engines creating a magnificent thermal plume they could see from where they were at. Was there any point to trying to remain hidden at the point?

"Tactical, go active sensors," he said finally. "OPS, put us back on the Link. Helm, I want—"

"I have that same echo!" the OPS officer shouted. "Just a hint of something when the actives came up. It's closing on us from the port, aft quadrant this time." Rawls's tongue stuck to the roof of his mouth while the relief tactical officer, who hadn't been on the bridge during the previous encounter, just looked confused.

"Tactical! Sustained NOTA fire! All port cannons, full randomized spread!" Rawls shouted, coming out of his seat a bit. To his credit the relief tactical officer turned immediately and executed the order. A non-target associated (NOTA) sequence overrode the tactical computer's desire to have an object or location clearly defined before firing weapons. Rawls had essentially ordered his entire port flank worth of pulse laser cannons to open up and continue firing wildly at all angles.

"Firing!" the tactical officer called.

"Impacts!" OPS shouted. "Target is twelve thousand kilometers off our port flank!"

"Target those impacts! All cannons, full power!" Rawls shouted, but it was too late.

"Target lock is lost," Tactical said. "Fifty-two separate hits on target confirmed, but nothing of sufficient duration or power to do much damage."

"Not exactly," OPS said. "CIC is reporting that we did moderate damage to the hull coating on the prow of the enemy ship and when it was retreating we could see it clearly on radar. The coating was actually almost one and a half meters thick."

"You ran them off right as they were coming in for the kill," the XO said softly before raising his voice. "Captain just saved our asses!" A hearty cheer came from his bridge crew and some people actually started applauding. Rawls, thoroughly embarrassed, waved them to silence.

"We're not out of danger yet," he said seriously. "Coms, inform the *Icarus* and the *Aludra Star* that we may have compromised the Specter's stealth capability, maybe temporarily, maybe not. Forward them the data from the engagement."

"Aye aye, sir!" the coms officer said with far more enthusiasm than was necessary for a routine ship-to-ship communique.

Rawls desperately wanted to escape the bridge even if just to go to his office and splash some cold water on his face. His crew was looking at him with a newfound respect that bordered on adoration and it made him want to throw up. The stunt with the NOTA firing sequence had been a bizarre knee-jerk reaction that had its roots in a running joke among his classmates in post-Academy training.

The command is usually executed when a CO wanted to test all his laser cannons with live fire and get real data on the power and control subsystems; it was why the relief tactical officer knew exactly how to do it. When he was doing bridge simulation training the instructors used to throw in ludicrous odds at the end of a session just for fun and, in a moment of levity, a young Ed Rawls had given the same order he had moments ago and claimed that he'd destroyed all the targets. They'd all had a good laugh and he'd never thought of it again ... so what in the hell possessed him to shout it out when he was about to piss himself with fear?

If he'd actually known what he was doing he would have ordered the power cranked up on his laser cannons; the pre-configured NOTA script had the projectors so dialed back that all he'd done with over fifty hits at relatively close range was burn away some radar absorbent hull coating. He felt like a fraud and he felt like a fool, but mostly he just felt drained and wanted to escape the burgeoning hero-worship he saw blossoming on his bridge.

"Sir, you okay?" his XO asked.

"I'm fine," Rawls nodded, swallowing hard. "Any word back from the other ships?"

"Both Captain Wolfe and Captain Wright send their congratulations on bloodying the Specter's nose," his com officer said, pausing the conversation he was apparently having in his headset. "The *Icarus* is reporting that they've cleared the planet and are going hunting and that they'll try to box the enemy ship in between us and them."

"Excellent," Rawls said without much enthusiasm. "Very well … let's maintain alertness everyone. If Captain Wright chases that bastard back our way we want to be ready to finish the job." This was met with another round of cheering and another wave of self-loathing from him, albeit smaller than the last. In truth he was hoping that Celesta Wright ran the son of a bitch down and ended the fight with her more powerful ship before he was forced to square off with it again. He had to imagine the enemy commander was pissed and embarrassed by his maneuver and might right now be working his way back to take another shot at the *Relentless*. Damn the luck.

****

"*Rawls* did that?" Jackson asked, regretting the tone the moment the words left his mouth.

"Yes, sir," Dole said.

"Not bad," Jackson said. "I wonder when he came up with that move?"

"Unsure, sir," Dole answered the rhetorical question. "Commander Chambliss reports that all shuttles are loaded and green for launch. Lieutenant Colonel Beck has also checked in and said his Marines and equipment are secured and ready."

"Very good," Jackson said. "Tell Flight OPS they are free to clear and open the launch bay doors."

"Aye, sir," Dole said. "The *Star* is on course and we've reached our target launch velocity."

"The *Icarus* is holding position above and behind us, sir," Simmons said. "No sign of the ship that attacked the *Relentless*."

With the *Star* having slowed to a veritable crawl in order to safely launch her drop shuttles the crew was on edge; they'd yet to pick up any sign of where the Specter may have retreated to. Nobody truly thought that the danger was over just because the *Relentless* had managed to knock some of the hull coating off, and they were now right in the middle of the most dangerous part of their mission, not to mention when they'd be the most exposed and helpless.

Jackson knew the crew expected that once they launched their shuttles they'd be able to push out at full power to their jump point and head home, but the longer the Specter remained hidden the less likely he knew that would be. The ship might have been making repairs to its specialized radar-absorbing hull coating, or it may be loitering out near the outer system, content to let them come in as they tried to escape. The Darshik seemed to have a pretty good idea where most of their jump points were and had no issue camping out and waiting for a Terran ship to transition in and then pounce on it.

"OPS, make sure we're able to get a good look at the secondary target," Jackson said, looking at the planet on the main display. "Specifically, I want to see if there's any support infrastructure being set up that we might be able to target from orbit."

"Secondary target is locked in, sir," Dole confirmed. "We'll adjust our course slightly once the last shuttle is away and that should take us almost directly over the site."

"I'm giving Flight OPS the authorization now to launch when ready," Jackson said, providing the biometric reading on his terminal to authorize Commander Chambliss to launch when ready. The course, speed, and release point had to be precisely controlled so what he was doing was essentially authorizing the *Star's* computers to fly her to the launch point and spit the shuttles out at the exact instant they need to be.

"Flight OPS confirms launch authorization," Lieutenant Epsen said from the com station.

"OPS, give a warning on the shipwide to stand by for launch," Jackson said. "Tactical, keep an eye on the horizon as we're coming across the terminator. The *Icarus* won't be able to cover us completely from where she's at off the stern."

"Eyes on the horizon, aye," Simmons said.

Jackson had no issues taking a starship in close to a planet at speed; he'd even dipped his previous destroyer down deep into the murky layers of what used to be the habitable planet of Xi'an, but he'd never performed launch operations while being so close. He'd only had two opportunities to deploy drop shuttles out of the *Star* for training purposes, and both times it was only two shuttles and they did it deep in the DeLonges System, far away from any stellar bodies.

Commander Simmons had served on assault carriers and the much larger fleet carriers his entire career, so Jackson was depending on him to speak up if he was about to screw up too badly. The truth was that the ship, despite being a vintage design, had been fitted with state of the art avionics and computers and she required very little operator input to successfully launch the shuttles and come around the other side without incident.

He could feel the engines running up and down on their own, fine correcting the ship's insertion vector as the final seconds counted down. The main display automatically opened a new window that showed a real-time view of the ventral hull looking aft so that they could watch the shuttles as they dropped out of the bays.

"*Drop Shuttles One and Two ... deploying.*" The voice of Commander Chambliss came over the overhead speakers as two sleek, lifting-body cargo shuttles were lowered from the belly of the *Aludra Star* on a series of rams that held the craft for a split second before releasing them. Jackson watched for a moment, fascinated as the smaller ships fell away and began maneuvering on their own attitude jets towards the planet below.

The process repeated in rapid-fire succession until all twenty-seven shuttles had been released out of the cruiser and the armored bay doors all swung up and locked with a series of *booms* that resounded through the hull.

"*All drop shuttles successfully deployed, Captain,*" Chambliss said. "*Relinquishing helm control now.*"

"Helm, execute our pull-up maneuver and get us over the secondary target," Jackson ordered. "Coms! Inform anyone you can get a hold of on the ground that their reinforcements are inbound and tell them where the shuttles will be landing. Let the *Icarus* know that we're continuing around the planet to get eyes on that atmospheric processor and then we'll be pulling up into a higher parking orbit."

"Aye, sir," Epsen said. "I've already been in touch with Colonel Rucker's people and have handed them off to the lead shuttle's copilot. Contacting the *Icarus* now."

It galled Jackson to have to leave the processor intact on the west coast, but the enemy had forced his hand when they began attacking Neuberlin in earnest. The obvious answer would be to strike the enormous machine from orbit with the *Star's* lasers or let the *Icarus* take a crack at it, but they'd put the damn thing right in the ocean. If they destroyed it he had no idea what sort of contamination nightmare he'd release into the water. It'd be conceivable that he would have fought all the way down to the planet to reinforce the Marines only to kill everyone anyway by contaminating the ocean. His hope was that the low-altitude pass they were executing would allow them to take detailed multi-spectral imagery of the machine and from that find a better way to eliminate it. Barring that, he was hoping for a safe way to disable it. He had to assume that any alien terraforming machine would be releasing some type of microbial life into the atmosphere that wouldn't be compatible with Terran flora and fauna. Keeping that contained would need to be their highest priority and he now had serious doubts about what he'd just done in deploying the only fresh ground troops within a hundred lightyears to defend a single city.

Chapter 25

Willy Barton was in excruciating pain. Major Baer was motionless on the ground to his right, and he didn't know where Castillo was. All he knew was that getting hit with one of those fucking Darshik weapons hurt as bad as it looked when he'd seen others take fire. The initial impact wasn't so bad, but whatever they used it burned and burned once it was inside you.

He coughed wetly and he knew he was done. There was still sporadic fighting around him, renewed pockets of resistance where Marines had met up and banded together, but the enemy had found them and was now advancing in earnest. Not only were the defenders falling quickly but there was nowhere to be medevac'd to so his wound, though not initially fatal, was surely mortal since he could go nowhere for treatment. After another bought of coughing he bit down on the emergency pain relief tab he'd pulled from a pocket on his harness with shaking fingers, chewing through the packaging because he knew his bloody hands would have no luck tearing it open.

"Ahhhh," he sighed, lying back and staring at the clouds above as the powerful narcotics coursed through his system. He pulled his sidearm from its holster and rested it across his chest, ready to take at least one more of those assholes out with him when they came to make sure of him.

A dull, throbbing rumble had begun after he'd taken the pain tab and he'd assumed it was a side-effect of the drug, but now he could definitely feel the ground shaking. Maybe the Darshik were finally bringing up mechanized units to finish them off quickly. Good. He hated waiting.

Soon the rumble had increased to a harsh roar and Barton caught movement off to his left. When he turned his head he had to blink a few times because he was sure he was hallucinating. If he wasn't, it sure as hell looked like there were at least a dozen Terran fast-assault drop shuttles descending out of the clouds and lining up for a landing somewhere to the east. He vaguely recalled there was a private airfield over that way. He was so engrossed in what was happening over to his left that he didn't hear the footsteps until he saw the shadow fall across him and knew it was time. When he tried to yank up his pistol a heavy boot came down and pinned it to his chest. It wasn't an alien boot.

"Easy, Sergeant," Colonel Rucker's face appeared over his head. "Don't want you getting jumpy and shooting me just before Colonel Beck rides in to the rescue. Where are you hit?"

"My … my side, sir." Barton squinted and fought against the mind-fogging effects of the drugs he'd popped. He was now ashamed of his own weakness, sacrificing his edge in order to minimize his physical discomfort, and he didn't want the old man to see him like that.

"Looks nasty," Rucker said, probing gently around the scorched area of his uniform top before turning his head and bellowing, "Corpsman!"

"Sir!" a Fleet corpsman in Marine fatigues ran up, sliding his kit off his back as he saw Barton.

"Sergeant Barton was hit with one of those damned plasma rifles, or whatever the hell they shoot." Rucker stood up. "Patch him up enough so that he's stable to move. Word's come down that if Beck can secure his airfield and advance enough to relieve us we're going to try and fuel a few shuttles up and push for orbit. Captain Wolfe has agreed to try and make it back around to extract us."

"Yes, sir!" the corpsman and Barton said simultaneously. The corpsman then looked at Barton almost apologetically as he pulled a canister out of his kit fitted with what looked like a stainless steel straw.

"This is really, *really* going to hurt, Sergeant," he said before plunging the straw right into the wound and pressing the top of the canister. There was a gurgling hiss of something filling the wound cavity and then a white-hot, searing pain lanced up Barton's side. He swung and tried to punch the corpsman in the face but the Fleet puke just batted aside the fist with a negligent swat.

"That's the normal reaction," The corpsman nodded. "This is going to take a few minutes to set, but it'll keep your blood and guts in place while you're moved. Once it quits hurting, you can go ahead and move around."

"Thanks, Doc," Barton said, lying back and breathing shallowly even as the pain began to fade.

****

"Wow ... this is bad." Pike leaned back in his seat, reading the synopsis his ship's advance computer had pulled out of the ether and compiled for him and his passenger.

The Broadhead II had popped into real-space just inside the heliopause and had been sitting silent, listening, for nearly thirty-two hours. They'd immediately detected the presence of a Link broadcast and Pike had wasted no time ordering his computer to break into the *Aludra Star's* Link archive and pull out the events that had happened since the assault carrier transitioned in, or at least the highlights.

Even without it being spelled out he and Amiri were able to tell that Ed Rawls's cowardice had almost cost the mission. If Celesta Wright hadn't arrived unannounced and pushed him in the right direction he might still be up near the system perimeter. Pike felt a pang of guilt at his uncharitable thoughts as he read further and saw that the 508th had lost two ships and the *Relentless* had actually executed a rather brilliant bit of strategy against an unconventional enemy and prevented their own demise.

The computer was savvy enough that it had provided a separate synopsis for Amiri Essa that focused on all the communications from the Marines on the ground as well as the eventual deployment of the drop shuttles to relieve the beleaguered force. The two men read in silence for the better part of an hour before Pike felt he knew enough to come up with some sort of plan of action.

"The com platform is gone," Essa said. "I don't know why we thought that would've survived the assault."

"The ships here should still have been able to get word back to New Sierra," Pike shook his head, picking up on what his associate was saying. "This is an established system; normal com drones wouldn't have even passed through the platform on the way out. Hell, the *Icarus* is carrying point-to-point drones."

"But in this system com drones and starships use the same jump point on the way back to the DeLonges and Columbiana Systems," Essa argued. "The Darshik picket ships might have intercepted any Wolfe or Rawls launched."

"Maybe." Pike was clearly skeptical something as small as a com drone moving at transition velocity would have been picked off by the Darshik cruisers they'd seen. "So now the question is what do we do? Technically I've completed my mission and the smart thing to do would be to haul ass back for New Sierra and try to get Admiral Pitt to commit more forces since it seems thanks to Wolfe and Wright this system might actually be tenuously back in Terran hands, but they can't hold it alone."

"That would be the smart thing to do," Essa said noncommittally, not looking over at Pike.

"Fine, you stubborn pain in the ass," Pike snarled. "We'll head down and put eyes on the planet while we're here."

"I didn't say anything!" Essa protested as the throb of the Broadhead's RDS coming up gave them both a moment of vertigo.

"I can feel the waves of condemnation radiating off you at the thought we'd just do a sneak and peek," Pike said. "That's why I can't stomach operators. No sense of perspective. You're all blunt instruments that get sent into situations that require a surgeon."

"Present company excluded, of course?" Essa frowned.

"I said it how I meant it," Pike said. Essa gave him a rude hand gesture from his homeland as Pike programmed an aggressive descent into the system. "I guess we'll see who has the better tech; whoever built that one-off ship for the Darshik or Tsuyo's ship designers."

****

"These images show that the machine is still dormant," Lieutenant Maan said, indicating the images she'd put up on the main display. The CIC officer had picked out a few images in different parts of the spectrum to highlight the points of her quick brief as the *Star* moved up into high orbit over Juwel.

"We can clearly see the inlets and the exhaust vents for the processor and there isn't any moving air around these areas. Thermal graphs show the exterior of the machine is only slightly warmer than the surrounding water it sits in; no hot spots or increase in temperature that would indicate a power source or that it's even preparing to start up."

"What about this line here?" Commander Simmons indicated a black line that stretched from the machine that was sitting fifteen kilometers offshore and ran up onto land near a flat spot of desert beach. "What's that?"

"Inconclusive," Maan said.

"It's a power cable," Lieutenant Commander Sharpe said confidently. The chief engineer had come up for the technical brief at the behest of the captain. "That machine isn't so big that they'd have a reactor buried down in it somewhere, at least not one of sufficient size to power something like an atmospheric processor. We've assumed the thing was in the water to hide it, but that never really made any sense. It's most likely immersed to provide cooling and then the power source will be located ashore where it's easier to manage and defend."

"So what would you use to power something that big?" Jackson asked. "There's nothing in the local area they could easily commandeer even if the power was compatible."

"Easy." Sharpe shrugged, appearing bizarrely disinterested. "I'd land a starship right on that flat spot the cable comes up to and run it off the powerplant."

"What?!" Simmons scoffed, rolling his eyes.

"That's actually not that outlandish," Jackson held up a hand. "We can land our ships in the event of an emergency and the Darshik seem to be at least on par with our Gen III starships ... but we can't get them back into orbit. Once they're on the ground that's it. We can control the decent but they'll never fly again afterwards."

"So?" Sharpe asked. "You're invading a planet with the intent of transforming the atmosphere to the point that you can live on the surface and all indigenous life dies off. A single cruiser to act as the powerplant and a base of operations for the terraforming effort seems reasonable."

"Word has come in from the surface, Captain!" the relief com officer called across the bridge. "The shuttles are almost fueled and the wounded have all been loaded up. It will be four shuttles in total coming back up. Colonel Rucker and twelve hundred or so of his Marines are staying behind to augment Colonel Beck's force."

Jackson thought about ordering Rucker back up so that he could go back and brief CENTCOM in person but relented. He'd earned the right to see the mission through to the end and he assumed he'd send some officer up that would be prepared to pass on the same information.

"Very well," he said. "Inform the *Icarus* that we won't be here much longer."

"So what do we do about this ... thing?" Simmons asked, gesturing to the display. "I still completely agree with the captain that destroying it from orbit is too risky given our lack of knowledge about what's in it. Since they haven't been able to power it up yet do we just leave it for the ground forces to handle?"

"The problem is that we don't know if any of the cruisers left lurking about in this system will do the job or if it takes a specialized ship," Sharpe said. "Keep in mind that what I said was just an educated guess. There could be a heavy hauler bringing in a powerplant even now from Darshik space *or* I could be completely off the mark and there's some sort of compact powerplant built into the thing *or* we could all be wrong and it's not an atmospheric processor at all. Honestly, unless they're playing a fifteen-year plan I don't see that single machine being able to do the job quickly enough to keep us from moving in everything we've got and destroying it."

"Speculation for another time and likely different people," Jackson said. "Let's get ready to grab our wounded Marines and get the hell out of here."

"Heading back to Engineering now, sir," Sharpe said, walking off the bridge.

"*Icarus* is breaking orbit, Captain," the com officer said. "Captain Wright wants to get out away from the planet where she can better maneuver in case the enemy stealth ship appears."

"Understood," Jackson said, still looking at the images of the alien machine on the screen. Sharpe had brought up a point that had been bothering him since they discovered it sitting in the ocean: as impressive as it was, it wasn't enough to modify an entire planet within a timeframe that was useful for the Darshik. So what was the point of it?

The four drop shuttles were able to safely launch from the airfield they'd landed at and made orbit without incident. Jackson opted for a slower, standard approach for rendezvous since there wasn't anybody actively shooting at them at that particular moment. No point putting everyone at risk doing a full combat extraction when Celesta Wright had effectively cleared the skies. He knew that the Specter was still out there, but its commander had watched the *Icarus* tear through four Darshik with ease and hadn't been able to destroy her in their first engagement. Jackson felt confident that the *Starwolf*-class destroyer's impressive speed and firepower would keep the Specter at bay long enough for him to collect his wounded and be on their way.

He assumed that the Marines could probably find treatment somewhere along the string of settlements surrounding Neuberlin, but he understood the tradition of the service and their desire to extract their own people to care for them. He also wanted to take back as much firsthand knowledge of fighting the Darshik on the ground as he could as he doubted this would be the last planet they tried to establish a beachhead on.

"Lead pilot has made contact; we're ready to being recovery operations, Captain," Ensign Dole said, stifling a yawn with his hand.

"Very well." Jackson sat down. "Configure the *Star* to recover spacecraft. Inform Flight OPS they're green to capture."

"Aye, sir."

Jackson took one last look at the images of the alien machine before they were cleared away and views from the recovery operations were put up in their place. There was something nagging at the back of his mind about why the Darshik would put it there.

Chapter 26

Alarms began chirping softly from the console, forcing Pike to incline his seat back up and see what was happening. It wasn't an actual alert so he wasn't worried that they were about to be fired upon or even that the sensors had detected anything in their vicinity.

"What've we got?" he yawned. He frowned as looked at the data his passive sensors were feeding him. "Hey! NOVA! Get your ass up here!"

"What?" Amiri Essa said irritably. He'd only gone back to the living spaces in the small ship to get some sleep an hour or so before.

"We're picking up another reactionless drive that isn't the *Icarus*," Pike said. "It's not very close, but it's up ahead and roughly along our current course."

"Our elusive Darshik ship that punched holes in your lady's destroyer?" Essa said, drawing an irritated look from Pike.

"It keeps popping up intermittently so it's not under power; probably making fine corrections to stay hidden but it's definitely drifting back towards Juwel," he said.

"I thought RDS ships were virtually undetectable," Essa said.

"Who the hell told you that?" Pike laughed. "Starships are made of metal still. Radar will pick them up unless they're stealthy like our friend here, but even a ship like that will show up using a magnetic anomaly detector depending on how close it is to you and how close you both are to a stellar body like a planet."

"So how are you seeing it as none of those conditions are currently true?" Essa said.

Pike hesitated before going on. "This is highly sensitive," he said. "The fact you're even on the flightdeck of this ship during combat operations is probably a pretty serious violation of half a dozen regs, but I operate outside normal channels so I'm taking a chance you're not going to screw me over and blab everything you see. You really want to know or just take it on faith that it works?"

"May as well tell me."

"This ship has the ability to detect minute fluctuations within the distortion fields of its own gravimetric drive," Pike said. "It's basically like an accelerometer but accurate to a degree unheard of in even the most sensitive electronic devices. I don't know how to explain it much further than that because, frankly, I don't understand the science behind it. I'm a spy, not an engineer. To keep this on point all I'll say is that I can easily track anything which moves by distorting space-time like an RDS regardless of how well they want to stay hidden."

"I can see why that's classified," Essa said.

"Exactly," Pike said. "The ESA is only now experimenting with gravimetric propulsion. We'd rather not let on that we have a way to detect them even more accurately than thermal detectors are able to pick up plasma thrust engines."

"You're not going to kill me now that you've divulged such a sensitive secret, are you?" Essa seemed more curious than concerned. Both he and the CIS agent operated in a world where people, even allies, were killed for less.

"Probably not," Pike said as he continued to work the controls on the large, curved glass console. "But I may report that you were made privy to it and it will limit your assignments to places where you can't be captured by anyone who would want that knowledge."

"I'd rather you just kill me," Essa said sourly. "So what are we going to do?"

"We're going to hope the Darshik don't have the same capability and try to get up close enough to get some intel on this bastard, and then we'll let the *Icarus* know where it's at," Pike said. "I assume it can also perform intra-system hops like its ugly cousins so I don't want to tip our hand too early."

"But what if it just decides to hop and we're still trailing it?" Essa said. "It'll arrive before our transmission does."

"Good point," Pike conceded. "We've already been transmitting limited data on the Link without drawing any interest. Let's use that and then start to move in."

****

"Sir, we have a new node that's popped up on the Link," Accari said. "No ship registry, but it's giving all the correct codes to access the stream and—ah, these are high level CIS codes. Stand by … I'll have to have the com section verify these."

"Verified," Ellison called out. "CIS access codes, level five, all properly authenticated."

"That narrows it down to either the director himself or a full-blown Agent," Barrett said. "Coms, call the captain to the bridge if you please. I think we can guess who the new arrival is."

It took a full five minutes for Celesta to come onto the bridge. She'd been sound asleep when Ellison had called her, allowing herself a few hours off while the *Aludra Star* wrapped up recovery operations and prepared to break orbit and head for home. She trusted Barrett even if the ship came under attack, so she left him on the bridge as the *Icarus* protected Captain Wolfe's ship while it was so vulnerable.

"Report!" She failed in her effort to contain her irritation.

"New node on the Link, ma'am," Accari spoke up. "Given the codes used to access the telemetry stream we're assuming it's Agent Pike or some other high-level CIS operative."

"Let's not assume identity based on non-specific codes," she warned. "CIS could have had a Prowler out there this entire time that's just decided to make its presence known. Is it providing information?"

"Not continuous updates," Accari shook his head. "Just a single burst with a packet that I'm not authorized to open."

"Send it to my terminal," Celesta said and crossed the bridge to her chair. She quickly logged in, found the encrypted packet, and used her command level authorization to access it. She read through it quickly, her eyes widening just a bit as she did.

"OPS, put a confirmation of transmission to the unknown node up on the Link," she said. "That was a CIS asset in the system and they've spotted our Specter. The ship is sitting out beyond the orbit of the fifth planet and there's a risk that it may be prepping to jump in close and take us by surprise."

"What do you want to do, ma'am?" Barrett asked.

"I'd say with the element of surprise gone we sit tight and be ready to fire on anything that approaches us or the *Aludra Star*," she said. "Coms! Tell the *Relentless* to start heading for the jump point and that we'll escort the assault carrier away from the planet once they're done."

"Aye, ma'am."

"And call first watch back on duty," she said as almost an afterthought. "If anything is going to happen it'll likely be soon. Coms, let the *Aludra Star* know that things are likely to get hot as they prepare for departure."

"Aye, ma'am."

****

"So we're all agreed this plan involves minimum risk to the population?" Jackson asked his senior staff one more time. "The *Star* will be clearing the planet for the last time in forty minutes, so now is the time to speak up and I encourage anyone who has the slightest doubt to do so."

"No, sir," Lieutenant Commander Sharpe spoke up. "I think this will at least give us some time to get more troops and ships here without them getting that machine operational in the meantime."

"Very well," Jackson said. "Everyone back to your stations. Tactical and Coms, coordinate one more time with Colonel Rucker about their requested fire mission and tell them we're less than ten away."

"Aye, sir," Simmons said as he nodded to Epsen.

The *Star* had recovered the outbound shuttles without incident and had then accelerated to climb up through two transfer orbits. She was now at departure altitude and carrying enough velocity to break away, so this would be their last trip around the planet. Colonel Rucker had called and said that he wanted a few pockets of Darshik troops hit with the orbit-to-surface guns in the *Star's* belly to give Colonel Beck's forces more time to disembark and organize before pushing on to Neuberlin.

Jackson had cleared the area of human presence on the previous orbit; thankfully Darshik combat suits read as much cooler than humans, so Simmons should have little trouble aiming his cannons and at least disbursing them. This was the first time they'd bunched up into large enough numbers to make an orbital strike feasible. Jackson assumed it must be in response to the Marines also clumping up as they were pushed back.

"Flight OPS has declared the launch bays completely secure," Ensign Dole reported. "Shuttles are locked down and all personnel have cleared the area."

"Targets confirmed by ground spotters and thermal imagery," Simmons said. "Ventral cannons deployed and tracking."

"You are cleared to fire when ready," Jackson said, watching the main display.

"Firing! Two volleys," Simmons said. "Firing program complete."

"OPS?" Jackson asked.

"CIC confirms good hits on target area, sir," Dole said. "But we'll overfly the target zone before the smoke and debris clears."

"Understood," Jackson said. "Tactical, next target is coming up."

"Cannons locked onto location, waiting to come within optimal range," Simmons said. The *Star* streaked over the continent at over sixty-two thousand kilometers per hour and was almost on top of the alien machine sitting off the west coast within minutes.

Jackson held firm in his belief that there was too much risk involved in firing directly on the unknown construct, but the power cable was very large and looked like it could be easily destroyed with wide-beam fire to the point that it would have to be replaced. It was based on the educated guess from his chief engineer that the dark ribbon in their imagery was indeed a power cable meant to connect to some as-yet-unknown power source on the coastline.

"Target within sight," Dole said.

"Computer has verified our position and adjusted our firing pattern ... stand by." Simmons was staring at his own displays without blinking as the alien machine began to take shape on the main display. "Firing!"

Jackson saw the distortion and vapor clouds left by their laser fire along with the billowing clouds of steam as the cannons fired into the ocean to hit the cable that was sitting a meter below the surface. The pulse lasers executed the preprogrammed pattern meant to maximize their coverage and damage the cable to the point that a simple repair would be impossible. Like with their first fire mission, the ground was soon too obscured with debris and water vapor for them to confirm they'd done anything useful or not. Jackson realized the effort may have been akin to pissing into a hurricane for all the good it would do, but he felt marginally better knowing he'd at least tried to do something while he was here.

"Firing sequence complete," Simmons said.

"Helm, come onto your new course," Jackson ordered. "All ahead flank. Coms, inform the *Icarus* we're departing Juwel's orbit and tell Colonel Rucker we wish them luck."

"All engines ahead flank, aye."

"The *Icarus* is reporting that Captain Wright sent the *Relentless* ahead of them towards the DeLonges jump point and that they're going to be our escort on the way out," Epsen said.

"Let's stay sharp, everyone," Jackson cautioned. "This isn't the easy part. Far from it. We're a bit lighter now, but the element of surprise is gone and any enemy cruisers left in this system will know exactly where we're going. It's a long way back up to the jump point and we have an unknown enemy presence out there not to mention our Specter that has yet to make another appearance."

Despite what he said to his crew Jackson could feel a palpable sense of relief as his ship pulled up and away from the planet. Part of it was from the fact he'd persevered, completed his mission, and that the Marines he'd brought to Juwel were vital to protecting the citizens on that planet. But being a destroyerman at heart he preferred to be out away from planets and moons when it came time for a fight. Large bodies in space hid things from view, threw off interference, and forced him to take their gravitational pull into account when pursuing or fleeing. Far better to be out in the open with some room to swing.

"Tactical, bring up all our weaponry, even the orbital strike cannons," Jackson said after a moment. "We don't have the drop shuttles aboard hooked to umbilicals anymore so we can spare the power. Set up a script that automatically brackets and tracks anything that comes within twenty-five thousand kilometers, but keep your fire control manual."

"Yes, sir," Simmons said, his hands dancing over the controls. "I think I know what you want, Captain ... they won't be able to jump in on us again without being fired upon instantly."

"You've got the idea, Commander," Jackson nodded. "Slave the Shrikes into that targeting control program as well. They have enough brainpower to be constantly updated without locking up and malfunctioning when you try to fire. The closer we get to actually getting out of this system the more desperate I feel they're going to get. Coms! Did you hear what I just said to Tactical?"

"Affirmative, sir," Epsen said.

"Good. Then pass that on to the *Icarus*. Make sure Captain Wright knows to give us at least a thirty-thousand-kilometer buffer," Jackson said. "We don't want any misunderstandings."

"Yes, sir."

Jackson settled back for what he hoped would be one of the longest, most boring watches of his career. He knew it wouldn't be … but he hoped for it nonetheless.

Chapter 27

"Incoming transmission from the Marines on Juwel," Epsen said. The *Star* was now fifteen hours away from the planet and still pushing hard for the outer system as the *Icarus* loafed along behind and well out of Jackson's "kill radius" he'd had programmed into the tactical computer. The theory was it would mitigate the risk of being taken by surprise by a Darshik warp hop, but the *Star* wasn't really able to take on another warship head-to-head and win regardless of how much prior warning they got.

"Ground-based BDA teams have rated our orbital strike as seventy-six percent effective against enemy positions," Epsen continued. "Zero civilian casualties, zero friendly-fire casualties. Colonel Rucker personally sends his thanks and wants you to know that with the material and personnel we dropped they're already pushing back on the Darshik troops."

"Put me on the shipwide, please," Jackson said.

"Go, sir."

"Attention everyone, this is the captain," Jackson said. "We've just received word from our forces on the ground that our mission has been a success. The loaded shuttles you deployed have turned the tide of battle from almost the moment they landed and the *Star's* orbital strikes decimated enemy forces while causing zero collateral damage.

"This is why we're here, everyone. Your efforts have had a direct impact and will make sure Colonel Rucker can successfully eliminate the alien threat on Juwel. We took a big risk staying here and going back in for a second pass, and we probably won't get out of this system without a fight, but we did our jobs and we made a difference. I'm proud of each of you. Now let's dig down just a little deeper and we'll get this ship home. That is all … carry on." He made a chopping motion to Epsen and waited until the intercom chirped to confirm the shipwide was closed before going on. The faint sounds of cheering could be heard coming from the open bridge hatchway.

"That goes doubly so for all the bridge crew pulling double watches and working at positions you're not fully trained at," he said. "OPS, do we have a position for the *Relentless*?"

"She's just finished her final course correction and is accelerating to transition velocity," Dole said as he manipulated his station to make the icon representing the ship in question flash. It was a green dot with a yellow halo around it to indicate the position was assumed based on an extrapolation of what had come through the Link while also accounting for the com lag.

Jackson just nodded without expression, but he was quite pleased with how far Dole had come along on this mission. When they left New Sierra he'd wanted the young officer replaced, but now he was able to honestly say he depended on him.

"*Icarus* has detected two—no, three—transition flashes on the far side of the system," Epsen said. "Their

OPS officer is telling me they're consistent with Darshik cruisers *leaving* a system."

"So there were two more that we hadn't accounted for," Jackson mused. "And we still have to assume the stealth ship is setting up an ambush for us. Coms, tell Mr. Accari we appreciate the heads up."

"You still know the *Icarus's* bridge crew, sir?" Simmons asked without taking his eyes off his displays, his hands poised near the controls that would allow him to react instantly should he need to.

"Most of them," Jackson said. "Idris Accari was a young navigation specialist on my last ship that showed promise. We fast-tracked him into a commission and Captain Wright swooped in and grabbed him for her OPS officer. He's a sharp kid. Her XO used to be my tactical officer and she herself used to be my XO way back when."

"I knew that last part, Captain," Simmons chuckled. "Why do you think those cruisers are leaving, sir?"

Jackson took a deep breath before answering. "Short answer is I have no idea," he said. "My first assumption is that those ships aren't at one hundred percent and the *Icarus* has already proven how adept she is at wiping out Darshik ships at greater than three-to-one odds. But, they put a lot of effort so far into holding this system and they've shown they're not afraid of a fight, so realistically I'd say they're going to get reinforcements. Three ships could mean they're pulling forces from three other locations … not a pleasant prospect."

"No sir, they—Contact!" Simmons shouted just before the tactical computers automatically locked onto a weak return that was coming up from behind and below them. "It's him! Point defense firing!"

The point defense laser batteries, some of the few weapons the ship had in the aft quadrants, opened fire well beyond their effective range. Jackson didn't care, however, as the lasers weren't a heavy draw on the power MUX and he knew that even if they weren't blowing bits of the hull off the incoming laser fire was playing hell with the enemy's sensors.

"Range?"

"Eleven thousand kilometers," Simmons said. "It jumped in *close.*"

"Snap fire aft tubes!" Jackson said. "Give the Hornets room to turn in on him. Manually detonate them when they're between it and the *Star* if they're going to overshoot."

"Firing tubes seven and eight!" Simmons said, referring to the two aft-facing missile tubes. "Hornets away!"

"*Icarus* is coming in hot from behind!" Epsen called loudly. "They want us to go to full power."

"Tell her we *are* at full power!" Jackson snapped, his ship's mild performance rankling him yet again.

"*Icarus* is firing Shrikes!" Epsen called. "Stand by!"

"Target has jumped," Simmons said. "It's no longer on our sensors ... sending destruct codes to the Hornets."

"This is going to be a long trip if that bastard is going to harass us the whole way out," Jackson said, standing. "Excellent work, Mr. Simmons. Giving him a face full of laser fire was probably distracting enough that he never got a shot off."

"Yes, sir," Simmons said. "I doubt it will work again, though."

"It won't," Jackson assured him. "He won't come in again without a better plan. OPS! I'm going to send you some parameters for another in-system warp transition, but this time we'll be going *away* from the primary star so the risk is exponentially less."

"Yes, sir."

"Let's get the ball rolling on this and have it ready in case we get boxed in," Jackson said.

Even as he sent over the basics of the maneuver he and Celesta Wright had perfected during the Phage War, a series of short warp flights that angled away from a system's ecliptic before eventually coming back up into an accepted warp lane, he knew it was just busy work for Dole. The *Star's* warp drive wasn't so robust that he wanted to risk more than one short hop; the risk of blowing out more than two emitters meant being stranded in interstellar space. He also couldn't charge the drive with all his weapon systems being powered up; the drive took the better part of twenty minutes to fully charge and the emitters would be deployed and vulnerable. So in that window if the enemy ship were to appear they'd be a sitting target with their most delicate system fully exposed.

The reality was that the *Vega*-class assault carrier was not the type of ship he would prefer to be on in this situation. It was supposed to come in once the destroyers and battleships had cleared the area and established orbital superiority over a planet and deliver ground forces for the second phase of CENTCOM's doctrine for retaking captured planets. Not only was the *Star* herself a bit behind the times, the tactics they were using were established as a hypothetical scenario on the off chance one human enclave made a move on another. Jackson found himself, yet again, at the mercy of Fleet procedure and hardware developed by people long dead for scenarios that had nothing to do with his current situation.

It would be easy to lash out at bureaucratic incompetence for not having quickly applied the lessons learned in the Phage War, but that would be a bit hasty. They just didn't have enough time between when they'd killed the Phage core mind and when the Darshik dragged the wreckage of the *Ares* back to the Xi'an System and blew it up. They'd suffered massive political upheaval, they still weren't very efficient at quickly building starships, and it was impractical to just purge Starfleet of its entire officer corps despite the known deficiencies. No … they'd have needed another fifty years to be fully ready given their current pace of rebuilding.

"Keep scanning for any new transition flashes," he said. "Maybe we'll get lucky and see where he hopped out to so we'll have an idea of which direction he'll be coming from."

"Aye, sir," Simmons said.

The feeling of being hunted was distinctly unpleasant and Jackson began working on a strategy that would allow him and Celesta Wright to work together in order to get both ships out of the system intact.

"Transition flash!" Dole reported. "The computer spotted it and matched it to the enemy ship. It's ... shit! It's down by Juwel! Delay accounted for and corroborates that it likely hopped from here to there."

Jackson's blood ran cold as he realized how stupid he'd been. The enemy didn't need to chase him all over the system. It could just go back and open fire on the defenseless planet they'd spent so much effort clearing.

He knew the *Star* had zero chance of coming around and making it back down to the planet in time. Hell, it had taken them twenty-six hours just to get as far as they had and it would be another thirty before they were even close to the jump point. Even if he had a way to get down there in time he held no delusions that his supposed tactical prowess would in any way level the field; that specialized Darshik warship would carve the assault carrier up at will in a standup fight.

"Coms! Patch me through to the *Icarus*." He tried to keep the defeat out of his voice as he sat down.

****

"—*over the planet. The Star can't get there in time. Break formation and try to take that son of a bitch out, Captain.*"

"Understood, sir," Celesta frowned. "But if we leave and this is a ruse we won't be able to get back up here in time. It could reach you before you can get to the jump point."

"*I'm well aware of that, Captain*," Jackson said over the channel. "*It's a risk I have no choice but to take. Get down there and kill that bastard.*"

"Yes, sir," Celesta said crisply. "*Icarus* out. Helm! Bring us about on a reciprocal course, all ahead emergency, everything she's got."

"Coming about, aye!"

With the capability provided by the upgraded RDS pod the *Icarus* swung about sharply, completing the turn in less than three thousand kilometers and actually *accelerating* during the turn. Her favorite helmswoman had skillfully rolled the destroyer ninety degrees like an aircraft pilot would to allow the inertia to be more easily nullified as the g-load evenly pressed them down instead of the system having to fight asymmetrical lateral acceleration.

A quick mental calculation showed under maximum acceleration they could be back at Juwel in under three hours, but even with the RDS she'd have to decelerate some or they'd overshoot the target.

"Tactical, kill the active sensors. OPS, secure Link transponder," Celesta ordered. "That ship knows where we're at but let's not advertise that we're charging back at full speed. The longer it takes for it to know what we're doing the further the *Aludra Star* gets and the better chance we'll have to take a real shot at it when we arrive."

A chorus of affirmatives met her orders as she settled down for a tense few hours. Despite having been on an extended mission when taking into account their failed effort to reestablish contact with the Ushin, the ship was ready to fight as was her crew. The RDS required significantly less power than magneto-plasma engines under normal operating conditions so they were still carrying plenty of fuel and their expendables were still in the green. The only thing she had to worry about was engaging the enemy and getting it to hold still long enough for her to shove a Shrike down its throat. It had taken her by surprise before, but she was more than confident that her ship would drop the hammer on it if they met head-to-head.

As the frantic activity subsided and her crew settled in to prepare for the coming engagement, a random thought flitted through her head: Where the hell was Pike and why was he even here?

****

"Well ... this was unexpected," Pike said to Essa as they stared at the sensor readings. They'd been drifting in high orbit over Juwel, scanning the surface, talking to the ground forces to get their unofficial report on the campaign, and checking out the alien construct in the western sea that Wolfe had fired upon. As the Broadhead completed its third orbit they were nearly blinded by a flash and then, *below* them, the Darshik stealth ship was also over the planet.

"So, what do you want to do?" Essa asked. He almost sounded bored as they recorded every detail of the ship from close range including all the battle scars inflicted by the *Relentless* and the *Aludra Star*. It looked like some effort had been made at repairing the hull coating, but there were still gaps where bare metal was visible.

"Other than perform a Jackson Wolfe special and just ram it there's little we can do," Pike said. "This thing doesn't carry enough firepower to bring down a capital ship even if it was a lucky shot *and* I knew where to target to hit something vital."

"I wonder why it's just sitting there," Essa said. "It's within range of Neuberlin … why not start hammering the Marines while it can?"

"It's going to try and either draw the two ships left in the system back or get them to split up," Pike said. "If the crew is half as competent as they've appeared to be then they know the *Aludra Star* isn't going to be able to get back—and there we go." He indicated the alert that had just popped up on the display. "The *Icarus* shut off her active sensors and dropped off the Link. Wright is going to come about and try to sneak in here for a shot."

"There has to be something we can do to help out," Essa insisted.

Pike didn't answer, just kept poring through the details of the running analysis his ship was performing on the Specter while the Broadhead sat silently above it.

"Well …" He scratched his chin and frowned. "The drive sections in the aft part of the ship are oddly exposed. If you look it's almost like the ship wasn't completed and the outer hull stops amidships. The guts of the entire aft end are exposed."

"Why don't they show up on radar?"

"Must be some sort of composite," Pike shrugged. "Do you see the two large blocky things on either side, sorta angled out away from each other?"

"Yeah."

"I'd bet you a case of very expensive Earth whiskey that those are the RDS field emitters," Pike said. "And that would mean that thick, armored bit connected to it that doesn't look like it's part of the frame would be the command and power lines."

"How expensive are we talking?" Essa asked.

"It's actually from Scotland, so very," Pike said.

"Okay, say I take the bet. What's your point?"

"I can't take this ship out as in destroy it completely, but I bet I could sever one or both of those cable assemblies," Pike said.

"Why the hell would someone build a ship like that?" Essa asked.

"Maybe they never expected to take a hit, maybe there's issues with their drive, maybe—Listen! Do you want to do this or sit and argue about ship building methodology?" Pike said irritably.

"Keep your shorts on." Essa raised his hands. "So if this is so easy, why not just do it and be done with it?"

"This isn't without risk," Pike said. "We'll be exposed and we're well within weapons range. I'm banking on the fact they'll be as surprised as we were when they showed up and it'll give us the time to get the hell out of here."

"I'm in," Essa said. "So when do we spring our trap? I'd think you'd want to give Captain Wright time to be close enough to take a shot if we manage to disable it, but if you wait too long you risk the ship moving off out of range."

"It's been just under an hour since the *Icarus* dropped off the Link," Pike said. "I don't know how fast that ship actually is now as it's highly classified, but I think if we take the shot within the next ninety minutes she'll be able to hit it while it's disabled."

For the next hour the Broadhead's powerful computer used the data from the optical sensors to create a targeting sequence that would simultaneously use the attitude jets to move the ship into the proper orientation and fire its four modest forward laser cannons. Pike would have loved to take a quick snapshot with the active sensors just to get a half-assed density reading on their target, but he couldn't risk it given their proximity. It was borderline miraculous, not to mention a testament to the Tsuyo engineers, that they hadn't yet been spotted.

"Looks like we're ready," he said as another forty minutes elapsed and the computer let him know it was as ready as it could be given the constraints on it.

"Let's do it," Essa smiled, causing Pike to scowl.

He pressed the flashing *EXECUTE* icon and the ship instantly pitched forward and over as the ionic jets spun them around to the proper orientation. There was a high-pitched whine as the cannons fired over and over. The lasers were invisible in space, but through the transparent forward canopy they could see the effect of their weapons fire as sparks exploded from around the areas they'd targeted.

Pike looked at the magnified view on the curved console and saw that they'd severed one of the power conduits and were now burning through the other one as the enemy ship began to move. It slowly rotated down and away from them, bringing its prow to bear on them as the Broadhead easily matched movements now that it could use its own RDS with all thoughts of hiding gone.

"That's it!" Essa cried. "Second one just burned off!"

"Then let's get the hell out of here!" Pike executed the second program he'd set up and the lights dimmed perceptibly as the ship's drive pulled an enormous amount of current. In the blink of an eye the small infiltrator shot away, leaving the floundering cruiser behind and soon out of range.

"Ship, open a channel to the *Icarus*," Pike said as the Broadhead climbed up and away from Juwel once it was on the other side, its diminutive stature and powerful drive allowing it to pull away without transferring to a higher orbit first.

"*Channel open.*"

"This is Agent Pike currently pulling away from Juwel. I believe we've managed to disable the enemy stealth ship by disrupting power to its main drive," Pike said. "Recommend you switch to active sensors to acquire and destroy target. Pike out."

****

"—*destroy target. Pike out.*"

"Tactical, active sensors," Celesta said after the channel had closed. How had Pike managed to get close in his little spy ship and take out the main drive?

"Actives up." Adler looked up as the threat board populated quickly since they were so close to the planet. "Target acquired. It … appears to be just sitting there, ma'am. We're not seeing any significant damage at this range, however."

"Lock on two Shrikes and standby forward laser batteries." Celesta was now on the edge of her seat. "Helm, brake now!" The *Icarus's* relative velocity was too great for the Shrikes to be successfully deployed. They would fire, but would be unable to maneuver to the target.

"Braking maneuver, aye."

"Velocity threshold reached," Adler reported.

"Fire missiles!"

"Missiles one and two away!" Adler said. "Tubes reloading, laser batteries charged and locked on target … fifty seconds until we're within range, but it will be a quick shot at this speed."

"I'm hoping there won't be enough left to shoot at," Celesta said. She watched, fascinated, as the target spun around but made no effort to evade the incoming missiles. It was going to be like shooting fish in a—

"Target has disappeared," Adler said. "Transition flash detected. I'm sorry, Captain, it jumped away right before the missiles reached it."

"Damnit!" Celesta snarled, slamming her palms down on her armrest in a rare overt display of emotion. "Did we detect a secondary flash? Did it hop somewhere close?"

"No, ma'am," Accari said. "The computer is constantly looking for a flash with that signature and nothing has been detected."

"Coms, ask Agent Pike if he sees anything from where he's at." Celesta struggled to remain calm. "It *has* to still be in the system."

"No, ma'am," Ellison said after a few seconds. "The Broadhead didn't pick up a second flash."

"Tactical, spin those missiles and have them brake to a stop." Celesta sounded suddenly weary. "We'll need to retrieve them, CENTCOM can't waste two Shrikes given the loss of Bespitd Depot the last time these bastards hit us."

"Signal sent," Adler said. "Missiles braking to a stop and entering recovery mode. Warheads safed."

"Tell Flight OPS to send a Jacobson drone to go get them." Celesta stood up. "Stand down from alert. Mr. Barrett, you have the bridge."

"Would you like the *Icarus* to begin a patrol pattern, Captain?" Barrett asked.

"No need, XO." She shook her head, glaring at the main display that now showed the night side of Juwel. "It's gone. It'll hide in the outer system and repair its drive and head home. It'll come at us again when it has the advantage. The First Battle of Juwel is over."

Chapter 28

It was three full days since they'd last seen the Darshik ship and Celesta's prediction had held true. There hadn't been a reappearance of the Specter, but Pike's ship had detected a transition flash well out in the system that indicated it had indeed fled, heading back for friendlier skies. The fact the ship had escaped her a second time had put Celesta in a foul mood, and her crew generally tried to avoid her as the *Icarus* monitored local space and provided occasional fire support for the Marines on the ground, who continued their seek and destroy mission for the remaining Darshik ground troops.

Pike had left right after the *Aludra Star* had transitioned out. He'd messaged one more time on a private, encrypted channel to tell her he was impressed that she'd come out with a single ship and had salvaged the Juwel mission, but he could tell she was in no mood to talk. Before he signed off he had mentioned going to Admiral Pitt and lobbying to get a more robust taskforce sent out to hold the system when Fleet R&S sent a team out to find out what the hell was plopped down in the ocean off the west coast.

"Captain Wright to the bridge! Captain Wright to the bridge!" It wasn't the computer's voice coming over the intercom, that was Accari and he sounded a bit distressed. She left her office and jogged to the bridge to find her OPS officer and XO leaned over the tactical station, jabbering away animatedly.

"What is it?" she asked brusquely.

"Transition flash detected within the system," Barrett said. "It's not the Specter, it's not a standard Darshik cruiser, and it's not one of ours."

"Transmission coming in," an ensign manning the com station said.

"Put it on the overheads," Celesta said.

"*This is the Ushin ship, Vol'a'atar,*" the artificial voice said smoothly. "*We have come in search of the Terran delegation that came under attack near the planet of our initial meeting and would continue our discussions if possible. We understand that trust is not guaranteed from your side given recent events.*"

Celesta stood stock-still for a long minute, well-aware there were many eyes on her as she thought over her options. There had been no attempt at direct communication with the Ushin that hadn't led to the loss of human lives at the hands of the Darshik. Would this be the same or would they finally be able to open a dialogue with their supposed allies? She knew it was at least important to get a toehold *somewhere* to put recent battles into context.

"OPS, tell Ambassador Cole he's about to earn his paycheck," she finally said. "Coms, reply back that they are to approach the planet slowly and halt at a range no less than seven hundred thousand kilometers and hold position while they talk to our ambassador."

"Aye, ma'am."

"Having them come closer here allows us to keep the planet under our protection and keep them in range as well," Celesta explained to Barrett when she saw his furrowed brow. "To meet them further out in the system to alleviate the com lag would leave Juwel defenseless."

"Is it really them?" Cole burst onto the bridge looking like he'd been in the middle of dressing when he'd been called.

"It appears to be," Celesta said. "Maybe this time you'll actually get to complete your mission."

"We can only hope, Captain," Cole breathed.

****

For the next two weeks Ambassador Cole sat through marathon sessions in an enclosed, secure com room while talking to the Ushin representatives. Celesta was invited by the Ushin to sit in on a few sessions, but her fear that the Darshik would attack while they were distracted kept her on the bridge as much as possible. She received daily briefs regarding the information she was cleared to hear from the ambassador over the evening meal they'd begun taking together in her office.

For her it was an efficient method to get the information coming from the Ushin almost as soon as it happened. For Cole it was a way for him to organize his thoughts from the day and better prepare himself for the next round of talks.

"They're far from a homogenous society," Cole was saying over a meal of overcooked pasta and a bland, almost tasteless tomato-based sauce. The galley crew were having to get creative with the dwindling food stocks. "They're a fractured and fractious people, even more so than our own enclaves though they've been a spacefaring people far, far longer than we have."

"How is that possible? Their ships aren't any more advanced than our own save for a few specialized capabilities," Celesta said. His sonorous voice and tendency towards oration over conversation had begun to wear on her nerves.

"The same reason *our* ship design had stagnated for centuries before the Phage: lack of need," Cole said. "Only recently have they even had a need for a martial force."

"Because of the Darshik?" She saw the reaction when she said the name and her eyes narrowed.

"I actually meant because of the Phage." Cole said, recovering quickly.

"The Phage attacked the Darshik, not the Ushin," Celesta pressed. "What aren't you saying? Or more specifically, what are you not allowed to say?"

Cole set his napkin down and leaned back, looking her in the eye. "You have to understand that I'm a one-man-show on this mission," he said finally. "I'm creating classification levels on information as I get it and usually arbitrarily. It'll likely all be gutted and reclassified when we get back to Terran space."

"So technically nothing you tell me is above my clearance level since you're setting the classifications," she reasoned. "Unless there's a specific reason *I* can't be trusted with this information."

"Well played, Captain," Cole sighed. "Very well … there is no such species as the Darshik."

"You have my complete attention." Celesta set down her utensils.

"We misunderstood during our initial meetings," he continued. "The word *Darshik* roughly translates to *worshipers* in our language, but it's a bit more nuanced than that. The Darshik *are* Ushin that have only recently splintered off and built their society around key people who learned their lessons from events so horrific—"

"The initial Phage attack," Celesta finished.

"Precisely," Cole nodded. "Only four planets were attacked by the Phage when they met the Ushin, and those societies were found to be of little threat so the core mind decided to use their systems as staging areas, breeding grounds, and logistical hubs.

"Swarms of Alphas would stream through their system and once in a great while the Phage would deign to talk to the Ushin there. It … changed them."

"We become what we fear most," Celesta repeated a line she'd always remembered from her time in school.

"Indeed," Cole said. "When Jackson Wolfe killed the Phage and all the individual units became inert, refusing to talk to the Darshik, they became increasingly agitated, convinced they'd displeased their overseers. You have to understand that many generations of Ushin were born and died with Phage units in their skies and along the way they began to deify them despite being a society that had evolved well past base superstitions."

"But in its death throes the core mind got a message to the Ushin, telling them who was responsible for killing it," Celesta argued.

"Yes, but only a select few ever actually talked to the Phage in their system. And those Ushin, now Darshik, interpreted that message as a call to arms," Cole said. "You know where the story picks up from there as you're the one who found the *Ares* in the Xi'an System.

"When the other Ushin found out about what their reclusive violent sect was about to do they made plans to reach out to us. The Darshik found out and razed two Ushin worlds to the tune of *billions* dead. The Ushin leadership was shaken to the core. It was no longer about trying to warn the humans of Darshik aggression, it was now about trying to enlist our help in dealing with what had become a grave threat to their very existence."

"I can only imagine the conversations," Celesta said. "Entreat the species that had wiped out the Phage to deal with the cult that worshipped it. This is ... a lot to take in. But it does clear up a lot of things that never made any sense in our interactions with either side of this little sibling rivalry."

"Oh, it's well beyond that," Cole said seriously. "I know you were being glib, Captain, but make no mistake:

This is a war for survival in every sense of the word. Either the Ushin will win, or the Darshik will. They've continued to grow in strength and technical prowess and with each victory they feel emboldened. If Starfleet was at pre-war strength it might not be such a worry, but we both know that isn't the case."

"So, have all your conversations with the Ushin been so profound?" Celesta suddenly wanted to lighten the mood in the cramped office.

"Unfortunately, no," Cole said wearily. "It's been quite trying. I have to deflect often as they want committed answers that I'm not empowered to give."

"On a more practical side, how much longer are we going to be required to stay here?" Celesta asked. "The *Icarus* has plenty of fuel but water, air, and food may become an issue soon and I don't think Juwel is ready to provide for us just yet."

"I will try to expedite things." Cole's tone clearly indicated he had no such intentions.

****

"Incoming priority transmission, sir," Accari said. He'd routed external com functions to the OPS station while the com officer ran down to the wardroom for a quick meal.

"Source?" Barrett asked.

"Huh. It's a com drone," Accari said. "It's not a point-to-point so it's probably going to fly out of the system since the platform was destroyed. Sending it to your—"

"Just tell me what it says, Lieutenant," Barrett said.

"We're being relieved," Accari paraphrased as he read. "A taskforce is inbound from New Sierra to take up defense of Juwel and oversee the study and dismantling of that machine they left in the ocean."

"Who drew the short straw and had to come out?" Barrett asked. "And what are they defining as a 'taskforce?'"

"The anchor is going to be the *Dreadnought*-class battleship *New York* commanded by Captain Lee," Accari said. "A fleet carrier full of science crews and more Marines, four First Fleet destroyers and three missile frigates."

"Wow." Barrett whistled in approval. "A proper taskforce with one of the new boomers coming in to squat over the planet. Captain Wright will be pleased to see our efforts will not have been for naught. The Darshik would struggle trying to recapture this planet from that."

"Yes, sir."

It was another seven days before the leading elements of Captain Lee's battlegroup began filtering through the DeLonges jump point. Mercifully, the fleet carrier had been loaded with replacement expendables for the *Icarus* before departing New Sierra, and the cargo containers containing fresh food and water were left along the flightpath she'd take leaving the system. Terran starships did an admirable job filtering the water and scrubbing the air, but there was still no such thing as a truly closed loop system and eventually things needed to be purged and topped off.

By the time the *New York* arrived the Ushin had concluded their conversations with Ambassador Cole, a new meeting time and place was tentatively set, and they made a discreet withdrawal before many more Terran warships arrived. For his part Cole simply looked overwhelmed. A lifetime of being ready for a first contact scenario and the first aliens they met, the Phage, weren't all that talkative. Now he was finally realizing the pressure involved in bridging the language, cultural, and biological gaps without any missteps and it seemed to be taking a toll on him. Celesta couldn't remember him looking so gaunt and drawn when he'd first boarded some months prior.

"Flight OPS reports that the cargo containers have been brought into the hold and secured," Accari reported. "They're going to let them warm up a bit before trying to open the pressure hatches."

"Coms, send word to Captain Lee that the *Icarus* is departing the system." Celesta stood up. "OPS, deploy and charge the warp drive. Helm, you are clear to accelerate to transition velocity plus ten ... steady as she bears. Let's go home."

Chapter 29

"And you believe them?" President Augustus Wellington asked his ambassador, hands crossed over his expanding paunch.

"They seem sincere," Cole nodded. "They also transmitted petabytes worth of evidentiary data that—"

"Yes, yes," Wellington waved him off. "The Diplomatic Corps, Fleet R&S, Fleet Intel, CIS, and Tsuyo Research Division are all tearing though the digital data you brought back like a pack of scavengers.

"I'm asking *you*... Do. *You*. Trust. *Them*. Don't clam up on me now, Cole. You were given this job for a reason ... apparently."

"I do trust them, Mr. President," Cole said stiffly at the thinly veiled swipe at the end of Wellington's remarks.

"Then I think our business is concluded." The President heaved himself out of the chair. "You may go. Go get drunk, go get laid, just don't leave the area. You'll likely have your ass dragged in front of at least a dozen discovery committees once Parliament gets word of all you agreed to."

"Yes, Mr. President." Before Cole reached the door Wellington had one more parting shot.

"Good job, Cole," he said, sounding genuine. "That wasn't an easy assignment and you brought back positive results. When the politicians get ahold of you, stand your ground … I don't think anybody else I could have sent would have done better."

Cole went from looking stiff to almost embarrassed. "My thanks, sir," he said before quickly retreating.

Once the door boomed closed to the executive office one of the other occupants spoke up, his voice like an abrasive grinder on the President's nerves.

"*'When the politicians get ahold of you?'* Did that little interrogation not count?"

"Shut up, Pike," Wellington sneered. "I have to be sure he won't buckle at the slightest harsh word when the opposition begins tearing into him. Now … what do the three of you think about what he said regarding this Darshik ace? Would taking him out really break down the last remnants of this Phage cult?"

"Seems tenuous, at best, Mr. President," Admiral Marcum said. "But they are aliens. They worshiped that Phage Super Alpha and now it seems that void has been filled by a military leader that promised them he could lead them to fulfill their destiny. Now that I think about it there is precedence for this sort of thing in human history."

"I think the issue we should be discussing is not *if* we'll be going after this ace, but *how*," Admiral Pitt said.

"I take it you have some ideas in that regard?" Wellington asked.

"The admiral and I are *not* in agreement on this," Marcum said sourly before being silenced by a look from his boss.

"Our newest generation of warships are ready for active deployment, Mr. President," Pitt said. "These four new designs include our newest destroyer. I want to send one out to hunt this bastard down."

"Why would you be against that?" Wellington asked Marcum, perplexed.

"Let him finish," Marcum said.

"It's time to put aside the publicity stunts, the petty paybacks, and the borderline bigotry, sir," Pitt said, ignoring Marcum bristling beside him. "Put Captain Wolfe on the bridge of a destroyer and let him off the leash. Give him six months to get acclimated and pick his command crew, then get the hell out of the way."

"I'm going to pretend none of that earlier business about bigotry or PR stunts was directed at me." Wellington sat on the edge of his desk. "He's your man for this job?"

"It's between him or Wright," Pitt nodded. "Between the two I still think Wolfe is the more naturally gifted tactician and leader. I feel Wright can be needlessly reckless at times and still tries to outshine her mentor by taking unsound risks."

"Make it happen," Wellington said before pointing to Marcum and Pitt with his two index fingers. "*Both* of you make it happen. Now get out of here and let me talk to my wayward aide in private."

"Yes, sir," both admirals parroted before walking out of the office, Marcum glaring daggers into the back of Pitt's head as they exited.

"Like fucking children sometimes, these Fleet officers," Wellington griped after the door shut.

"That's why I never joined the military," Pike said lightly. "Please tell me I'm going to get a break, sir. The inside of that Broadhead smells like old socks, spilled beer, and the shattered dreams of my youth."

"I need you to become Lynch for a time," Wellington said. "And I mean really become him again, not just put on the expensive suit and haughty expression. I want you shadowing Ambassador Cole."

"To keep him on the straight and narrow while navigating these august halls of power?"

"Partially," Wellington said. "I also want him under close observation by someone I trust. Just call it a precaution. He's been in contact with an alien species of unknown capability for weeks on end, alone, and I'd rather have some sort of warning if he's been compromised in some way."

"Understood," Pike nodded. "Anything else?"

"So between the two admirals that were just here I have one that would like to see Wolfe drummed out of the service and another that thinks he can singlehandedly win the war," Wellington huffed. "Which one is right?"

Pike considered his words carefully before answering. "I think Marcum's dislike of Wolfe is borne out of frustration at not having been able to fully control him. Maybe even a little jealousy that almost every time he bucked the chain of command he came back covered in glory, and not a drop of that glory splattered onto Marcum even though he was in the trenches trying to do the right thing … most of the time," he said. "Pitt doesn't necessarily love Wolfe either, if you hadn't realized that. He's angry he left Starfleet when they could have used his experience and mentorship after the war to help rebuild."

"You didn't answer the question," Wellington said.

"I think you know the answer, sir," Pike said. "Wolfe may disregard a command structure that has proven itself inept at times, but his loyalty towards the Federation is unwavering despite how he's been treated, and most of that just because of where he was born.

"I've seen him in action many times and I can tell you he'll never tire, he'll never quit, and he has sudden insights as to how his enemy thinks that makes him seem lucky … but that couldn't be further from the truth."

"So you'd put him back in a destroyer to go wreak havoc in someone else's backyard?" The question was asked with a half-smile.

"Hell, sir … I'd almost enlist just to go with him."

****

"Is this the last one?" Jackson asked.

"It is," the orderly said. "He asked that you be the ones to pin his medals on personally."

"I've never met the man," Celesta said. "But it's an easy enough request to fill."

The two starship captains were in full service dress and had been making morale calls on those that had been wounded in the Battle of Juwel. Most of them were Marines, but there were a few Fleet officers and enlisted that had been wounded in the exchange of fire. Unbelievably, six of them had been scooped up floating around in lifeboats that had deployed from the *Racer* and the *Resolute*.

Neither Jackson nor Celesta had ever been particularly comfortable in the role they were forced into at the moment. Most of the time it was their action or inaction that had caused someone to be injured, and to have to turn around and give that person comfort was exceedingly awkward at times since the wounded spacer would still look at them as the captain and, thus, infallible.

"Sergeant Barton, you have visitors," the orderly said loudly as he opened the door.

"I'm decent."

"How are you, Sergeant?" Jackson said as he came around the hanging partition and looked upon a young Marine who was heavily bandaged but looked otherwise intact.

"Sir, ma'am," Barton said, nodding to each captain. "Thank you for coming. I know you both have to be very busy."

"I'm stuck here waiting for a ride to the Arcadia System for two more days," Jackson forced a smile and shrugged.

"I won't keep you long, either of you," Barton said. "I just wanted to say thank you ... I know you stayed in the system and fought your way back to the planet a second time to deploy our relief force when you'd have been well in the right to say it was too dangerous and fly right back home.

"Without Colonel Beck's force we'd have all died. You saw my friends already?"

"Corporal Castillo and Major Baer?" Celesta asked. "We talked to them this morning. Castillo is quite the character."

Barton just smiled. "That he is," he said.

After a bit more uncomfortable small talk Jackson pinned Barton's medals for valor onto his hospital gown and stood with Celesta for some pictures with the young man. He was on his way out when Barton stopped him.

"I hear you're getting another ship, sir," he said. "A destroyer. I hear you're gonna hunt that fucker down."

"That's ... highly classified," Jackson said, not bothering to deny it. He was always amazed at the accuracy and speed of scuttlebutt aboard New Sierra Platform.

"I want to be on that ship if I can, sir," Barton said. "I want to try to be on your Marine detachment ... watch your back like General Ortiz did back on the *Blue Jacket* and the *Ares*."

"We'll see about that when you're up and about, Marine." Jackson nodded to him and fled the room as quickly as he could.

"You never could take the hero worship," Celesta teased as she came up beside him in the corridor.

"Never will, either," Jackson said after failing to think of a sarcastic remark that wasn't simply mean rather than funny. "So, Captain … when do we leave?"

"The *Icarus* will be departing for the Tsuyo-Barclays Shipyards in the Arcadia System at 0430 station time where she will be refitted with updated tactical computers and point defense batteries," she said. "I take it I'll be heavy one VIP?"

"No, just a broken-down old spacer," Jackson joked, looking down at his antique watch that was far outside Fleet regs. "Got time for a drink?"

"Why not?"

Epilogue:

"Mr. and Mrs. Wolfe, it's truly an honor. My name is Gyo Hamaski. I'll be your technical liaison."

"I'm here in an unofficial capacity, Mr. Hamaski," Jackson said. "I just wanted to see her before the official orientation and my wife happens to have connections here on the shipyards."

"Please, call me Gyo," Hamaski bowed. "And yes, Mrs. Wolfe's team has done marvelous work getting the training program ready on both the *Juggernaut*-class battleships and *Valkyrie*-class destroyers. I'm afraid it won't be possible to step foot on the ship just—"

"I just want to see her," Jackson assured him.

Soon the three of them were in a small, autonomous tender with a bulbous, transparent passenger compartment and zipping along the spindly web that made up the shipyard complex. Hulls of varying degrees of completion were all around as were thousands of workers, human and robotic, all going around the clock to get as many starships completed as they could, as quickly as they could.

After a moment they were past the rough construction yard and moving among completed ships, the shapes of which took Jackson's breath away. He'd been given images of the new ships, of course, but it was never the same as seeing them in person for the first time. His wife looked up at him and seemed to be enjoying his reaction.

"I think you'll find the *Valkyrie*-class ship a worthy successor to the *Starwolf*-class destroyers, Captain, even if they're not named after you," Jillian said in a light, teasing tone.

"And there she is," Gyo said, commanding the tender to slow down and circle a ship that was nestled into a fully enclosed berth with multiple gangways and umbilicals still attached. "She's the second operational hull to come out of the yards, third in the class counting the proof-of-concept prototype that we used to shakedown the drives."

"Spectacular," Jackson breathed. The ship was sleek, dangerous-looking. There were few protuberances to break up her lines, continuing the trend started by the *Starwolf*-class, and a shorter, less pronounced superstructure. The hull was dark silver and looked substantially armored. He couldn't make out too much detail as she was backed into the berth and they were sitting outside in a tender, but he liked what he saw so far.

"What'll she be called?"

"She was originally going to be christened the *TFS Endurance*, but that name went to the first hull that's already doing her shakedown run. You'll actually start out on that ship to begin training your crew before this one is fully operational," Jillian said, squeezing his hand. "Admiral Pitt sent word ahead that he'd pulled some strings in the Fleet Operations Subcommittee and had this one renamed to something more appropriate for her mission and her future captain."

"And that is?" Jackson asked.

"*Nemesis.*"

Thank you for reading *Iron & Blood,*

Book Two of the Expansion Wars Trilogy.

The story will continue with Book Three:

Destroyer

Due in fall of 2017

Subscribe to my newsletter for the latest updates on new

releases, exclusive content, and special offers:

http://tiny.cc/dalzelle

...and connect with me on Facebook and Twitter:

www.facebook.com/Joshua.Dalzelle

@JoshuaDalzelle

Also, check out my other works including the bestselling

Omega Force Series available on Amazon,

Barnes & Noble, and iBooks

From the Author:

Thanks for reading everybody, hopefully this continuation of the Black Fleet Saga is living up to expectations. I'll keep this short as I'm working as quickly as I dare to get this book wrapped up and released and press ahead with other projects. While it was with the editor I was plugging away on the next Omega Force book so look for that this spring.

With this book I wanted to get away from the story being on such an epic scale like the survival of the entire species. I thought it might be interesting to concentrate on the comparatively small story of fighting for a single planet and all that goes into that. Sometimes writers fall into a trap of making each subsequent chapter of a long-running series bigger and grander and far more complex than it needs to be and in the middle of all that the entire point they were trying to make gets lost.

This brings me to my next point: While Omega Force is pure escapism and adventure sci-fi without much of a message past having some fun, with this series of books I've tried to lightly touch on some of ethical and practical issues around using force to gain a political objective. I've tried to make sure it doesn't come across as heavy-handed or that a reader starts to suspect I'm using a sci-fi book as a soapbox to talk about my own political views (something I don't inject into my writing) and puts it down. The title and quote at the beginning of this book may raise a few eyebrows, but I assure you that it's meant to be taken at face value *and* completely within the context of this story, not as a statement on Otto von Bismarck's entire political history.

Anyway … this is book five so we have four more to go after this before the entire saga is wrapped up. The next book is titled *Destroyer* and following that will be The Unification Wars Trilogy. Thanks for the patience as I know this one is a little late from the initial planned release date.

Cheers!

Josh

CPSIA information can be obtained
at www.ICGtesting.com
Printed in the USA
LVHW090954071120
671027LV00052B/635

9 781542 870351